PRAISE FOR *THE HEAVY SIDE*

"The Heavy Side *is a devilish joyride of a novel, a literary thriller that's as original as it is mesmerizing. From Tahoe to Mexico, a star-crossed couple can't escape their coiled fates, even when--especially when--they most need to. Ben Rogers writes like a maestro--readers won't be able to put down this book."*

–Matt Gallagher, author of *Empire City*

"A vivid thriller made all the more engrossing by its narrator...Lyrical... Haunting. Very, very highly recommended."

–Midwest Book Review

"Fantastic...an absolute page turner."

–The Biggest Little Library Podcast

"The Heavy Side *will be one of the smartest and best literary works you will read this decade. Rogers updates traditional literary themes...through the languages of literature and of programming code. In doing so he blends an authentic love story and an intense thriller into a unique, gripping human story."*

–**Caleb S. Cage**, author of *Desert Mementos: Stories of Iraq and Nevada*

"Original, modern and refreshing."

–The BookLife Prize

"This is carefully crafted fiction that springs from the well-organized mind of an engineer with the soul of a storyteller."

–Mark Maynard, author of *Grind*

"Rogers' precise language makes the twists of Vik's code as involving as the particulars of his getaway plan in this astute thriller."

–Jenny Shank, author of *The Ringer*

"Filled with tremendous writing about the meaning of code, and what coding a masterpiece might be like, as well as a primer on the economics of the illegal drug markets with deep insight into how drug cartels operate."

–Joseph G. Peterson, author of *The Rumphulus*

PRAISE FOR *THE FLAMER*

"A story of love, told like an explosion–a novel not only about a boy's romance with fire, but also with language, people, and the whole wide world. Rogers has crafted one of the wisest, funniest, strangest novels I've ever read, narrated by one of the most unique characters I've had the pleasure of meeting in American fiction. I treasure this book."
–Christopher Coake, author of *We're In Trouble*

"The Flamer *is a diabolically funny, explosively tender portrait of youth, a mad scientist's coming-of-age story. Brainy and splendidly profane, Ben Rogers's writing is incendiary and hypnotic. We watch with an arsonist's glee as his boy genius lights the fuse of his own volatile adolescence. A sizzling debut."*
–Claire Vaye Watkins, author of *Battleborn*

Named one of Five Overlooked Books It's Impossible Not to Love.
–Barnes & Noble

"A highly original and delightful debut."
–High Country News

"Like Harper Lee and Mark Twain, Ben Rogers has tapped into regional America to scribe a coming-of-age story that is universal in its truths."
–H. Lee Barnes, Member of Nevada Writers Hall of Fame

"A witty, Nevada-based coming-of-age story."
–Las Vegas Review Journal

"Rogers gives us a precocious young man with fiery tastes and curious charm."
–Don Waters, author of *These Boys and Their Fathers*

"Rogers gets the coming-of-age novel right."
–The Nevada Review

THE HEAVY SIDE

a novel

Ben Rogers

C Q B o o k s

www.readrogers.com

For Jill

"We can see now that information is what our world runs on: the blood and the fuel, the vital principle."

--JAMES GLEICK

"The future is already here — it's just not very evenly distributed."

--WILLIAM GIBSON

"A new analysis of 234 banknotes from 18 U.S. cities...found cocaine on 90 percent of the bills tested."

--SCIENTIFIC AMERICAN, AUGUST 16, 2009

PART I: TAHOE, 2015

1

I know now that there was a young Hispanic man on the hillside above the cottage, watching through binoculars as Vik, a young Indian man, oblivious, did pushups on his Persian rug. I know about the man on the hillside because Los told me when I was his hostage. I know about the Persian rug because Vik told me how he always tapped out his reps with his nose against one of the trees in the rug's pattern. The tree had an extra leaf compared to the other trees, and this was an intentional flaw: we Persians know that weavers cannot create perfection, only God can. Vik told me he did not know whether there was a God, only that there was a Steve Wozniak, who'd designed every circuit and authored every line of code in the original Apple II computer, and to this day not a single bug found in any of it. But what if perfection isn't divine? What if bugs are?

We might know that, Vik and I.

The cottage sat at the terminal switchback of a mountain road above Incline Village. I'd like to think that there was a moment during which both young men—the one on the hillside, the one in the cottage—despite their separate vantages—paused together in mutual awe of the aquamarine wonder far below, a lake two-thousand millennia in the making, a small alpine sea. Lake Tahoe.

Vik tapped out a text—*1PM still good?*—then set his phone down, knowing better than to expect the gratification of an instant reply. He had big plans for us that day, but I had gone out the night before, and though at 29 I was still too young for bona fide hangovers, Vik figured (correctly) that I would be sleeping one off. He sometimes joined me and my friends on our nights out. No longer in his invincible twenties, he played the part of The Older Guy, invariably ducking out before the wee hours. A few times that doomed summer he'd offered to take me home, but I am not the type to leave before everything that is going to happen, does. I have to be the last kid out of the pool.

However. By late August we had twice found ourselves alone together—once in a hot, dark hallway at a party, once in a moonlit parking lot—and had done the things single people do. We had kissed each other frenetically and lay hands upon each other and confided secrets, only to downplay the significance of such things when the sun came up. Or, I had. Vik would send me a heartfelt text, and I'd send back a picture I took of a squirrel eating a Cheeto.

Electronic conversation plays to our mutual strengths. We can craft a message, shoot it out, get a reply, interpret it. Think. Craft another. It gives us breathing room. Face to face, we can take each other's breath away. Especially in those days.

The saving grace of my forced estrangement from Vik has been the time and distance it's given me to write with him, and about him. To codify his story. I have hundreds of pages of his letters. By now he's divulged to me most of the dots; here is my attempt, then, to connect them. Any bugs are mine.

Vik used to do sit-ups, too, on that Persian rug. Pull-ups from the wood cross-beam overhead. The rug, the beam, they are no longer. But there may always be a man on the hillside. We know that.

2

The cottage was really a single-bedroom guest house. It had been built in haste by the prior owner to establish legal residence in the tax haven of Nevada while he fussed over plans for an accompanying mega-mansion to be built adjacent. However, soon after ground was broken on the main house, the SEC caught up with the man. He went to prison for illegal junk-bond trading. The property hit the market in early May, priced for rapid liquidation. Vik swooped in.

He'd been living there ever since. He never minded the half-finished eyesore to his west, with its 15-foot, concrete retaining wall and exposed foundation. Trees had been cut down to make room for the house; a copse of 12-inch support beams stood in their place, supporting nothing. The foundation collected rainwater. Pallets of lumber lay warping in the Sierra sun. Bouquets of multicolored wires bloomed here and there from exposed conduit like wildflowers after a forest fire.

Still waiting on my reply to his text, Vik stood in the kitchen, tamping espresso grounds into a dense brown puck so as to leave the water no path of least resistance. He pulled a shot. The espresso machine was industrial grade. The manufacturer's vice-president had been Vik's roommate at Caltech. Years later, over lunch, the man had casually mentioned a temperature overshoot issue plaguing their product's boiler.

Vik had scribbled down three lines of code for a low-pass filter that could smooth out the boiler's thermocouple signal —three lines subsequently included on every machine the company produced. Months later, a delivery man wheeled a dolly up to Vik's doorstep and held up a clipboard for signature. Vik cut into the cardboard and liberated a gleaming, aluminum marvel. He'd never much cared about espresso before. Now he wondered if he could even think without it.

He stood leaning against the counter, gnawing his lip, staring out at the lake without really seeing it. An urgency building. In the corner of the room was a semicircular workstation with a 27-inch iMac workstation and beside it a MacBook Pro laptop. Both monitors blank, the processors hibernating. The file basket piled with unopened mail addressed to the junk bond trader, which Vik had been gradually repurposing as scratch paper.

If he didn't start soon, the vaporous ideas in his head would swirl off, unable to nucleate. He rubbed his whiskered face. He'd once been the type to grind away late into the night. Since coming to the lake, he did his best work in the morning.

He crossed the room, tapped the keyboards, sat down, logged in. Back straight. Navigating menus, opening files, repositioning and resizing terminals. His posture deteriorating. Hunching toward the screen, counting with his finger the arguments nestled inside a set of parentheses: 1 argument, 2, 3, 4, 5, 6—*ah, that's the problem*. Typing in the missing seventh.

Coding.

To the young man with his binoculars, watching a magnified, trembling, silent-movie version of Vik, time expanded: the next three and a half hours felt like a day. As they would to anyone from his POV. Very little seemed to be happening. There was a man in a cottage, staring at a computer, cracking his knuckles, looking occasionally at the ceiling.

To Vik, though, time imploded. He'd fallen under another of his self-induced spells. Thinking, typing, compiling, running. Erroring out. Scrolling back. Oblivious to the world beyond the one he was writing, line by line—the world he'd created, and controlled. Lines of text spooling past in a blur, slowing to a halt.

I know exactly the feeling.

When he'd first started coding, he'd worn headphones pumping EDM to stay in a trance. He didn't need them anymore. He moved through his program function by function, watching the variables change. Rarely touching the mouse, relying instead upon keyboard shortcuts to auto-complete filenames, to search backward, to place the cursor at the ends and beginnings of lines.

He rubs a hand across his face, smells the coffee on his breath, the rug on his palm. Repositions his cursor, kills a bug with a single keystroke. Recompiles, reruns. Feels a fleeting jolt of satisfaction. Seeks another.

Patches of sunlight on the floor compress toward the windows.

At some point he got thirsty. Realized his wrists ached. His back was tight. He knew he ought to go outside and walk around, but sensed he was on the verge of a small breakthrough. There was just one more variation he wanted to test out...

Half an hour later he was still at the computer. The only sounds in the room the soft rat-tat-tat of the keyboard, the occasional sniff, the compulsive jiggling of a foot against the desk. Finally, he went back through the new work and tidied up. Saved a working snapshot of the code to the hard drive and went to the kitchen for a glass of orange juice. Drank it in gulps, looking out the window at the lake. Seeing it this time.

He unhooked a frying pan from a rack and set it on the stove over a blue flame. The remaining block of butter in the refrigerator door was thicker than he needed but too thin to divide, so he peeled away the wax paper and dropped the whole thing in the pan. Broke in a pair of eggs, put a slice of bread in the toaster. The eggs crackled and sputtered. He leaned both hands against the counter and hung his head. It is difficult for him to escape the confines of a problem space. He flipped the eggs and lay slices of cheese over them and when the cheese had melted he spilled the crackling, steam-

13

ing contents of the pan out over the toast. So much to think through.

Coarse ground pepper, coarse ground salt.

Variables, functions. A girl.

He went out on the deck and ate standing up, without a fork, licking yolk from his fingers. When he was done he went around to the storage closet located just off the front deck. Inside was a full-suspension mountain bike and an un-plumbed water heater tank filled with cash. The bike dangled on a hook in the dark like a curing carcass. He lifted it off.

The young man in the forest shot off a text: *Listos.*

3

While the young man slipped into the vacated cottage, Vik drove down the hill with his bike strapped to his beater Mercedes. The bike was worth more than the car. It had been Vik's gift to himself upon moving to Tahoe. He'd had a bike in the Bay Area, but had worked so much in those days that he never really rode it. In the mountains he'd grown legs, lungs, *cojones*.

He stopped at a supermarket. Bought a baguette, a wedge of brie, an avocado, a mango, a salami, and a bar of dark chocolate. Then drove south, skirting the lake. Perhaps recalling the day we'd met. He'd been sitting at the bar at Gordon's, eating a cheeseburger, trying to look cliché—trucker hat, board shorts. But he wasn't local. His brim wasn't flat enough. His skin wasn't brown because of the sun. I materialized beside him, ordered some pitchers.

Nice bike out there, I said, for I'd noticed him when he rode up.

Thanks, he said.

You should lock it up, I said, or one of these assholes'll steal it.

I gestured to the men at the bar, the bartender. All of them knew me. None took offense. Vik offered to help me carry the pitchers.

Face to face, he put me on my heels. He had a physicality like honesty.

Soon he was throwing darts with my friends. His intro-version was taken for modesty, his bike as proof he liked to ride, and by the time we parted ways he'd been invited along on a group ride the coming Saturday. Not by me. Though I had no objections. Quite the opposite.

Now we were going on another ride together. Just us.

He parked at the trailhead. Tore the baguette in half and stuffed it in the bag along with the rest of the food and a bladder of water. Plus the thumb drive upon which he ha-bitually backed up his work. An unseen Mountain Chickadee whistled its signature three-note call from the forest: *high-low-low*. We've all heard the local kids putting words to its tune: *Hey, stu-pid!*

On the 2-lane highway, a shuttle van towing a trailer of bikes was waiting to turn left across the endless string of traffic circling the lake. I pedaled alongside it, balanced for a moment on my pedals, peering up the highway, then shot a gap in the traffic, leaving the van in limbo, its blinking turn signal reiterating a desire it couldn't fulfill. Not me. I rode right up and kissed Vik, my hand on his waist.

By this time he knew that my tender features—my button chin, my dainty feet—were false advertising. He'd noticed the slide-tackle scars on my knee; my crooked nose —broken while grappling with my brother one Thanksgiving. He knew that story because he'd asked me a lot of questions. He, on the other hand, had deflected all such attentions. As such, our understanding of each other at that point was asymmetrical.

And who are *you*? he asked.

So I curtseyed, acknowledging that, *yes*, I'd been caught a little out of character, I'd taken something seriously. On all the rides we'd gone on, I'd worn some version of a 'wife-beater' tank and running shorts—amateurish gear that set me apart from the expensively-clad bros we inevitably passed on the trail. I don't know what I had against 'bros.' I'd dated more than a few in my years at the lake. They were, after all, the abundant game. I think I've always wanted to think of myself as picky when it came to men, but that I wasn't truly so until I picked Vik.

Therefore. High-cut bike shorts, tight riding jersey, low-cut sports bra. My signature ponytail split into pigtails. I was going for 'sexy-mischievous-schoolgirl-jock.' Feast your eyes out, Vik Singh.

A girl can't buy a new outfit? I asked.

He asked if the shorts came with the usual, built-in, padded chamois.

Check, I dared him.

He flicked idly at his bike gears. Shifted subjects.

Who was out last night? he asked.

The Usual, I said. Everyone but you.

He smiled, channeling some hidden frustration into his handlebars as if merely testing his suspension. Said he'd had to work.

I ignored this excuse: it, too, was The Usual. You were missed, I said.

We both knew this wasn't true. My friends hardly knew him. They called him 'The Brown Recluse.' Nobody at Tahoe really knew him. Except me. Or, I was getting there.

At least, I said, *I* missed you.

There wasn't a trace of sarcasm in my voice, and he had to look away. It was the most nakedly sentimental thing I'd said in a long time. After all, I was a card-carrying member of a new strain of woman. We donned wife beaters. We cage fought. Hashtag fuck you.

He smiled snidely at me. It wasn't fair. He had so much more information than I did.

We rode abreast up the fire road, our pedaling pace conducive to chitchat.

How's work? I asked.

Decent, he said. Made good progress this morning.

Who'd you say it was for again?

I don't know if I did, he said.

Oh. Okay.

It's the same client I've had for awhile. It's just a new

version of their app.

What's it do?

Same thing it already does, I guess. Just, more efficient now. More secure.

Fixing what somebody else wrote, I said. I've done that before.

Actually, he said. I wrote the first version, too.

I started to apologize. He laughed.

It's okay, he said. I'm a hack.

Bullshit, I thought. When he'd first told me he was a programmer, I'd told him: Oh. I dated one of those, once.

And? he'd asked.

I told him I'd had a turtle once, too.

And he'd smiled, because, well, I didn't know what the hell I was talking about. Coders weren't like turtles at all. They were more like roosters—territorial, cocky, flaming one another on message boards. To them, a man who'd scrapped and won money was a successful man, with reason to strut. The richer and geekier, the holier. Linus Torvalds was a god. Woz, too. Jobs was cooler than Gates, but Gates actually wrote code, as did Zuckerberg, and that meant something. Coders were cliquey, too—Indian, Chinese, Californian. Money was the only equalizer, entrepreneur the only true ethnicity. 'Heard Yeezy was racist, well, I guess that's on one basis: I only like green faces.' –The gospel, according to Kanye West. So was Vik a rooster? He didn't strut. His heroes—Babbage, Lovelace, Morse, Turing—predated Silicon Valley. However, if the pigeonholes were indeed binary—turtle or rooster—then he'd have to let my turtle comment glance off his shell unrefuted, and that's exactly what he'd done.

You're not a hack, I said. The trail we were on was starting to steepen.

Vik considered that. How would you know? he asked.

True, I said. You don't tell me shit. I haven't been to your place. Maybe you work for some spook agency. Oh my god. Are you a spy, Vik Singh?

Nope, he said. Just a hack.

Hacks don't put a drop of lube on every single link in their chain, I said.

Thank you?

So, who's the client?

They've got me under NDA. Sorry.

It's fine.

How about this. It's a big, international conglomerate. I can say that.

So...Wal-Mart.

He laughed again, but I went quiet. I wasn't satisfied with his half-answers.

It's just number crunching, he said. Price optimization.

Mm, I muttered. And I pedaled off, pretending I was no longer curious. He caught back up and changed the subject to my job. I was at that time still a 'youth concierge' at the Ritz Carlton in Northstar. Coordinating nature walks for 'tweens, private ski lessons for toddlers. I hated it. But I needed the money.

Sometimes I wonder how *anyone* affords to live at Tahoe, I said.

By all means necessary, he said.

Like that guy who built your house.

Exactly.

I'll whore myself out before I move back to Iowa.

You've got a Ph.fucking.D., he said. You could teach at Sierra College.

Ugh.

What about this novel you keep threatening to write?

I've got a couple chapters, I said.

Can I read it?

Sorry, bro. NDA.

Message received. We pedaled on. I asked if he'd brought any brie, and when he shrugged noncommittally I glared at him over my sunglasses, both of us in on the joke. Of course he'd brought it: he knew me. And he liked me. It was plain now where things stood.

Our pace picked up and conversation dropped off, leaving space for other sounds: our breathing, the creaking of my poorly-lubricated bottom bracket which drove him insane, the faint wash of traffic on the highway far below, the crackle of tires over granite, the inescapable taunt of the Chickadee.

I stared ahead at the ceaseless pistoning of Vik's legs and worked to close the gap he'd started to put on me. I wasn't going to let him get away.

We paused at a panoramic view of the lake and the undulating Sierra—ranges to the south toward Yosemite and to the west toward Donner Pass. Half a dozen ski areas in view. Far below, boats unzipped the surface of the lake. I rested my helmeted head on Vik's shoulder. It was an awkward gesture, and for this all the more touching.

I rode off and he followed me across the face of the mountain, high above the impossibly turquoise coves and jumbled boulders of the east shore. Yellow pollen drifted out from the treetops. In a former century, timber bound for Virginia City had traversed this selfsame route in V-shaped flumes; billion-year-old water carrying hundred-year-old trees felled by twenty-year-old men—an enterprise powered by the ageless forces of gravity and greed. I tried to keep focused on the trail's treacherous contours, but the view distracted. The view and Vik. The feeling of his eyes on me.

The climb crested at Marlette Lake. Fir and pine carpeting the slopes, stands of aspen at the creek mouth and in the gullies. The windblown faces of the peaks were dotted with manzanita and sagebrush. The lake was dark blue, the sky light blue. The breeze cooled the sweat on my neck. On a prior ride, we'd followed the main road around the eastern shoreline. I started off in that direction but Vik turned across the dam. I braked to a stop.

Where're you going? I yelled.

I think there's a better spot, he said. This way.

There's no trail over there.

Exactly, he said. He stared at me. A stare like a depth sounding.

You're a curious motherfucker, Vik Singh. I wonder about you sometimes.

Well, ditto, motherfucker, he said.

He beckoned; I hesitated. For I had only just seen it— the thin strand of possibility he'd stretched across the dam. He'd known this moment was coming; it had been sitting in the pit of his stomach all morning. I, however, was confronting it for the first time, puzzling over its many facets and implications. The young man inside Vik's cottage had by this time gotten what he wanted.

Not Vik, not yet.

I turned around. Pedaled daintily across the dam in the direction he wanted to go. The one lacking a trail. Of course, I had to make light of my acquiescence.

You have the brie, I explained.

4

Neither of us had ever gone that way before. The terrain was not suited to riding, so we walked our bikes. Our cleats crunched in the pine needles. I let Vik lead, and mirrored his every cutback and route adjustment, as if to make it clear that whatever trouble we got into was entirely his doing. We contoured along the slope separating Marlette from Tahoe. We came to a fallen tree. Left the bikes. He kept the backpack.

Across the hillside we continued, still parallel to the shore. Jays screeched from the trees and glided in arcs through sunlit spaces. I could see the lake through the trees but Vik didn't cut downhill. The waterline was one long rocky ridge with steep banks. I veered around a patch of manzanita and when I came back alongside him our hands met, our fingers entwined. Neither of us commented.

We emerged from the forest into a sunlit cove. Small waves were lapping at the rocks. An osprey was perched in a dead pine tree near the shore. It cocked its head to peer at us, then returned to staring out over the world.

There really is no one over here, I said.

Vik shook his head, *nope.*

He crouched and started removing things from the backpack. I pulled my jersey up and over my head. Unstrapped my cleats and kicked them into the brush, then shimmied out of my riding shorts. They bundled at my ankles and there was no turning back. I took steps in place to free myself. Pulled my sports bra up and off.

The sunlight had not yet mellowed toward afternoon. There were no shadows to hide in. This was the unflinching light of an operating room, and I felt Vik's eyes on the constellations of moles across my back and shoulder, the stubble on my legs, the lines imprinted in my skin by the elastic of my fancy new outfit. I had dust in my hair. A breeze kicked up from across the lake. Goose bumps.

Brrrr, I said—I had to say something, anything. I picked my way down to the rocky bank. The water was crystal clear near the shore and darkened to cobalt a few feet out, the underwater slope an extension of the steep hillside we were on. I hopped up on a rock just wide enough for my bare feet and stood, balancing. I have been told (by my mother) that I have a tendency to slump my shoulders. I made sure not to. Waterlogged sticks and pinecones bobbed in the pollen-coated water near the shore.

I dove. The cold took grip of my body. A luscious sensation, the way the water melded to my skin. Eyes open, I followed diminishing vectors of sunlight into the cold dark before arcing back to the surface for air. I whooped, and the sound echoed across the water. The osprey lifted off from its branch. In a few impatient wing-beats it caught an updraft and curled out over the lake.

How's the water? Vik shouted.

Deep, I said.

He undressed, as quick as I had. Quicker.

I swam slow strokes along the shore, pretending not to see.

The precise demarcation at his sock line between his clean feet and his dusty legs.

The smudge of chain grease below his knee.

His skin, like mine, a shade or two lighter where the sun don't (typically) shine.

He crept down to the jumping rock and perched. I treaded water. I whistled at him.

He dove. Disappeared into his splash and didn't surface right away. When at last he did, his head sleek as a seal's, he was facing me. Those white teeth sparkling. That jet black hair.

Hi, I said, as if for the first time.

Hi, he replied.

Floating. Heads at the same height. Face to face in a way we'd never been. His brown eyes, their green auroras. His lashes slicked wet. I wanted to tell him all the truths bubbling up in me; how it felt to share the desolate side of the lake with him, like a secret. I wanted to thank him for getting us there.

I kept my mouth shut. It felt right to be quiet. Nor did he speak.

He kissed me, or I him. I don't know for sure. Bodies entangled. Our skin all slippery and cool, the water like silk, and when I detached and stroked toward shore, he followed. We reached a spot where our feet touched down in silt. I tied my arms around his neck, my legs around his waist. We kissed with our watery mouths. He held me up, though the water took most of my weight. We started moving against each other, his mouth at my ear. He made a noise that sounded like pain, but wasn't. I recognized it. I'd been feeling the same ache. We rid it from ourselves together.

I took a knife to the mango. Vik sat cross-legged on the ground, watching me make one cut, then another.

You're butchering it, he said.

I just started, I said.

You just started butchering it, he said.

I passed him the fruit, the knife. No offense taken.

Cradling the mango in one hand, he made a slice from top to bottom, the blade flat against the seed. A boat-shaped slab fell away and he lay it skin-down on a rock. He cut a matching cheek from the opposite side, then handed the big seed to me. A fibrous yellow corona clung to its edges.

Gnaw on that, you animal, he said.

Which I did, making a show of my uncouthness. Ignoring me, he took one of the mango cheeks face-up in his palm and made a tic-tac-toe of crosscuts that penetrated neither his nor its skin. One by one, he flayed off little yellow parallelepipeds and ate them directly from the glistening blade. I cleared my throat. He skewered one for me. I took it between my teeth. He slid the blade out clean. I handed him the avocado.

For your next trick, I said.

While we ate the things he'd brought we talked about places we'd been, places we wanted to go. We argued kind-heartedly about Radiohead and broke off squares of chocolate and lay against each other watching the osprey kiting on thermals.

He asked, Is that the same bird from the tree?

The osprey? I said. Yes.

Ah. But how do you know for sure? Have you been watching it this whole time?

No.

So you can't be sure, he said.

It's got the exact same mustache, I said. I was always trying to make him laugh.

Growing up, Vik had been led to believe that we can program ourselves, that the sole boundary condition to our success is our willingness to work. So he'd put in the time: the perfect grades that got him into Caltech; the masters degree in statistics that got him the research position at the University of San Francisco; the proposals; the papers; the moonlighting for start-ups in exchange for stock; the 70-hour workweeks; the midnight oil burned by the gallon; the appetites suppressed; the gratification delayed. He became a disciple of the cult of overwork. His father's cult. His grandfather's.

An infinite loop, as he called it.

He'd come to a small epiphany while at a conference in Boston. He'd just given a talk, and as the audience milled away, he found himself at the front of the room. I picture his acknowledgement slide still up, projecting some university-mandated collage of a campus life he never really enjoyed: a happy couple in conversation along a tree-lined walkway, a trio of cheering coeds in cutoff tops, their taut bellies painted

U, S, and F. A young woman approached the lectern. She'd been accepted to grad school in the Bay Area. She asked Vik what there was to do there, and if the weather was nice.

Vik pretended to know.

At that point, he had precious few pals and zero girlfriends. He subsisted to an unhealthy degree on fast food and energy drinks. Masturbated with a regimen not unlike exercise. His paychecks went largely unspent: he was too busy working. He dabbled in amphetamines: adderall before work, cocaine on the weekend. He tried microdosing LSD on the recommendation of a fellow programmer who insisted it made him more creative.

Vik felt nothing.

Then his father called. His father never called. Three months later he was dead of pancreatic cancer.

The two men hadn't been *estranged*, exactly. They were both just hard-working men who shared little of themselves. Men did their work. Suffered in silence. There was dignity in that. That *was* dignity. Standing over the casket—his father's scrawny body shrouded in a white sheet, his forehead smeared with ash, his withered hands pressed palm-to-palm in prayer—Vik bore witness to his own death. Or, more acutely, the life he was wasting.

He chuckles at his Hindu relatives for believing in reincarnation. But he *does* believe in Silicon Valley, where they preach the 'pivot': start-ups usually re-invent themselves, or die.

Vik's father, then, granted Vik the gift of life two times over.

Of course, I did not know any of this as I lay against him in sunlight. Vik 2.0 was the only version I'd ever known. The Vik I knew was not the type to hold his palms together in supplication. He grabbed life by the handlebars. He'd steered us into unknown territory. And though he would always look the part of a 'dots-not-feathers' Indian, he identified more with the 'feathers' lot. Given the choice—and who's to say we aren't?—who wants to be the starving yogi, humming in a hut, when they can be the wild-haired Comanche, flying across the prairie atop a hand-painted horse?

I looked out across the sparkling lake and declared: Let's never leave here.

Deal, Vik said.

But we have to, I said. Why does life have to be that way? Even when we know we're in the good parts, we know they have to end.

Vik nodded.

That time at the lake—that would be our *locus amoenus*—look it up. Or don't. It's some English Lit major bullshit.

One time, I said to Vik: You see everything as software, I see everything as literature.

Codes either way, he said.

Riding back down the mountain, we were granted the same spectacular views of Lake Tahoe we'd had on the way up, but this time we didn't stop to look. We rode until we reached the parking lot. While he loaded his bike back on his rack, I said what had been on my mind the whole ride down: I think we should eat dinner together tonight.

Like consenting adults, he said.

Like a date, I said. Yes.

And I smiled and spanked him, then pedaled away, shouting out the time and place I wanted to be picked up.

At that point, I might have argued there was no better sensation than hope; that anticipation is better than consummation; that our minds trump our bodies in this regard: we can imagine fantastic futures we can never realize. This outlook, however, dooms us to disappointment. The physical world—meatspace, as Vik sometimes called it—is never what we hope it will be. It is not virtual, and therefore not programmable. It is what it is.

Vik returned to his cottage and took a hot shower. The water rekindled the feel of our slippery bodies in the lake. He shaved. Put pomade in his hair. He wandered into the kitchen and drank two glasses of water—one to recuperate, the other to prepare. Days and nights with me can require hydration. Finally, he walked around the main room and lowered the shades on every window. Then fetched his magnifying glass.

He swiveled the iMac ninety degrees on its stand and re-positioned the desk lamp such that it shined at the row of interface ports on the back: a headphone jack, an SD card slot, four USB ports, two display ports, and an Ethernet connector. He held the magnifying glass up to the headphone jack and immediately found what he was looking for—two particles of cocaine, resting like crumbs in the bottom of the little canal, right where he'd placed them with a toothpick two months ago. He shifted his attention to the SD card slot. Two particles there, too. The USB ports were fine as well—including the first one, where he'd replaced fresh particles that morning after backing up his latest work to his thumb drive. In the Ethernet port there was a single fleck. It was absolutely miniscule, at the limit of what he could discern, and looked to be the pulverized remnant of one of the original particles.

Realization crept up the hairs on Vik's neck and over his scalp. He glanced at the front door, expecting to see someone staring in, watching.

He'd been following this routine for months; it had become perfunctory, like typing a password. And the particles were *always* there.

So maybe they'd fallen out. Glassing the desktop, he found a few bread crumbs and a layer of grayish dust toward the back, but no white particles. He adjusted the light to peer deeper into the Ethernet port and found one of the larger particles at the back, lodged in the miniscule gold teeth.

Both computers were password protected, but logins can be lifted, backdoors kicked in. In grad school, a student in Vik's research group had gone so far as to leave a webcam-enabled laptop near Vik's desk to record him typing his password—all as a prank to replace Vik's beloved Fedora operating system with Windows 95.

Vik kept his iMac an island, cut off from the internet and every other network. The ports on the back were the only way in or out.

He opened an application that kept a log of port traffic; there had been no activity all afternoon. Still, he knew how to scrub such records; anyone worth their salt would too. Hence his crude but foolproof method of detecting an intrusion.

Think.

On his way out the door that morning, he'd made one last change to his program. He rarely logged out after coding, since the computer did so automatically. The default wait time was five minutes, but he'd upped it to twenty because sometimes he sat and pondered for that long before typing again, and logging back in had gotten annoying. *Annoying!*

Vik was enraged at himself.

Had someone been waiting outside the cottage that morning?

The room swirled. The sense of good fortune he'd been enjoying all afternoon was gone in an instant. He racked his mind. He'd locked the front door when he left, but not the French doors. For someone to get in that way entailed scaling a 15-foot deck in the light of day. To do so would be brash, but not overly difficult.

He'd lulled himself into complacency. And now he was—*what?* What kind of trouble was this? He was afraid to answer that for himself.

He mapped the computer's drive. His work had last been saved at 12:25 pm. He opened the script and scrolled to where he remembered adding a final snippet of code on his way out the door. And there it was, right where he'd put it —the naïve, cavalier fool he'd been, then; a traitor to himself. Any B&E thug could have plugged into the machine and created—for anyone, anywhere on earth—a wormhole into his work. All they would have needed was a wireless hub and a few feet of CAT5 cable.

Heavy silence in the room. Vik had to swear aloud just to break it. *Fuck.*

The air felt breathed, violated. His cozy space, which had for months served as his refuge...suddenly the walls felt like windows.

Was he being watched at that moment? he wondered. Had they tracked him on the trail? At the lake?

He felt a foreignness to everything, a slipping in his gut, and before he knew it he was vomiting chocolaty bile and strands of mango into the wastebasket. He crossed the room to spit in the kitchen sink. Tried to steady himself. *Was there a reasonable explanation? Could the coke have fallen out? A breeze, a tremor?*

No. He refused to delude himself. It was the system he'd used because it was the system he trusted. He'd been compromised by someone intending to go undetected. It followed, then, that if someone was still watching, they'd want to see that all was well, that Vik remained unaware. Until Vik knew something more, he needed to act as if he knew nothing at all.

He needed to go on a date with me.

5

Nearing six o'clock. The sun still up, the roads busy, people heading wherever they wanted to be when it got dark. Vik pulled up to the condo I shared with my friend and co-worker. I waved to him through my kitchen window and moments later emerged wearing my light blue cocktail dress. I'd even put on a dusting of makeup. My hair was in a bun skewered by a black chopstick. He got out and opened the passenger door for me. He had on a gray button-up shirt and charcoal slacks.

You look so nice, I said when he got back in the car. He didn't immediately reply.

That guy back there, he said. Leaning on the car.

I turned in my seat to look out the back window. Don? I said, almost laughing.

You know him? Vik asked.

Yeah. He lives next door.

He's been staring at me.

Stares at me too, I said.

Vik looked at me for a moment. Then smiled. I took his hand.

I'm thirsty, I said with a wink.

We drove straight to a bar of my choosing, where we found plenty of my drinking buddies. Vik bought us pints of beer, then hung on for dear life as I worked the room, hugging and hazing the gathered cliques in turn. He kept trying to hold my hand, but I kept needing it, to gesture. His thumb drive dangled out of sight on a lanyard around his neck.

The bar was loud. Vik was out of his element. I was, admittedly, perfectly in mine. He was trying to follow the conversations, smiling when he should. On our drive over he'd thought about sharing at least the surface details of his situation with me. It already felt to him like too much trouble for one mind to handle. He craved empathy. Counsel. The bitter beer sloshed around in his recently purged stomach, alarms kicking on in his head.

What did Remi even see in me? he asked himself. Diving deeper, he concluded that he was only cool by association, with *me*. And didn't he have to weigh the possibility that I was in on this, whatever it was? That he might be nothing but a fool-hearted mark, seduced away from his computer. He knew the scope of the organization he was dealing with. He knew its reach.

He was standing beside me at the head of a crowded booth, watching with everyone else as I pantomimed something. The group erupted in laughter. I felt his hand at the small of my back.

Mind if we get out of here? he said.

I cocked my head at him, asking, *Really?* I recalled our earlier juncture at the dam: once again, he wanted us all to ourselves.

Sorry, he said. I'm just—I'm starving.

So I said my goodbyes. We headed toward the door together, both overdressed for the bar. In that tight-knit town, the sight of a paired-off local couple is cute enough to deserve a little ribbing. '*You kids be good.*' '*Get her home early.*' I basked in such attentions. Vik endured them.

As we drove away he monitored his mirrors.

Did you see Melissa and Sarah are fighting again? I asked.

Is Lone Eagle Grille okay? he asked. Because I need to turn...

Of course, I said, patting his leg. Mister Fancy Pants.

He put our name in with the hostess. I suggested he fetch us drinks, then excused myself to 'powder my nose,' an innocent and unintentional turn-of-phrase. He headed to the bar.

What'll it be? the bartender asked.

Lacking the mental bandwidth to peruse a cocktail menu, Vik said: Just, something with vodka. Two of them. Please...

To which the bartender nodded conspiratorially—*I got just the thing*—making a show of squeezing, shaking while Vik turned to scan the faces in the room, the garrulous groups, the quiet couples. What was he even looking for: some loner leaning in a corner? No one fit that description. And no one would. He wasn't dealing with amateurs. *He* was the amateur.

A particle moves and the whole world slips out of orbit.

Standing there felt to him like acting. He *was* acting. This awareness of his own expression. This trying to look engaged, or dumb, or drunk, whatever it took—all these people seemed to be doing a fine job of it. They were smarter than Vik in that they knew the trick. He watched sailboats through the window, crisscrossing the lake in the low-angle sunlight. Finally he noticed me, waving to him from a cocktail table I'd scored. He brought over the drinks and I pulled out a low-slung leather chair for him, the one facing the lake, but he took the one across the table instead. For he sought a different view. He handed me my drink. Its rim encrusted with sugar.

Looks good, I said. What is it?

Not sure, he said.

Didn't you order it?

It's the special.

Looks like it.

I lifted it in a toast. To Eden! I said, my eyes twinkling with firelight, my cheeks rosy from mirth and sun, my guard down. Vik glanced around. No one was in earshot.

He looked me dead in the eye and said: To Vicente Gamboa...

Our tumblers clinked. He kept his eyes locked on mine

and waited out the ensuing beats of naked silence, watching to see how the name landed in my unguarded psyche.

What he saw was...*nothing.* I looked as if I hadn't even heard him. Brought my glass to my lips. Sipped. The name he'd dropped had fallen right to the floor.

Wait, I said, licking sugar from my lip. What'd you say?

Vicente Gamboa, he said. *El Luchador.*

I don't get it, I said. I took another sip, swallowed. Sincerity incarnate.

He couldn't help but smile, he was so pleased. My reaction had been all he could have hoped for. I was either a profoundly gifted actress or legitimately unaware of this particular monster's existence in the world. I looked the part of what I must therefore have been: a happy young woman, enjoying a fancy drink with Mr. Fancy Pants himself. His toast had come off like a misfiring joke; I'd taken it perfectly in stride.

He runs a drug cartel, Vik explained. (Ha ha?)

I see, I said, holding up my glass. So, this isn't sugar on the rim?

He shook his head, no. I widened my eyes to a fiend's intensity. I started glancing around the bar, as if to see who else might have succumbed to this criminal prank by the bartender. Suddenly this was *my* joke; I was going to run with it.

And that was that. He knew: I was his ally. He got up, switched to the seat I'd originally offered and said, I want to tell you a story.

Good, I said. It's about fucking time.

So..., Vik began. I was at this party. This was a few years ago. Six, actually. *Wow...*

It was Fourth of July, he continued. This guy from work takes me to this gigantic house up in Hillsbourough. Sunny day, place is packed. Big pool out back. Definitely a Silicon Valley crowd—I talked to this anesthesiologist for a long time, I remember, and these two sisters who were starting a venture firm—but I end up in the master bathroom with two girls

I've never met and this guy: *Los.* That's his name. Mexican dude. Super skinny. He's wearing this *bright* pink polo shirt. No shoes. The three of them are doing lines of coke off the side of the bathtub. Los asks me if I want some, and I sit down on the floor with them.

At this, Vik studied me. I sat sipping my drink. I'd never felt so close to another person. I could see he was worried. We'd now shared our whole bodies but not yet our whole stories—not the intimacy of information.

So Los and I, Vik said, we start having this intense conversation. And at some point it becomes clear that he's a dealer. Or, more of a wholesaler. I start asking him all kinds of questions—how he got started, how it all worked. The girls were kind of laughing at me. Los was an open book, though. He said he'd started out selling meth to tweakers, but tweakers were unreliable. He said he preferred selling to *his kind of people*—that's how he put it—by which he meant, like, professional types, like the people at the party. *People with something to lose*, he said. By the way, back then it was five years in prison if they caught you with five grams of crack, or *five-hundred* grams of coke... Which one would you deal?

Neither, I said.

Fair enough, Vik said.

He went on: One of the girls starts telling me how Los' stuff is the best. How it's super pure. Earlier, this same girl had been complaining about a waiter who didn't know if the soup was gluten free or not...and I'd asked her, Do you know if this coke is gluten free? And she goes, It's *coke.* So I suggest that, maybe, Los cuts it with a little bit of flour... I was kidding, kind of. And Los was laughing. He told me he only bought from someone he'd known for years, and that you can tell by looking at it, that when it's pure it has a sheen, like fish scales. He showed me.

I think that's when it struck me, Vik said. You buy a box of cereal, there's a label with every ingredient, but you spend a few hundred bucks on coke, it comes in a plastic fucking baggie, and you just have to take some asshole's word that it's pure... It just seemed insane to me. Not that I'd ever really thought about it. But, I mean, these people in Palo Alto go to Whole Foods before Burning Man and stock up—organic this, non-GMO that—and then they stop in Oakland on the way out of town and give some stranger on the side of the road a thousand bucks for a baggie of white powder. And I thought, *I'd* be willing to pay a little extra, to know if it's pure. Wouldn't you?

I didn't answer. I gestured at the woman standing over Vik's shoulder. He turned, jumpy.

Singh? she said. Party of two?

I took the final sip from my drink and gathered up my purse. Vik left his drink on the table, nearly untouched. I picked it up. I handed it to him.

You can finish it, he said.

Oh, I said. I take it you're having coke with dinner?

The hostess had now stopped to wait for us, wearing a look of disinterest. I drew the twin red straws between my lips and puckered. The liquid level plunged once, then again, all the way to the bottom of the glass, the ice clinking as it stacked, the suction gurgling. I set the tumbler down and blotted coquettishly at my mouth with a cocktail napkin. Vik shook his head.

The hostess led us to a table beside a double-sided fireplace. The calm of the room was a welcome contrast to the flux of the bar. Vik ordered potato-encrusted halibut and water; I ordered a 14-oz ribeye and a glass of merlot. I draped my napkin across my lap like a story-time blanket. I was utterly enthralled with the man sitting across from me.

Go on, I said.

6

Vik continued: I took some of Los' coke to my stoner friend who worked in a chemistry lab at UCSF. Told him he could keep the sample if he tested it for me. He called the next day. Told me I could have the shit back, he didn't want it. Said it was loaded with all kinds of shit. Solvents, vitamin C, sugar, caffeine. Lidocaine. Something we later figured out was teething powder.

Like, for babies? I said.

Numbs the gums just like coke, Vik said, tossing up his hands and deploying his best smile—one rather poorly aligned with the disclosures he was making.

I eyed him with motherly concern. What'd you tell Los? I asked.

The truth.

And?

He got mad. Not at me, necessarily. He wasn't the one cutting it, it was his supplier. Still, he's out there telling people his product is super pure—because he'd never, you know, run it through a mass spectrometer. So I pitched him. I said, next time you make a purchase, get me half a teaspoon and I'll test it within an hour. Let you know if you should buy it, or walk. Los just laughed. He said that was a great way to piss people off. Powerful people.

I nodded.

Vik said, I told Los I was happy to give the test results to the *San Jose Mercury News* instead, let them do an exposé on the dangerous impurities of coke in Palo Alto. Get the whole Bay Area paranoid—all Los' dot-commer clients.

So, you blackmailed him, I said.

I got him listening, Vik replied. Sure, I didn't want to go that way, but my thinking was, *this is just good business*. I was on to something, I could feel it, and soon Los started to see it too.

You're quite the salesman.

I talked numbers. No bullshit. Los liked that, I think. From the start, all I ever told him was the truth. Eventually, he started to trust me.

He'd probably never worked with someone like you, I said. With your qualifications.

He *dealt* to people like me all the time. But, yeah. He was used to working with criminals.

Not coders, I said.

Vik smiled back. He explained that, in India, his grandmother had picked tiny white stones out of the rice she bought by weight at the bazaar, stones the sellers intentionally put there. In college, he'd learned to call this 'information asymmetry': when buyers don't know what they're getting, crooked sellers win. But the opposite can be true. Arm the buyer with information, and honest sellers win. That's what he was trying to get Los to see.

It helped that Los was young, Vik explained. Not set in his ways. Actually, he reminded me of some of the entrepreneurs I've worked with—very Bay Area bohemian, talking free love *and* free markets, with that same distrust of government, that same talk of *disruption*...

Sounds like you had a crush, I said.

Vik was taken aback by this. He smiled, but clammed up. Sensing I'd struck a nerve, I peeled back the napkin on a basket of bread and offered it across the table. He accepted a roll.

Yeah well, he said, chewing. Eventually we got the quality dialed on the supply side, but we needed a way to differentiate ourselves. People needed to know they were getting something better than the street stuff, or else why pay a premium? I had this idea to sell the coke in these cool glass vials that I got in bulk from a chemistry supply place. We put a drop of red wax on the cap to seal it. Like a tamper-proofing thing. I mean, Los was a high-end dealer already, but once this shit hit the scene, people in the valley went nuts for it. They started calling it 'red-dot' coke. It became something of a status symbol.

That was you? I said. Red Dot was *you*? Now I was the one looking around the restaurant. I was in the palm of Vik's hand.

You've heard of it? Vik said, excited.

Of course, I said. I've never had any, but everybody *knows* about Red Dot.

Vik nodded. It was gangbusters there for a while, he said. Los paid to get the rights to 'red dot com.' I hosted the site anonymously from some Russian server. I wrote a little app where you could text a picture of the label on the vial and see a print-out of the analytics from that particular batch. It was about as legit as we could be without being legit, or giving away who we were. And I still went to the newspaper—it was Los' idea, actually—and they bit on the story. They actually included Red Dot in their little report, and of course it came up pure as hell. It was a fucking PR coup!

I still can't believe that was *you*.

Sometimes neither can I.

Weren't you afraid you'd get caught?

A little. But I never had much in my possession. I audited a class at UCSF to get access to the lab, and found a way to scrub all our tests from the instrument's memory. At first Los had us running a sample a week, then pretty soon it was a sample *a day*. I pulled in almost two-hundred grand that year, working like 20 hours a week.

Jesus.

I know. Los was sending just *insane* amounts of cash back to Mexico, on flatbed trucks. He was bankrolling this huge extended family. He went to church every Sunday. He said he prayed for his country. *Poor Mexico*, he'd say. *So far from God, so close to the United States...*

Can you still buy Red Dot?

Oh I'm sure, Vik said. But it won't be ours. Our packaging was too easy to copy. Eventually, imposters started selling their stepped-on shit with red wax on it. But by then, Los' customer base had grown exponentially. He was fine.

I could only shake my head.

Crazy, right? Vik said. Trust me, Remi, from that side, everything looks different. *Everybody* is using. I'd be in a grocery store and I'd look around and try and guess our customers. Even the dealers were…well, some were thugs, definitely. But there was this honors student from Redwood City. He said there were so many kids on Ritalin at his high school that coke wasn't a hard sell. There was an ER doc. A mom in Oakland, she was a florist. For her, it was crossover clientele: rich white ladies.

The way you describe it, it's almost like…

Like it's *legal*, Vik said.

Exactly.

I straightened up as a waiter arrived tableside with steaming plates in hand. He mistakenly delivered the ribeye to Vik. Vik pointed across the table.

She eats like a man, he said, trying to catalyze a little laughter. I wasn't laughing though. I felt caught in transition, outpaced by the quick changeover Vik had made from clandestine to cavalier. I couldn't tell, yet: did his revelations make him more alluring, or newly frightening? I leaned across the table. The candle flame tilted with my breath as I asked: Why are you telling me all this?

Are you upset?

No, I'm just… It's a lot to take in, that's all.

Vik was disappointed by my primness, and looked it. Over the years, he'd become frustrated by the hypocrisy of the 'party line,' as he called it: coke being cool to snort, just not to sell. Getting high being somehow nobler than getting rich.

I've hidden a lot of things from a lot of people, Vik said. I don't want to hide anything from you.

I don't want you to, I said. It's just…this afternoon at the lake, I thought I knew you on some level. Maybe that was naïve. You never really know anybody, do you? Not if they don't want you to.

But I *want* you to know me, Vik said. I'm sure there's things you haven't told *me* yet.

I cut into my steak. I have some scar stories, I said. But, I never dealt coke if that's what you mean.

That makes two of us.

What do you call it, then—what you did?

Consulting.

Ah, I said. My dad used to say a consultant is someone you give your watch to, then ask what time it is.

Yeah, well, Vik said.

I guess nobody trusts themselves, I said.

Vik nodded at the truth in that. The sadness of it.

This latest client of yours, I said. Is there really a non-disclosure agreement? Or...

Or...what? Vik asked.

Please, I pleaded. I'm not *judging*. I have no right.

I lowered my head, incapable of reflecting the intensity of Vik's gaze. It was my turn to talk.

I used to steal, I said.

7

Steal what? Vik asked.

Everything, I said. My bike...

You stole that?

My skis, I said—and, wanting a worthy counterbalance to Vik's confession, I added: And stuff from the rooms.

At the hotel? he asked, astonished—surely wondering: *What happened to the prudish Remi I sat down to dinner with?* He'd gambled on my trust. And I'd called his bet.

We had a little scheme, I said, keeping my voice low. Have I introduced you to Alex, the girl I work with? You'd like her. She's smart.

Vik didn't know what to say to that.

I went on: These rich kids get dropped off, their parents go skiing or head into town, whatever. Sometimes they're gone all day. So one of us takes the kids, the other goes through their stuff. They almost always have room keys, and we know the room numbers from the sign-up forms. It's just a matter of sneaking upstairs for a quick look.

You're still doing this?

Well, not anymore.

Why'd you stop?

Nerves, I said. It was like backcountry skiing. Eventually, I was going to trigger an avalanche.

I don't ski, Vik said.

It's a matter of odds, is all. You understand *that*. My number was going to come up.

I see, Vik said.

Problem was, I said, it kept *working*. I think because we never took very much. I'd peel a few bills off a roll of cash, or take *one* diamond earring, or write down a credit card number. Shit that wouldn't be missed, at least not right away. And if it was, it'd be hard to prove it wasn't just lost. Maybe I'd nab a kid's iPad. These people—there's so damn rich they leave behind brand new skis all the time. Bottles of Dom. The maids pocket stuff too. And yet the lost and found still looks like an Apple store. Hardly anyone ever calls to claim any of it. It's probably less of a hassle for them to just buy more stuff.

It felt cathartic, telling Vik all this. He was relishing it. He asked what we did with all the stuff we stole.

Alex knows a guy, I explained. He fenced it all. Down in Reno.

Whatever means necessary, he said, quoting our earlier conversation—a chat between two very different people, clearly.

Exactly, I said. This is *Tahoe*. These are some of the richest people in the world we're talking about. So, what?—a pair of Manolo Blahnik's goes missing and they shrug it off, but I cover half my rent. They *need* people like me to watch their little brats, just like they need a bunch of bros to load their chairlifts, and some *senoritas* to change their dirty sheets, but the insane thing is, none of us can afford to live here. Not without taking steps.

It's true, Vik said.

It *is* true, I insisted—because I wasn't sure he believed it.

But then I hesitated: all of this confessing smacked of one-upmanship. I was ready to just stop talking, call a stalemate. I sensed that Vik was of similar mind. I picked up my fork and knife and sawed back into my ribeye.

Damn. Delicious. I skewered a piece and held it across the table on my fork. Vik lowered his head like a supplicant, accepting into his mouth the meat of an animal he'd seen roaming the streets of New Delhi with impunity. He returned to picking at his fish, which paled in comparison. He'd been out-ordered. I lifted my glass of wine and sat back. We eyed each other across the table.

What? he asked.

Nothing, I said. Just, what's our plan?

For *us*?

For *tonight*. This little date. Are we going to take a romantic walk down the pier? Get a milkshake with two straws?

I take it you think those are bad ideas, Vik said.

Not necessarily, I said.

But you have a better one.

Depends, I said.

On what?

If you've got any Red Dot.

I brought my napkin to my mouth to hide my smirk. I took my time wiping it off my face, knowing I wouldn't be able to get all of it.

We left the restaurant hand in hand, thick as thieves. The valet bid us a polite 'goodnight', which we returned in kind. Ahead of us on the path was a well-dressed elderly couple, helping each other down a granite staircase. Vik escorted us politely around them, his hand on my back. At the Mercedes, he opened my door for me. I pinched his ass.

Vik was trying all the while to keep himself reined in. Was pleasure even possible in his foreseeable future? Or would he need to remain forever on edge, watching the sky for hawks like a vigilant rodent?

The parking lot was nearly full. Rows of luxury hoods gleamed under the overhead lights; darkness had settled into the forest.

This is just a ruse to finally see your place, I said, my hand on his thigh as he sped up the hill.

It's quaint, he said.

The cottage glowed warmly through the windows, all the curtains drawn. As soon as we got inside, I kicked off my shoes and floated around, taking it all in.

The main room was anchored by a stone fireplace, the focal point of a deep-seated sectional couch upon which

Vik had the previous night, after two days working almost without a break, fallen asleep half-watching TV (while being half-watched himself). The TV had been stolen from a drug dealer, who'd stolen it, more or less, from Vik. White bookshelves flanked the fireplace. On the wall was a framed drawing of a placer miner kneeling beside a creek and staring into his pan with a look of shifting fortune on his filthy face. The cottage had come furnished with art. This drawing was the only piece Vik had kept.

I wandered over to the computers and stood, contemplating.

Vik opened the French doors. I followed him outside. The deck was littered with pine needles. He knew he needed to clear them off: we'd all seen the flyers stapled outside the post office, Smokey Bear pointing accusatorily: *DO YOU HAVE DEFENSIBLE SPACE?* We stood there together, looking over the lake, inhaling the mountain air.

Hideous, I said.

Mm, he said.

You're *way* up here. You can look down your nose at all the snobs.

They're not snobs, he said.

Oh? I said. You know these people?

He did not reply, and I regretted my tone.

In fact, he'd always felt like a squatter. Rumbling up the hill in his aging diesel, he'd registered his neighbors' inquisitive stares and half-hearted waves, the vigilance of their Labradors, and wondered why they'd never stopped by to say hello, nor invited him to one of the many soirees he'd glimpsed through the trees on weekends. At the very least he'd expected someone to come by under auspices of neighborliness and peek inside the cottage, confirm it wasn't a meth lab or—worse?—tackily redecorated, all Punjabi-ed out, the air thick with incense. But no: they'd left him alone. He'd wanted to call this prejudice, but suspected it was something milder, some congenital allergy to the nouveau riche. Maybe his neighbors saw no point in befriending someone who surely couldn't ski. He'd rented a P.O. box in town; still, mail came daily to the cottage—catalogues and junk mail addressed to the prior owner's wife, or to his more fittingly anonymous designation, 'Resident.' He'd recently installed a flagpole beside the front door from which he flew the stars and stripes, lest there be any doubt.

I felt closer to Vik at that moment than I'd ever felt to anyone.

C'mon, he said—leading us back inside. He left me in the kitchen while he went to get one of the two remaining vials of Red Dot he kept in a bathroom drawer. As he did, he felt jealous of the lucky bastard he saw reflected in the mirror —*that* guy got to have all the fun. The one in his head had to do all the worrying.

So do I just?..., I said, leaning over the inch-long white line Vik had laid out on the granite countertop using a piece of the junk-bond trader's junk mail. Vik nodded. I plugged one nostril with my thumb and vacuumed the granite clean. Righting myself, I coughed, one eyelid quivering. Vik squared up a line for himself.

It had been awhile since Vik had partaken. More had gone into computer ports than noses that summer.

The high came on immediately. I hadn't known what to expect. Los once summed the feeling up for Vik as: *you can bench press the world.* I've never bench-pressed anything, but I think I know what Los meant. I felt...tremendous. For Vik though, the cottage closed in like a cell. The light turned harsh. He went to pour himself a glass of water. Meanwhile I went to the stereo cabinet, and summoned Kanye West: a hoarse taunt, a teasing beat, the bass not yet let off its leash. Then, silence as I skipped ahead to the next song. The next. More beats beginning, only to be truncated. Finally I found the one I wanted. I let it play. The room filled to capacity with the music. It rattled things.

I'm starting to feel good, I yelled—gyrating back across the room, one hand in the air. Like, really, *really* good!

For thirty minutes, Vik yelled back.

That's all? I said.

I stepped directly in front of him.

That's all, he said.

My fingers are tingling, I said.

Vik smiled. *Fuck it*, he thought. *Let the bass thump.*

He reached up, past my ear, and tugged the chopstick out of my bun. My hair tumbled down. We kissed, soft at first but then with aggression. We hastily undressed each other. Our senses heightened to unnatural registers. Our eyes and mouths and hands taking turns, taking each other in.

In removing Vik's shirt, I found his memory stick lanyard. Vik thought I was going to tease him about it, but I simply draped it around my own neck. Vik stared down at it—all those precious bits flashed into its silicon, bits he'd been mining for months, the sole source of his income and his moxie and his present danger, dangling like a summer-camp charm in my cleavage. The only thing I had on. Mind-blowing.

He looped a finger through the lanyard and led me, practically purring, to the bedroom.

Later, with me fully done for—diagonal and naked, hair in my gaping mouth, hoarding all the available pillows, making little hums—Vik lay awake. He stared out the window at the moonlit mountainside, where denuded ski runs looked like the clawings of some colossal beast—marks made in claim of territory, or in violence, or merely to encode proof upon the world that it too had passed through it. It was ten o'clock at night. Vik pulled on clothes and slipped back into the main room.

Kanye had played himself out. A hum of static issued from the speakers. Vik fell into the couch, where the ideas seemed always to come looking for him, with or without his consent. He had never found an 'off' switch. The vapors started to swirl. It was either trap them then and there, or lose them back to the ether. With a few more solid days of work, he could deliver something. But what would that mean, he wondered, in light of recent developments?

He got up and went into the kitchen. The vial of Red Dot was still open on the counter. He laid out a bump. Hit it. Fired up the computers.

8

Vik awoke on the couch. The sunlight in the room seeming to him out of sync. He checked his phone: 11:15. *Damn.* He'd worked until the sky had gone pink before succumbing. Under the circumstances, sleep had seemed self-indulgent.

He spoke my name. No reply. He went to the bedroom, found it empty. Went out to the street. His car was right where he'd parked it. Went to the storage closet. Found himself staring up at an empty hook.

I was standing in my bathroom with a towel wrapped around my head, getting ready for work when my phone buzzed.

Hey, I answered. It's my dealer!

I'm calling to report a stolen bike, he said.

I steal things, I said.

I heard you quit.

I lie.

I see.

I needed it to get home, I said. I'll bring it back. Soon.

No hurry, he said. On the bike, that is. As for you...

I miss you too, I said.

Vik peered casually over his deck railing at the hillside

below. In the soft black soil was what looked like a boot print. He rushed back inside and got all the way to the front door, ready to circle around the cottage on the ground for an up-close look, but stopped. He would just have to trust his hunch, haunting as it was. Snooping around would only prove to anyone watching that he knew they were there.

The next two days were for him a blur of code. He didn't eat so much as consume calories. When he did sleep, he napped on the couch, never in his bed, and upon waking would feel the buzz of new ideas. He chain-drank espressos. The work kept his mind off looming things. He'd decided it was the only thing he *could* do. The only way to be proactive. He showered on the second afternoon, and ran the water so cold he could only *sense*, not *process*. He stood there shivering until his skull ached.

I knew he was going hard, and kept in touch with him via text. I was fine with some space after such an intense day together. It seemed, actually, to be the perfect move on my part, though it wasn't a 'move.' I wasn't playing cool; I wasn't playing at all.

On our second afternoon apart I texted him: *can we hang out?*

i wish. got momentum, have to keep crankin. almost done tho...

k.

soon!...sorry...

An hour later his doorbell rang, and there I stood, wearing a pink spaghetti-strap bikini and cutoff jeans. It was a warm, beautiful evening. I could smell the stale air of the cottage come wafting out. Vik looked around, almost squinting. My friend Alex sat in the driver seat of her idling pickup. Vik waved, Alex waved. Alex never likes my boyfriends. The ragged t-shirt Vik had on was the same one he'd been wearing the morning I slipped out.

I handed him a warm paper bag from which emanated the locally-famous aromas of *T's Mesquite Rotisserie*. He pulled me partway into the cottage and kissed me. His ravenousness a revelation. He'd been starving for this.

Sorry to just show up, I said—not meaning it.

No, no, he said. Thank you for coming.

I ran a hand through his hair and glanced past, into the cottage. I worry about you, I said, up here all by yourself. How's it coming?

Fast and furious, he said. He looked down, ashamed: a prisoner in his little palace.

Go back to the matrix, I said. I'll be here when you come out. I have an idea.

Sounds dangerous, he said.

More dangerous than writing software, I said.

I kissed him, tugging at his waistband, then left him to his devices.

As Alex's pickup receded down the hill, Vik dug into the roasted chicken right there on the porch, tearing away the breast meat, gnawing at the bones, wiping his mouth on the back of his hand. I'd brought him a cold bottle of Coke and warm tortillas and little cups of black beans and rice.

Were we a couple? both of us were wondering, simultaneously.

Sunset was nearing. The shadows had crept halfway down the mountain. Vik went back inside and did as I'd commanded. By midnight, he could see the end. There was no more creativity required, only execution. A feeling of completeness swept over him. He sat back, eyes dull, neck tight, the room peaceful. He scrolled one last time through his work.

It was the best thing he'd ever written.

And yet all he could think about was me.

9

Thursday. Twilight. Vik and I tracing the northwest edge of the lake in his Mercedes. The traffic on the road light. In certain stretches the lakefront homes gave way to panoramic vistas, and we looked out upon the water to see it giving back the purples and blood-oranges of a cloudbank smoldering above the Sierra. Faintly visible above the far shore, the trail we'd ridden together.

We'd re-united earlier that day, after my half-day at work, and eaten eggs at a diner in town. Lots of coffee, lots of sidelong looks and good-natured joking. Both of us, it seemed, a little skittish and silly over our fledgling relationship, neither of us ready to get much closer just yet, having already revealed so much. At my suggestion we'd gone to an actual romantic comedy and shared an actual milkshake. Vik's nerves were fried. I could see it in his eyes.

For me, some long-festering cynicism had started to recede. I felt myself tingling back to life. I craved Vik so much it pained me; I felt like a lovesick teenager for the first time since actually being one, and this brought me great joy—pride, even. I felt open-hearted and vulnerable. This made it almost impossible to do what I was doing.

I'd cooked up a surprise for our evening out. All Vik knew was the destination: Tahoe City. Also that we were already running late.

He hit the gas and shot out across a double yellow to

pass a van. He kept glancing in the rear-view. I looked in the side mirror, saw a pickup there. Vik accelerated again, passed another car. I gripped my door handle.

We don't need to get arrested, I said. Or killed.

He patted my knee.

Or petted, I said.

Roger that, he said.

We reached Tahoe City just before seven. I pointed to a shopping center along the shore. Vik hadn't shut the engine off before I had my door open. He had to jog to catch up. I took his hand and steered us past restaurants and shops toward the waterfront, where rows of boats were moored to buoys. A sixty-foot cruise boat with twin smokestacks and faux paddlewheels was docked against a long pier. Some people were making their way across a gangplank to the bow; others sipped cocktails below festooned lights on the top deck. Music carried over the water.

You don't get seasick, do you? I asked.

No, Vik said, though—like the weather and the extracurricular opportunities of the Bay Area—he didn't actually know.

Good, I said, because this is like my favorite thing.

It was true: I used to go alone all the time. Pretend I was a tourist. I love being around people taking pictures. All that. I like seeing it through those eyes again.

I plucked Vik's wallet from his back pocket, then rushed away to buy tickets for the moonlight cruise.

Vik stayed put and let the world spin. A pair of men were wheeling cases of beer and wine through a door on the hull of the boat. He envied their honest job for honest pay.

I waved him over. A woman in an ill-fitting sport coat tore our tickets.

Ya'll made it in the nick of time, she said.

Are we last on? Vik asked.

Looks like it, the woman said.

We crossed the gangplank and took a place on the bow. Our little scramble was over. We'd made it. I snuggled up to Vik, my head to his heart. I saw a man arguing with the agent at the ticket booth. The man gestured at his watch, the boat.

He was fifty yards away, but I felt him looking right at us.

I said nothing.

Huge engines rumbled; lines were tossed free. The boat slipped its moorings and backed out into the open water, listing. We slipped away from the glimmer of the wharf and struck a southern course across the blackening lake. The bustling galley was lined with big windows. The walls were red; the carpet blue. Tables were arranged in rows like a cafeteria. A line had already formed at the bar.

I led us up a flight of grip-taped stairs to the top deck, behind the pilot house. More tables and chairs outside, plus plenty of my beloved tourist types with their sunburns and sensible shoes. I overheard a kind-looking family recounting a water-ski wipeout. An American flag angled off the stern. I picked out a table against the railing, its chairs facing overboard. The lakefront mansions glowed like jack-o-lanterns.

We took seats and were quiet for a spell. We stared at the moon's reflection on the water. I reached across Vik's lap to set my bag on an empty seat beside him.

Buffer, I explained. So we can talk.

More about our criminal pasts, he joked.

Is that what it is for you, then? I said. The past?

Vik looked at me, trying to get a read. All day long we'd managed to keep the conversation light. I, too, was weary about wading back into deep water. And yet, here we were.

You want to know if I'm still involved in that kind of thing, he said.

Sort of, I said. Yeah.

Damn, Vik thought. For he'd been enjoying our date, his paranoia suppressible. He'd even laughed at the rom-com. He watched the tranquil open water slip under the bow, heard the props scrambling it up. A girl at a nearby table was staring at us as if she too were waiting for Vik to speak. But the longer he held out, the more conspicuous he felt about saying anything at all. Every possible revelation, he knew, would betray someone.

I bent down, my hands came to my face. It came as a surprise to me, but I'd begun to cry.

*Remi...*Vik said, confused. He wanted to embrace me,

this hardcore girl who now seemed too fragile to touch. He lay a tentative hand on my back.

I spoke into cupped hands: This is insane. I shouldn't have done this.

Done what? Vik asked. He had no idea.

This, I said. I shouldn't be here. I shouldn't be asking you this. I feel like I'm trapped.

Vik let out a little laugh. You're the one who tricked me onto this boat, he said.

Suddenly, I felt enraged. At myself. At the situation. I felt myself coming unglued. I refused to raise my voice, but by the look in my eye I may as well have been roaring. I asked Vik a question he couldn't answer: How did I ever get myself into this?

What are you talking about? he said.

It's all just...*pressing in*.

He took my hand. We can trust each other, he said. Didn't we decide that?

But you shouldn't trust me, I said. I'm not honest.

Because you stole a few things? he asked. Because, that doesn't matter. Not to me. You're honest in different ways. You're honest with *me*.

I'm not, I said.

Okay. Well, it seems like you're trying to be.

I couldn't speak. The moon hung above the mountains on the eastern shore. Evening stars were blinking to life. The time had come to make a choice.

I don't know what's holding you back, Vik said. It's just you and me.

You'll hate me, I said.

That isn't possible, he said.

I looked him deep in the eyes, and I believed him. Tell me, he whispered. So I did.

I got caught two weeks ago, I said. Like, red-fucking-handed. Some parents came back to the room early, found me. I had a bracelet in my pocket, some cash. I got taken down to the police station in Truckee.

Vik nodded. It's okay, he said.

I went on: They put me in a room with this asshole cop.

I've seen him around. They hadn't caught my friend yet, but they seemed keen on linking me with a bunch of unsolved burglaries at the hotel. I was facing felonies, jail time. That avalanche I was talking about? It hit. But this dickhead cop —he starts asking me all these weird questions. Like, about my life. He knew things about me—*a lot*, actually. He knew about you.

Vik's whole face changed, from sympathetic to startled.

Really? he said.

He knew we were friendly, yeah. He started asking what *you* did, who *you* hung out with.

What'd you say?

I said it was none of his business. Then he made this face, like, *we'll see about that*, and he left.

Remi, I...

Vik, please. Just listen. This other officer came in. He's *DEA*, though. He starts asking the same questions. So I was like, what are you guys really after? I thought this was about *me*.

Vik's heart had become a fist.

So that's when it started, I said. This DEA guy, he asks: *How'd you like to fly out of this jail tonight, like a little birdie?* That's how he said it, I'll never forget. So stupid. Of course I told him I'd like that. But the deal was, I had to keep up my relationship with you. They wanted to know what you were working on, who you were working with, where you went...

Is this a joke? Vik asked.

No, I said. I'm dead serious. I asked them how long I had to do this, and they said as long as it takes. They said to get you to brag.

Brag? About what?

How should I know?

So, you agreed to spy on me?

I agreed to stay close to you.

So this is all bullshit? These last few days? You're just a —I won't even *say* it...

Vik felt the same stirrings of fury he'd felt at the cheating dealer's apartment. He'd thought he'd tamed it for good.

I felt like the lowest person on earth. I'd come to terms with being a thief. But not a liar.

I told you this would happen, I said.

Yeah? Well, what do you want me to say? I can't even think right now, this is so *fucked*.

I agree, I said.

So what *did* they tell you? Vik asked.

Almost nothing.

Vik stared at me.

Just, they thought you might be involved with a cartel, I said. Spoken aloud, the truth can sound ridiculous. Vik's chin fell to his chest.

I'm only telling you what they told me, I said. Apparently the DEA was tailing some guy—this was months ago, before I even *met* you—and they watched him go up to your house in San Jose and drop off a duffel bag.

And you believed them? Vik asked.

Why would they make that up? I said. They said they couldn't figure what someone like you was doing for people like them. I guess neither could I...

Someone like me, Vik muttered—remembering how it felt, counting the stacks of bills from that particular duffel drop-off—an odd amount, and more than he'd been owed. Probably because the money hadn't been counted, but weighed.

I'm just repeating what they told me, I said. They check in with me every few days, but it seems like they don't really know very much. And honestly, neither do I.

You know more than I've ever told anyone, Vik said.

But, can't you see how I got stuck? I said. I mean, we'd hooked up a couple times, but it wasn't too serious. The DEA made you sound, well—*dangerous*. Which didn't compute for me. But I figured, maybe they were saving me from something. I'd be stupid not to take a deal.

You know exactly who Vicente Gamboa is. Don't you.

I gave an embarrassed shrug.

Quite the actress, Vik said.

I sat in judgment. Guilty as charged. Not that Vik wasn't feeling something similar. Were our crimes so great, though? Sometimes, getting away with something can feel like license to continue.

We were far enough out on the lake now to see back to the quaint, twinkling hillside of Incline Village. Another world.

I spoke next, almost in a whisper: There was a bust in San Diego. This was a few weeks ago. Some IT guy at the DEA cracked into a dealer's phone and found some weird software...

At this, I turned to watch Vik's reaction, for my revelation had been more of a question. He wore a look of either anger or fear, or both. He seemed to be recoiling from himself.

I know how this all sounds, I said.

How it sounds? Vik said. How it *sounds!*

Heads turned at nearby tables. Two men eyed us, ready to intervene. Everything okay there? one of them said.

We're fine, I said. I reached out and took Vik's closed hand.

You have every right to hate me, I said. I understand if you never want to see me again.

But first we have to take a romantic cruise together, is that it? Vik said. Straight to federal prison...

Hold on, I said. I think you're seeing this all wrong.

Really? Vik said. What is it I'm not understanding?

I explained: When I signed on for this, I was being totally selfish. I was just hoping to save myself. And I didn't think there was much risk. I thought, *Vik won't tell me anything.* Because, why would you? I was just some girl. And you were so...smart. We weren't as close then.

What about Marlette? Vik asked. Our ride.

That had nothing to do with this, I said—knowing how untrue that must have sounded.

How could it not? Vik asked.

Because it was your idea, I said. And because I wanted it, too. These past few days, I've gotten in over my head. So many times I wanted to tell you everything. It felt like a lie, when I wanted so bad to be close to you in a real way. The more you opened up, the more overwhelmed I got. By *honesty*. Here you are, finally trusting me. But the more you tell me, the more I'm betraying you. I got scared you were going to tell me everything.

Are you wearing a wire? Vik asked.

A wire? *No.*

And I'm supposed to just believe that.

I guess you don't have to. I could show you...

Have you been wearing one? he asked.

You've seen me naked, I said—suddenly surly. Did you notice one?

I recalled that feeling of exposure at the lake, perched atop the rock at the waterline, before I took the plunge.

Why are you telling me all this? Vik asked. What do you gain?

Don't you get it? I said. I gain *nothing.* I'm in serious shit if they find out.

Wait: you think you're *helping* me?

Of course, I said. Because I did.

I went on: I mean, can't you just claim this is just a big misunderstanding? You're a consultant, right? You write software. So who's the victim? How is what you're doing even...

Illegal? Vik said.

Exactly, I said—relieved to hear him finish off the argument. I reached past him and grabbed my bag off the chair. Took out my USB memory stick.

A copy, I said, of *yours.*

Vik was completely lost for words.

That night, I said. I woke up early and your little nerd necklace was on the nightstand. You were crashed out. I figured it might be worth something. So I took it home.

Vik felt at his chest, feeling the drive there...

Well, I put it back. I thought I'd have to play it off, but when I rode back up the hill that morning you were still dead to the world, so I just put it back.

Don't worry, I said, reading the look on his face. I haven't given it to anyone.

Did you look at the files?

Yes, I admitted. They're all just Kanye West songs, right? (I'd even played one.)

Vik nodded. He seemed unsurprised.

I only made one copy, I told him. *This* one. The DEA doesn't know about it. I guess it was my insurance policy. But that was *before...*

Before what?

Before I started falling in love.

10

The word landed like a body punch. Vik wanted to pretend he hadn't heard it—but that's *my* trick (*To Vicente Gamboa!*). Vik can't act. While he'd kept his share of secrets over the years, he had trouble passing off lies. He could protect better than pretend. I, apparently, am quite the opposite.

Love? Vik thought. His head swam.

He asked, How can you possibly say that?

I know, I said. It's not fair. And I'm sorry. I'm *so* sorry. I didn't think it could come to this. I just thought...

You thought of yourself, Vik said.

I nodded—taking the blame right on the nose.

Meanwhile, Vik was struggling to catch up. For days he'd been trying to understand *why* his computer had been infiltrated. At least now it was making some sense. Time was of the essence. A continent of distribution channels were at risk, billions of dollars. He hadn't delivered his new code fast enough, so they'd stolen what he had, no payment made. He wondered: was there another coder, then?—someone good enough to tie tourniquets on his algorithmic loose ends? *Shoot the engineer.* So say the marketing guys when a program gets stuck in development. Because there comes a time to forgo perfection for profit and get the thing out the door. No one, it seems, thinks further ahead than the next score.

Love? Vik thought.

Earlier, Vik said. There was a man on the dock.

I noticed him, too, I said—a little overeager to please. But I haven't known the cops to be following me. Otherwise I wouldn't have...

It's okay, Vik said. For he was beginning to see that, regardless of what harm I'd already done—and I couldn't have done much: he'd only just started opening up to me—I *was* putting myself at risk. I *was* trying to help. It was at that moment he decided he ought to let me.

When we were riding to the lake, he said. Did something go down?

What do you mean?

Like an operation.

What?

Were you supposed to keep me away from the house?

Definitely not. (This, like everything else I'd told him since getting on the boat, was the absolute truth.)

Well, someone broke in, he said. I think they may have stolen my work.

Jesus, Vik! Why didn't you tell me?

I am.

Now.

Yes, *now.*

I chewed my lip and looked around. I didn't think the DEA had enough on you to *act*, I said. I mean, that's why they wanted my help, right?

The DEA would need evidence, you mean, Vik said. A warrant.

Exactly, I said with too much conviction, as if my surety on this matter was all the protection Vik needed. So he waited, watching as comprehension settled into my eyes, followed by terror, as I too glimpsed the beast he'd already seen charging us. The DEA was indeed bound by rule of law; Q.E.D., this wasn't the DEA.

Vik leaned into me, speaking in my ear: *I was falling, too*, he said.

I was unsure. Was that a reassuring, or utterly cruel, thing to say?

Was, I clarified.

He lowered his head to my shoulder. A half-nod, a half-truth. Perhaps that's all we were capable of, he and I. I pressed my forehead to his, our eyes inches apart, mine imploring, tearing up. His already seeing past me.

He straightened up. We need a drink, he said. He rubbed together the tokens we'd been issued. What'll it be?

I wiped at my cheeks. I guess it depends, I managed. What're *you* having?

Water, he said.

I looked at him askew, unaware that he'd encrypted a message. I wouldn't crack it right away, but that was okay. I would eventually. He knew me.

Surprise me, I told him.

The bartender was taking stemware from a wooden rack affixed to the galley ceiling and pouring drinks as fast as she could. Vik leaned against a support beam, as if waiting his turn. He listened to the muddled conversations and stared out the window at the scrolling shoreline. An elderly couple played cards at a nearby table, their reflections in the window creating a foursome. At the base of the woman's chair was a hiking backpack with a Nalgene bottle protruding from its side pocket. Vik started across the room, then kneeled to re-tie his laces. When he rose he had the Nalgene clutched against his body. He did a lap of the galley as if looking for someone, then slipped down a hallway.

He passed the humming engine room from which emanated a feint reek of diesel. The hallway came to a 'T' at the stern. Turning right led to a pair of unisex bathrooms. He exchanged polite glances with a woman waiting in the dim passageway. Turning left led to the man door he'd noticed at the dock, through which the booze had been carted aboard. Above this door, a sign: *EMERGENCY EXIT—ALARM WILL SOUND.*

He went to the door and peered through the window. One of the bathrooms opened up; the woman stepped in. Momentarily alone, he examined the door and located the sensor pair affixed to its frame. Traced the wire up the wall to the ceiling, then back along the hallway to an alarm keypad. He made this examination hastily, for he was now back in view of the galley. The keypad was mounted at shoulder height. He leaned back against the wall as if waiting for the bathroom, meanwhile blocking the view of the keypad, then reached up with his off hand and pried off the cover plate. A small speaker was mounted in the corner of the printed circuit board. He hooked his finger around the speaker's red wire, severed the solder connection with a yank, and replaced the cover plate.

Back at the door, he unfastened the deadbolt, gripped the knob and, glancing around again, pulled the door open.

The night air. The water, like obsidian.

A red light started flashing in the hallway, but no alarm had sounded. He replaced the door in its jam, but did not re-lock it. The flashing stopped.

The woman re-emerged from the bathroom. Vik stepped in. Poured iced tea out of the wide-mouth Nalgene bottle and wiped its inside dry. Lifted the thumb-drive lanyard from his shirtfront and lowered it into the bottle. Followed by his wallet. His phone was too wide. So be it: this was an inevitability. He considered tapping out a message to me, but thought better of it, knowing it might be used against me. He scrolled to my contact info and memorized it, then put the phone back in his jeans, re-capped the Nalgene, and lashed it to his waist with his belt.

Stay or go, he thought. *Fight or flight*. The binary choice men have faced for millennia, and choosing correctly often enough, it seems; the 3.4 gigabytes of code inside Vik's every cell was a proven algorithm. It had survived, leaping from body to body on twisted ribbons, down the generations, debugging itself. It was in Vik; he ran the script. Would it keep him alive, too? Could the code inside the Nalgene? He stepped out of the bathroom; a little boy ducked in.

With the hall momentarily empty, Vik opened the man door and stepped through, tossing it shut behind him as he fell.

The shock of the water. He made himself dive. The

cold clutching at him. Clothing compressing against skin. He heard the high-pitched whir of the propellers. He pushed himself out, away from the boat, floundering through the emptiness. Eyes open or closed, it didn't matter. When he could hold his breath no longer he rushed to the surface, sucked at the thin air, and floated for a spell, rocking on the waves shed by the boat. Hanging off its stern, beside an American flag, was a lifesaver, but he could hear only casual chatter on the top deck. Party lights danced upon the water. No one was missing him, yet.

The big boat glided away, trailing its white wake like the train of a gown.

PART II: SILICON VALLEY, 2012-2015

11

The year Mark Zuckerberg's New Year's resolution was to write code every day (the previous year's being to eat meat only from animals he'd killed), Vik texted Los out of the blue, offering to buy him breakfast at a greasy spoon in Sunnyvale where Los was partial to the French Toast. So there they were. Reunited. It had been three years. They sat in Los' usual booth near the rear door, across from a bank of decrepit payphones. Two of Los' men sat at stools at the counter, donning jackets despite the weather. Los had on green chino shorts, topsiders, and a white Tommy Hilfiger polo, the collar unbuttoned partway down his chocolate chestplate.

You look like you won the America's Cup, Vik said.

I dress nice, Los said, staring out across the main room. So people recognize.

Recognize what? That you own a yacht?

That I'm not a wetback.

Vik took a sip of coffee to sidestep the remark. Los, meanwhile, started cutting up his French Toast.

A few years ago, Los said, I was walking through a restaurant, and this old white lady calls me over. She says, 'My husband never got his soup.' The next day I bought this watch.

Los raised his wrist, from which dangled a silver Rolex. Vik had been wearing the same t-shirt and jeans for two days.

He pulled out his phone, tapped in the password, and slid it across the table just as Los tucked into his breakfast.

Take it, Vik insisted. Please. I want to show you something.

Los' expression was that of a man interrupted whilst enjoying one of the few things he still could. He read Vik's face, then lifted his napkin from his lap and daintily wiped powdered sugar from his lips. He picked up the phone.

Open the calculator app, Vik told him.

Los humored him. The GUI popped up. It looked like a common calculator. At Vik's instruction, Los turned the phone sideways. The interface expanded into a scientific calculator.

Cool, Los said, handing the phone back.

Vik chuckled. Hold on, he said. I'm gonna show you. See, the way this works is, when one of your people makes a transaction, they'll push 'log'. Vik pointed to the screen. Go ahead, he said.

Los just stared at him.

Vik reached over and pointed out the 'log' button. Los wouldn't touch it though, so Vik did it for him. Now if it's a sale, Vik went on, you'd enter a minus sign. If it's a buy, a plus. Then you type in the amount of product. In grams. Gotta make sure it's in grams.

Los lifted his mug and found it empty. Frowning, he tried to catch the eye of the waitress.

Vik had at this point spent three weeks writing this code, purely on spec. He pressed on with his pitch. It's simple once you get used to it, he said. Let's say you're buying five kilos... Vik reached across the table, but like a selfish child Los pulled the phone out of reach, then keyed in the entry himself. He held up the result for Vik to admire, and Vik was reminded of the entitled upperclassmen he'd tutored in high school. Perfect, Vik said. Now push 'exponent' and type in the price you're paying.

There is no exponent, Los said.

That one there, Vik said.

He waited as Los keyed it in.

That's it, Vik said. We're done. Just hit 'equals.'

Los did. The calculator displayed 'INFINITY.' Los' brow furrowed.

No, it's good, Vik assured him. The data you entered just got encrypted. And, now—well, here, I'll show you.

Vik brought his MacBook out of his bag and opened it on the table. Launched a terminal window that displayed a map of the Bay Area. The two men watched together as a little red pin fell from the heavens and stabbed itself into the map. See that? Vik said, zooming in.

Los looked closer. That's *here*, he said. This restaurant.

A text balloon popped out of the pin, displaying a price per kilogram and a date.

Every transaction gets logged, Vik explained. Purchases in red, sales in green.

It's pretty, Los said. He slid the phone back across the table.

It's *profit*, Vik wanted to say, but didn't. For Los was looking around as if for someone to commiserate with.

Hey fellas, he shouted to his men. You wanna know where we are? Vik's got a map here...

One of the men stood up from his stool and started over.

Sit the fuck down, Los muttered.

Vik rubbed his temples. I'm trying to help you, he said. I can take this to someone else.

Oh? Los said. Who?

Vik locked eyes with him for a long, empty moment.

Entonces..., Los said. How 'bout we speak *my* language now? And you tell me how your little *toy* makes me money.

Remember Red Dot, Vik said.

Yes?

So, *that* was about *what* we were selling. Our product was the purest. But after a while, we got copied, we got undercut. Fine. That's the new reality. You know that. Amazon, Wal-Mart—everybody sells the same shit. It's *how* you sell that matters. It's the *information* you have. How you track product, control distribution, set prices. Information's the weapon. It's how you win the war.

War, Los said, his eyes wandering out the window, a corner of his mouth curling ever so slightly.

Vik had set his hook.

Vik was all talked out. Los' two men had by this time gotten up from the diner counter and, with Los' blessing, stepped outside to lean against the gleaming chrome grille of Los' Chevy Suburban. Los owned five car washes in the Bay Area, three in Los Angeles, and two in Fresno—all fronts to launder money and provide him a legitimate business concern. The business was called El Camino Real, Inc., after the 600-mile road once linking the Spanish missions from Alta to Baja California. The 'Real' in the name was one of a precious few words that Los intentionally pronounced with a gringo accent; not *Ray-al*, but *Ree-ul*. Vik's laptop remained on the table beside Los' half-eaten breakfast. He had turned pensive, and made no comment when the waitress came to take his plate.

Get you gentlemen anything else? she asked.

You can take a look at this man for me, Los said—holding his hand out at Vik. Would you trust this man?

The waitress stood holding the plates. She was a little chubby, with a round pretty face and thick blonde hair. Amazing eyelashes. A pen tucked behind her ear.

I'd say he looks honest enough, she said, winking playfully at Vik.

Los, of course, got a kick out of that. I like you Debra, he said, reading her nametag. Do you mind if I ask you something else? Something personal?

Debra shook her head. Los rose from his seat and suavely wrested the plates from her hands. See the master salesman at work. See him stack the plates back down on the table, hold a palm out toward the open seat across the booth.

Debra tucked a strand of hair behind her ear. It tumbled back out. She sat down, leaving her legs hanging in the aisle. Nice to be off my feet for a sec, she said.

My sleepy friend here has been giving me ideas, Los said.

Debra said, You two been hatching quite the plan, by the look of it.

Perhaps, Los said. So, let me ask you. How big of a tip are you expecting from us?

Debra's chin retreated ever so slightly into the pudginess of her neck.

Leave her alone, Los, Vik said.

It's a simple question, Los said.

It's okay, Debra said. She turned to Los, willing to meet him head on, and said: I'm expecting whatever you think I deserve.

Ah, Los sighed. What an admirable answer!

Sure, Debra said. It's up to you, right? It's a *gratuity*.

Los frowned his appreciation of such earnestness. Debra, he said. Do you see those men out there? In the parking lot?

Debra looked out. One of the men spat on the asphalt as the other laughed. Los reached across the table and very gently slipped the pen out from behind Debra's ear.

If I may, he said. Then he took the check and, shielding his work with his hand, jotted something down on it. He flipped the check back facedown. I just wrote down a tip for you, Debra, he said. A very big one.

Okay, Debra said. Thank you.

Yes, but, here's the deal, Los said. The number I wrote is the most I'm willing to pay for you to walk out there—right now—and show those big, beautiful tits of yours to those two gentlemen.

Debra cocked her head at Los. His expression did not change. She let out a cackle of nervy incredulity.

You couldn't pay me enough, she said. She moved to slide out of the booth. Vik was glad to see her escape.

But that's just it, Debra, Los said. You get to name your price! If it's higher than what I wrote, then you're right, I can't pay you enough. But if it's lower, then you get *exactly* what you asked for—what you think you deserve.

Debra didn't move. Vik silently willed her to keep sliding out of the booth, out of Los' gravitational pull, and back to the remainder of her normal life.

I have a son, Debra said, placing a hand across her heart.
Los nodded, all empathy.

Debra turned to Vik. She re-posed Los' original question. Can *this* guy be trusted? she asked, nodding toward Los.

Unfortunately, Vik said.

Debra looked out the window. Two thousand, she said.
Los said nothing. Debra got up.

You boys have a nice day, she said.

Los reached into the front pocket of his shorts and produced a rubber-banded cylinder of cash. Peeled twenty $100's off onto the table, forming an arch that collapsed under its own weight.

This is a prank, Debra said. You're messin' with me.

Vik fielded this one, sadness in his voice: Does he look like he's messing with you?

No, Debra said. That's what's so scary.

She stared down at the bills, then glanced over her shoulder at the main room of the restaurant. And that was that. She got up, walked out the back door, and made a b-line across the parking lot. When she was standing in front of Los' men, Los picked up a cold strip of bacon. Bit into it, watching.

Debra put her chin to her chest and quickly unbuttoned her uniform from the top. When it was open to her navel, she gripped the cups of her high-capacity bra with both hands. The bra was light blue. Her milk-white chest heaved, she pulled the bra back. She was facing away from the restaurant. Los' men had Christmas-morning looks on their faces. Debra gave it a good three count, then buttoned herself back into a wholesome waitress. The men were ecstatic. They saluted Los through the window, not entirely unaccustomed to such gifts, such sights.

Debra came back in through the front of the restaurant, setting a bell jangling. No one seemed to have noticed the errand she'd gone on. A woman at a table held aloft her empty water glass; Debra ignored her. Retuning tableside, she snatched up Los' bills and tucked them into the pocket of her apron without a word. She flipped the check over. In the corner, away from Debra's shorthand, Los' had writ large: $5K.

How's it feel, Los asked, leaving money on the table?

Debra was at a loss. She looked appalled, and tried to compose herself, but Vik could see it in her eyes: she'd been cheapened by the exchange. He knew the feeling.

Money well spent, Los said.

I should have asked for more, Debra said. I—I had no idea…

Los pointed at Vik and said, That's exactly what this fucker's telling *me*, Debra! Neither of us charge enough for our goodies.

You're an animal, Debra said.

Now hold on a minute, Los said. I just made you—

…A whore? Debra said. Is that the joke here?

Not at all, Los said—taken aback. God, no. I was going to say, I made you two-thousand dollars. You should be very proud of that. Take that money home, to your son.

Well, I'm *not* proud.

Then give it back to me, Los said.

No.

Good, Debra, he said. Very good.

Fuck you.

Raise your son up right, Debra, Los said, looking out the window. So he won't have to hustle, like you and me.

I'm nothing like you.

Los ignored this, too. If you're lucky, he went on, your boy will be all smart and shit like my colleague here. In fact, take that money and buy your son a fucking computer. Pray he becomes a programmer.

12

I n the months following their fateful breakfast, Vik proceeded to piece together the jigsaw puzzle of Los' territory. Los continued to do all the buying, but his foot soldiers were made to download Vik's program to their phones, where it hid in plain sight. If a phone were to be confiscated, no one would be the wiser. The calculator app still worked. Its secret modification was undetectable to anyone less savvy than Vik.

Vik was so savvy.

The dealers were told to keep doing exactly what they'd always done: deal. Get the best price. Only, they were now expected to log every transaction. Los knew how many kilos each of them had been allocated, and every gram had to be accounted for, as did every penny brought in. He made it known that anyone caught logging a lie would be wholly fucked.

For the most part, the dealers were willing to humor Los. He told them it would mean more money, and soon. After all, that's what Vik kept telling *him*.

Vik had won Los' head but not his heart. Los had gotten to where he was in life on instinct. It was not easy for him to trust an algorithm. So when Vik said he wanted to add even more inputs to the program—that he wanted Los' dealers to start tracking the race, age, and gender of every buyer, even their sexual orientation (this being San Francisco), using other, newly repurposed keys on the calculator—Los could only laugh.

They can't be asking people that shit! he said.

They can make educated guesses, Vik said.

Remember, *amigo*. Most of them aren't educated.

They're street smart, Vik said.

Yes, Los agreed—turning reflective. People have called *me* that.

It's true.

It's *insulting*, Los said. Smart is smart. You went to college—who gives a shit? Someone taught you the names for things.

Can your people make good guesses or not?

I'm sure some of them can, Los said, and some of them can't. They're not all the same. Are all Indians good at math?

All the ones I know, Vik said.

All the ones you know went to college.

Because they were good at math.

El pollo o el huevo.

Vik threw his hands up. Fine, he said. How about this. Am *I* smart?

No, Los said. But at least you're *Indian*.

All I'm asking is we gather some intelligence, Vik said. The most valuable kind: the kind nobody else has.

I don't know why I put up with this shit, Los said.

Which Vik took as permission. And so his dataset widened, deepened. The map of California was soon carpeted in green pins, interspersed with red ones. It reminded Vik of a pox. Los said it looked like Christmas. He confessed that he'd begun staying up late watching the pins rain from the sky.

In an ideal world (i.e., academia), Vik would have collected far more data. But Los did not give a shit about statistical significance. He wasn't trying to publish a paper, he was trying to *get paper*. He told Vik as much one morning at a juice parlor in Palo Alto.

We've got two fucking months of data, he said—bolting down a shot of wheatgrass, making a whiskey face.

We need two *years*, Vik said.

History repeats.

Not every month it doesn't.

I can't buy shit with data.

That's where you're wrong.

So you keep telling me.

Tell me, then, Vik said. How do you know what to charge?

What the market will bear, *cabrón*. A hit should cost pennies.

If it was legal, you mean.

Yes. Without our markup.

Tabulator of blessings that he was, Los drew a hand from forehead to heart, shoulder to shoulder.

Back in the thirties, he said, cinnamon was illegal in Mexico. Did you know that? Motherfuckers got rich smuggling it in. From the *United States*.

Cinnamon, Vik confirmed.

Si, Los said, *canela*. It's not complicated. The border is our business model.

What the market will bear. Los' Law. Vik had been subject to it too, over the years. He'd spent his life writing only what code the market would buy. He'd never hit on an idea that was both marketable and, for him, magical. So this was once-in-a-lifetime. It was Vik's killer app, a mash-up of stats and software, borne of his curiosity and his imagination. He felt he alone could write this code. He awoke each morning hungry to do just that.

A month later, he released the second incarnation of the app to a subset of eight dealers—a beta test. By this time, the calculator had evolved. Now it solved a word problem:

Coca is grown on the eastern slopes of the Andes. Its leaves are refined into white powder which you can buy from various cultivators (Colombian, Peruvian, Bolivian) for $2,000US per kilogram. In Mexico City a kilo fetches $10,000. Further north—in dusty pueblos along the 1,989-mile border with the hungriest drug market on earth = half the world's total demand—the kilo is worth $15,000. Go north a few *more feet and the value doubles, to $30,000. Tricky though, that particular traverse. The US' annual wholesale cocaine market = $60 billion = Microsoft's annual revenues, but you divide your bricks into bumps, sell it retail. The street value of your kilo is now $100,000 (more than twice its weight in gold) so long as you know what you're doing. You meet a pediatric psychiatrist behind a 7-Eleven in Redwood City on New Year's Eve. What price should you charge this man for an eight ball? Do you know what you're doing?*

Vik did know, now. The data logged from thousands of sales and dozens of big buys had enabled interpretation, extrapolation. With each transaction, Los' dealers would code in the amount of coke they wanted to sell and the calculator would tell them the price they had to charge.

Think of it as a dynamic pricing engine, Vik told Los.

I'm trying not to think of it at all.

Why?

It's frightening, that's why. Now that we're really doing it.

Vik had never seen Los like this. He told Los to think of it as *cheating*. Like sneaking a calculator into a math test.

Los stared at Vik for a moment and said, We are very different people.

Before Vik's app, Los' dealers had bought coke from him and then re-sold it, squeezing out whatever margin they could. Prices had therefore fluctuated with the dealers' gut feelings and perennial financial crises. After the app, prices adhered to Vik's algorithm, which itself adhered to the only two variables that mattered: (1) supply, and (2) demand. Vik had massaged the numbers for months. With computational brute force, he'd pitted every variable he could get his hands on against the prices dealers were getting. He'd been hunting for predictors reliable enough to warrant his trust. On the supply side, he could only account for Los' own stock, and therefore was left to assume Los represented the market at large. This seemed reasonable: Los *was* a shark in the pond. Demand, meanwhile, was tested against all the demographic data, as well as a long list of sales-side variables: city, neighborhood, street, time of day, day of week, day of year, the Dow Jones Industrial Average, the Consumer Price and Consumer Confidence Indices, seizures/arrests elsewhere in the cartel's supply chain and those of competing cartels, proximity to Los' distribution hubs, weather. Vik was a placer miner, sifting pan after pan of sand for specks of shine. He'd learned from experience to be wary of over-complexity: he harnessed the data to the simplest functions he could, seeking linearity wherever possible. Los' data were noisy and sparse, but they were all Vik had, and after all his sifting he'd come to believe he'd found variables that correlated to a non-trivial degree with price.

Not all of the relationships he discovered made sense. Nor did he delude himself: he knew that correlation and causation are separate beasts—the first being the easier to hunt down, and the less precious for it. So be it. He'd decided that he needn't concern himself with *why* the price of coke ticked up on rainy days or after 8 PM in certain locales. It didn't matter why Tuesdays were the slowest day, or why (apparently) gay and Asian men over the (apparent) age of 40 would pay 8 percent more, on average, than other demographics. What mattered was, the data said so.

Theorists theorize; dealers deal.

13

Having tracked Los' finances for months, Vik became the *de facto* bookkeeper of his operation. He soon learned that Los' car washes were small change; the bulk of his profits were handled by black market brokers Vik never met; they took receipt of dirty cash in exchange for high-value items: gold, diamonds, PlayStations. Los then exported these things to Mexico and resold them, injecting the profits into other shell businesses there, including, as it turned out, a chain of car washes. To Vik's shock and amusement, Los used QuickBooks.

Vik made one key change right away. He insisted that Los start paying his dealers salaries, with commissions based on the number of deals they made. This way, dealers working turf where prices tended to be low didn't lose out; they were incentivized by sheer volume of sales. While many of the dealers immediately appreciated the steadiness of such an arrangement, four quit right away. Vik asked Los if he would re-assign some of his people to the vacated territories.

No, Los said. Let 'em fight over it. It's healthier.

Los adamantly refused to let the app tell him how much he should be paying upstream, to his cartel supplier. This had been a hard-won bridge, he said. He refused to risk burning it. Vik sensed this reluctance stemmed as much from fear as from logic, and told him so during one of their weekly meet-ups. They were sitting together on a park bench overlooking a pond. The Bay Area fog had been relentless all summer. It was pessimist weather.

Hell yes, I have fear, Los said. So do those ducks. That's why we're both still alive.

But, you can negotiate, Vik said. There's always wiggle room.

Los gave Vik a look of disbelief, then wiggled his ass on the bench. You know so much, he said. But you understand so little.

Vik wondered if this was true. His beta test was well underway. Before it began, he'd negotiated a 30 percent cut of whatever profit boost the app provided (assuming it provided one at all). However, he'd been poring over some frighteningly weak initial performance numbers, and was starting to lose faith that this beast could be wrangled. The new data blurred all his pretty initial curves, so he'd been making hasty adjustments. Parts of his mathematical model were proving useless, or worse—dangerous. Of course, he had no intention of sharing any of this with the apex predator of the California drug racket.

Let's say my supplier is asking thirty-two a key, Los said, but your little program says to pay twenty-nine. What then? Cross the street and buy a *different* semi-trailer of coke from someone else? This isn't SimCity, motherfucker.

I realize that, Vik said.

Really? Los said. I wonder sometimes.

There's repercussions.

There's *blood*, Los said. The wet kind. Los shook his head, then performed an encore of his belittling wiggle dance.

Vik was safe at least in the knowledge that Los liked him. It was clear from the way Los teased him. The app had been Vik's way of doubling down on this affection.

There was pushback from the dealers, too. Because the prototype app used a phone's current GPS location and time of day to determine price, the dealers had to arrive at each sale with the price still unknown. But customers wanted to know prices ahead of time. This was obvious in hindsight. So Vik added a function where the time and location of an upcoming sale could be input on the map, and the app would provide a price. The dealers used a growing set of repurposed function keys on the calculator to capture whatever demographic detail they could—the more the better, so long as it wasn't wrong. (Gender, for example, could be tricky in the Tenderloin, or West Hollywood). The main issue, however, was that the algorithm sometimes called for higher-than-typical prices, which left dealers powerless. In the old days, they'd just come down on price to close a deal.

The customer is always right, Los argued.

Wrong, Vik told him.

Sometimes you have to be flexible, Los said. To make a sale.

You mean?... Vik couldn't resist: he wiggled.

In the end, this was an easy battle for Vik to win. Los was a snob when it came to his product. He considered himself a luxury brand. As such, he was willing to charge a premium, especially if Vik said he should. He drew the line, however, when the app told dealers to unload product at what they considered too much of a bargain.

Now *this*, Los said. *This* is just wrong. They can't be giving my shit away, Vik.

And so again, Vik had to talk Los off a ledge. As part of his initial trial, he'd done an experiment in three territories: Hillsborough, Oakland, and South Central Los Angeles. Cities Vik picked for their property values, representing the full socioeconomic spectrum of Los' clientele. Midway through the trial, Vik manipulated the code to cut prices by 15 percent. Within two weeks, sales volume in South Central tripled compared to the other two cities—all the proof he needed that Los' poorest buyers were also his savviest, with the most acute awareness of price, and no 'brand loyalty.' They knew a deal when they saw one. And yet even at the lower prices, this was still good business. The boosts in volume made up for the slimmer margins.

Remember, Vik told Los. This is all preliminary. Let's just wait and see how it pans out.

So they did. And in the first month, Los' overall profits increased by $12k compared to the prior three months. The dealers in the test group made an average of $1.5k more than those without the app. Vik's cut of this was $3.6k. The next month, with Los' blessing, Vik did a full release to all 75 dealers. The numbers jumped tenfold. Vik's cut that month was almost $50k.

Goddamn gold mine.

Los started calling the app *Dora*, short for *La Calculadora*. Vik was okay with the name. For 'Dora' was to him its own double entendre, a tip of his hat to Fedora, the Linux Operating System (which itself abbreviated to LOS!) comprising 200 million lines of open-source code that to Vik ranked among mankind's greatest achievements. Dora, by comparison, weighed in at just 15,081 lines. But Vik had written every single one. She was his immaculate conception, born late one night on the margin of a take-out menu.

Los treated Dora like a goddamn oracle. *Un poco con la cabeza de Vik y otro poco con la mano de Dios*, he said.

It was autumn by that point, the summer fog having abated. Both men had emerged from their respective holes and were back to their favorite bench, overlooking the ducks. Vik having worked himself into oblivion once again. For the most part, though, he'd taken satisfaction in it. He'd dissolved into the work, and was sleep-deprived in a way that for him had always equated to happiness: too tired to give a shit. Einstein, after months of frenzied calculation, called himself 'contented but kaput;' Vik knew that feeling, but believed in a variant: *kaput, thus contented.*

Diego Maradona, Los explained, wistfully.

Vik yawned for the umpteenth time that morning.

Now *there* was a cheat, Los continued. Argen-*fucking*-tina. Maybe we should name this thing 'Dona!

Vik just stared at the ducks.

Wake up, Los said. I have something for you.

He made Vik lower his head, then draped him with a 3-inch silver crucifix on a matching chain. The pendant had conspicuous size and heft, a counterbalance for a conscience much heavier than Vik's. This was a boxer's crucifix, a gangster's. Los asked him if he liked it.

Yeah, Vik said, glancing around to see if anyone was

watching. He hated it. Upon further examination, he realized that Jesus' legs had been crudely amputated at the knees, along with the lower third of the cross.

It's a plus sign! Los said—clearly relishing this role reversal: explaining a math symbol to Vik.

I used crimpers, Los explained.

What'd you do with the part you cut off?

What? Los said. Like the legs and shit? You want that shit too, you cheap bastard?

Over the next year, Vik pulled in nearly $450k, more than half of it paid in cash. Untaxed. Rolled, wadded, bundled, and shrink-wrapped. The distinctive stench of it leaking out of whatever it happened to be delivered in that month: an army rucksack passed to him outside a mall food court; a poster tube mailed to his PO box; a plastic garbage bag slumped on his doorstep. Vik paid with cash for everything he could, and began slowly padding his bank accounts in deposits of less than $10k every month to avoid the scrutiny of the IRS. He re-plumbed the water lines in his house to reroute them around a 50-gallon water heater (having first installed a tank-less model further along the line). At the back of the empty tank Vik Sawzall-ed a slot wide enough to accept cash in whatever girth Los' bundlers happened to use. Vik later made these same modifications at the Tahoe cottage.

The rest of the payments came as checks issued by El Camino Real, Inc., where Vik put himself on the books as 'Consultant,' even going so far as to issue himself a W2 form. He paid $35k in taxes that year. This left him torn as to which political party he favored: the one for softer sentences on drug crime, or the one for lower taxes.

Meanwhile Los started demanding that the code do more. He wanted it to be easier for his dealers to input data, and for the data to be easier to interpret, especially by himself. Also, he wanted more data. More charts, more maps, and definitely more predictions. He wanted to track the prices of heroin and pot, too, and to somehow keep tabs on relevant news about The War On Drugs coming out of Mexico and South America and Washington D.C. and Sacramento. He wanted a way to measure customer satisfaction. He wanted to forecast profits for the coming summer so he'd know whether he should upgrade his yacht over the winter, while boat prices were low.

That it? Vik asked.

Sarcasm! Los said. Careful, man. That shit's corrosive. I avoid it with my kids.

I'm sure you're a wonderful father, Vik said.

You hardly know me.

Well that goes both ways, I think.

Yes, Los agreed. But we *understand* each other, don't we.

I'd say so. Yes.

And in the end, Vik aimed to please. He relished this opportunity. It was interesting and difficult work, and more than enough to keep his mind humming. Plus it paid five times better than any job he'd ever had. (*Eeees a plus sign!*) This is when the code began to branch out, and—like its author—become increasingly entangled.

14

Los arrived at the pre-arranged street corner at 7AM, the bass notes of a *narcocorrido* rattling the cabin of his chromed-out Suburban. He was slouched in the backseat alone, his two men up front. He bid Vik a good morning, but said little else as they drove through San Francisco. The bus stops were crowded with blue-collar types, kids in school uniforms. They drove south down the bay and arrived at a condo in Sunnyvale. Vik had never been there before. Los jumped out and bounded up a flight of stairs. Vik caught up, jittery with testosterone. One of the men stayed in the car, the other joined Los and Vik in a dim breezeway. Vik knocked. Los reached past him to knock again, louder.

Hard data, Los said, and Vik nodded acknowledgment: he'd been preaching the term to Los for months, probably more than he should have—hence this little errand they were on. Los' idea.

Moses' spies didn't conquer the Promise Land, Los said as they waited. Joshua's *army* did.

I wasn't aware, Vik said. He could hear his own heartbeat in his ears.

Book of Numbers, bitch, Los whispered.

The door cracked open. A young man poked his head out—a kid, really. Maybe 20. Sweat pants, Fila sandals, shaved head. One of Los' more prolific dealers.

Hey, he said, squinting into the light of day.

Buenos dias! Los replied.

The dealer glanced at Los' heavy, then at Vik. Vik looked into the dealer's beady eyes and saw just what he was looking for.

I brought a consultant, Los said. Okay if we come in?

The dealer pulled the door open. The condo reeked of fast food and pot. A 72-inch flat screen was perched atop a glass bookcase holding three different video consoles, their various controller cables running across the carpet to the deployed recliner of a sectional couch. A Sony Vaio sat open on the coffee table amongst scattered men's magazines. Vik spotted a mattress on the floor in the bedroom. The rest of the rooms were empty.

Los' man stayed by the front door while Vik and Los trailed the dealer into the kitchen. Vik leaned against the sink, Los the oven. The dealer stood at a perceptible remove from both of them.

You made a sale yesterday, Vik began.

I made like ten, bro.

Tall lady, Vik said. Bought quite a bit.

Yeah yeah, said the dealer. Bitch was throwing an after-party for some band…

We planted her, Vik said.

The dealer reacted to this with a sad smile. Los said nothing. Vik took this to mean the floor was his. His hands had begun to quake. He was a natural test taker, but had never taken this kind of test. He opened the cabinet below the sink and pulled out the garbage bin. Fished through it. Plucked out a soggy McDonald's hamburger wrapper. Peeled it open to reveal a mash of rotten pickles and tomatoes.

Picky eater, Vik said.

The dealer shrugged, and in the time it took him to do so Vik covered the ground separating them and landed a right hook to the dealer's jaw. It was the second time in Vik's life he'd ever punched someone. The first had been his oldest brother, who'd busted in on Vik and his only high-school girlfriend when they were kissing, naked from the waist up. The dealer crumpled to the hardwood floor, clutching his face.

What the fuck, you asshole!

Get up, Vik said.

The dealer dabbed at his lip, finding blood on his fingertips.

Vik repeated himself in exactly the same tone.

The dealer took his time. He glanced imploringly at Los, who said nothing. Vik picked the wrapper up from the floor, folded it like a taco, and held it out to the dealer.

Eat, Vik said.

His anxiety had turned to anger. He was channeling some other version of himself, but the boiling in his blood was now unmistakable: it was pure, righteous indignation. The piece of shit cowering before him had cheated them. The more the dealer cowered, the more Vik hated him. This hate was a godsend. It carried him through.

I will not ask again, Vik said.

The dealer tore off a piece of the wrapper and slid it gingerly over his split lip. His teeth pink with blood. He started to chew. The blood dripped and splattered the stripes of his Filas.

You sold that coke for more than you were supposed to, Vik said.

The dealer shrugged. Dry heaved.

Tell me, Vik said. Why is that a problem?

The dealer kept chewing, as if this were preferable to answering.

Vik asked again: *Why.*

'Cuz it don't work otherwise.

What doesn't work?

The whole thing, the dealer muttered, as if by rote. Your little system.

That's right, Vik said—disregarding, though not excusing, the dealer's cutesy injection of the word 'little' to describe something more sprawling and multivariate than anything he could likely fathom. Because he *had* seemed to recognize that the system was Vik's.

The data gets fucked, Los said—causing the dealer to look over at him.

Vik, feeling the need to reassert himself, grabbed the

remaining wrapper out of the dealer's hand and stuffed it in the dealer's mouth.

Garbage in, garbage out, Vik said. You hear me?

The dealer hung his head like a cow—dumb-eyed, mouth full of cud.

What did I say? Vik asked.

The dealer mumbled back, his mouth so full that the parroted phrase was recognizable only by its cadence. Vik crossed his hands atop his head and tried to calm himself. His knuckle throbbed, and he wondered if he'd broken it. *There's something bad in me,* he thought. *Some hidden bug.* He had lost control of his hate. It had turned on him.

Los appeared most pleased.

Vik turned for the door.

I think you're forgetting something, Los said. This gentleman still owes us two grand.

Of course, the dealer claimed he didn't have the money. He and Los began to argue. Vik had no patience left. He went over to the massive TV and unplugged it. Yanked out all the cables connecting it to the various consoles. Los' man took the cue and came over to assist. Together they hefted the TV off the bookcase and carried it out of the apartment under the mournful eye of the dealer, who said nothing more. The cords dangled over Vik's shoulder and down his back. Midway across the parking lot, Los' second heavy jogged over to take Vik's side of the load.

Vik stood watching the men cram the TV into the back of Los' Suburban when out of nowhere he felt a blow to his shoulder. Still amped, he swung around and threw a wild punch, barely missing Los, who'd only struck Vik in a congratulatory way—Los being a man for whom violence was communication and luck was currency. Los snatched Vik's wrist.

Calmate, Los said. *Calmate...*

Sorry, I—

That was *amazing,* man! Los said. It felt like communion in there! *Eat this in remembrance of me...*

Book of Numbers, bitch, Vik said, panting through his nostrils.

They climbed into the car. Vik was resolved never to feel this way again. He couldn't handle his hate; it got him way too high.

Let me buy you breakfast, Los said. And you can keep the TV. My kids have too many.

15

Vik's inquiries were met with vague explanations. Only one thing was clear: Los had gone to Mexico. To visit family, explained one of Los' lieutenants, to which he appended, And for business. As if this secondary motive was almost too obvious to speak, as if he were saying, Of course. Vik was led to believe that Los' return was imminent. But two more weeks went by, and Vik realized that he wasn't being lied to. It was just that nobody really knew what Los was up to. Vik didn't care enough to worry. He knew Los could neither stand, nor afford, to be away too long from the day-to-day machinations of his operation. Plus—of course—there was his beloved wife and children.

A year and a half had passed since the full-scale implementation of Dora. It was no longer an experiment, it was an unqualified success. The organization had been organized. Leaving Vik to question whether any strategy, plucked from any business book in the world, would also have been more profitable than the fend-for-yourself chaos upon which things had functioned before. Dora made things run like a fast food chain.

Dora the Exploiter.

Still, Vik couldn't help but think of ways to make the program better. An engineer to his core, tinkering toward perfection satisfied a certain restlessness in him. It kept him who he was.

Los, meanwhile, was a salesman. That's what kept him who *he* was. A high-school dropout himself, he'd gotten his start peddling car stereos—legitimate ones at Best Buy, soon followed by illegitimate ones. Then meth. And coke. Los moved product. He considered himself a bringer of chemical joy, the Santa Claus of Santa Clara, at a handsome profit of course, and fuck any un-American *puta* who faulted him for that. Therefore, it should have come as little surprise to Vik what happened next. But it did. Vik was shaving at his bathroom sink one evening when he got a phone call from an international number.

He answered, *Hi*—not a greeting, not a query; a deduction.

Veek! You miss me?

Nope, Vik said, switching to speakerphone so he could keep shaving.

And yet you keep asking about me.

There's work to do.

Yes. There is. I'm in *El Corazon*, Los said. His voice sounded strange, ecstatic.

Is that a town? Vik asked.

The beating heart of the beast, man. And I *am* working. I'm trying to make you rich!

I'm sure, Vik said—being delicate with the razor in the tricky spot under his nose. And are you high right now?

Claro. How can you tell?

You sound happy, Vik said.

Well, Los said, I *am* among friends.

No offense taken.

I'm sorry. Are we friends, Vik?

Vik rinsed his razor and didn't answer right away. Los *was* his friend. He was arguably (and sadly) Vik's best friend at that point, considering the sheer amount of time Vik spent with him relative to anybody else. Vik had deep respect for Los. They knew how to coax and cajole each other. Whether Vik liked it or not, he liked Los a lot. They were more than friends, even—more like battling brothers. Vik still hadn't answered when Los moved on.

I showed someone Dora, he said. Someone *muy import-*

ante.

You *showed* somebody? Los, are you—

He was very impressed, Vik. I think he wants it. There's a few changes to be made, but...

Vik stared at his double in the mirror. He could see his double was angry. An anger borne of deficiency; Vik wasn't accustomed to not being good at something, to not knowing things, but there he was. He didn't know product. Whereas for Los, supply and demand were not abstractions. Supply had weight; you could hold it in your hand, dent the baggie with your finger. Demand smelled like sweat-soaked twenties from a junkie's pocket. Los had spent a decade looking into ravenous eyes; he'd traded blow for blow jobs; he'd seen a toddler too malnourished to cry strapped in a car-seat on the balcony of a weekly rental while his mother got fucked for cash inside. Small surprise, then, that it was Los who realized first what should have been obvious to Vik all along: the product wasn't coke. It was code.

In creating Dora, Vik had done what he did best. Now Los had, too. He'd whored her out.

Vik tried to sound calm. *Changes*, he said.

Calmate, Los said. We talked about this, Vik. You're a genius, but you think so small!

I—

I understand, Vik, truly I do. Dora is your baby. We just need to help her grow, help her *mature*. I've got us a monster on the line. *El tiberon.*

Who? Vik asked.

Los was enjoying his high. He started improvising a song: *El corazon...del tiberon! El cor-a-zon...del—*

Los, Vik stammered. Give me a name.

I think you know, Los said.

Jesus Christ, Vik muttered, staring blankly at his own weary doppelganger, the only man on earth with whom he could commiserate.

Mas o menos, said Los.

Vik had seen the same grainy, surveillance-camera freeze-frame as anyone else who'd ever typed *Vicente Gamboa* into a search engine—wide face, thick mustache, receding hairline, paunch. It was apparently the best glimpse that anyone, including the three-lettered U.S. agencies, had so far been able to get. The man was a ghost. A ghost with an empire. It was rumored he spent $500 a week on shrink wrap just to bundle up his flow of cash. Vik had seen the story on *60 Minutes*: the money jammed into car fenders; palletized in shipping containers; zip-locked like bocadillos in the backpacks of schoolchildren passing daily between Tijuana and San Diego. All of it eventually funneled to the Mexican branches of crooked European banks who sheltered Gamboa and others like him at steep fixed rates. Gamboa had gone so far as to fabricate custom cash boxes that fit into each of the willing banks' teller window slots.

Of course, for all of this to flow freely, eyes had to be averted, or blinded outright. Gamboa mailed all newly elected officials a care package containing a bundle of cash and a single, shimmering bullet. *Plata o plomo*—silver or lead —was the choice. *Plata* reigned.

The price of doing business, Los had once explained, as if it were his own cartel.

Gamboa had his fans. The Mexican people, by and large, revered *and* reviled their cartel bosses, but tended to cheer the enigmatic ones, especially those who made fools of their first-world pursuers. Gamboa was both. The tabloids dubbed him *El Luchador*, The Wrestler—a moniker borne of his uncanny sense to don a *lucha libre* mask whenever cameras were present. Like all such masks, it tightly enshrouded the head, with holes at the eyes and mouth. Gamboa's was black, with a red cross upon the forehead and bony skeleton teeth. The popularity of the design had grown along with Gamboa's infamy: knock-offs dangled outside *tiendas* from Cancun to Juarez. Boys wore them while pedaling their bikes; old ladies donned them in jest on *Dia de Los Muertos*. For some, the mask was a fuck-you to the crooked government and its useless police force; for others it was a symbol not unlike the jersey of the national *futbol* team. This is us. He is us.

It was believed that even Gamboa's own men never saw him without the mask on, and that he kept certain men in his employ whose sole job it was to wear the mask around as a way to dilute the possibility that the man inside was Gamboa. Which, sometimes—statistically—it was. A man wearing the mask might expect to be saluted by calloused farmers or winked at by girls.

What impressed Vik, though, was Gamboa's logistical network. It was as sophisticated as FedEx's or Amazon's—doubly so, really, since he did it all in secret, at the risk of incarceration and death. For this reason, *The New York Times* likened Gamboa to Ginger Rogers, who'd done all the same steps as Fred Astaire, only backwards and in heels. Because the cartel's profits were injected into legitimate Mexican businesses, Gamboa was at one point estimated to represent one percent of Mexico's entire economy. He dabbled in philanthropy, footing the bills for churches and clinics and schools on his home turf. Meanwhile, the man himself was said to live as a blue-collar nobody, slipping amongst safe houses scattered across northern Mexico.

If *El Luchador* says your name, Los once explained, you either get rich or you get beheaded.

And if one believed the tabloids, the latter of these were promptly dissolved in vats of acid by a man more elusive than even Gamboa. A man Gamboa kept on retainer for just this task. No pictures existed of this man. Only rumors, and a nickname: *El Cocinero Estofado.* The Stew-Maker.

What's *he* want? Vik asked Los.

He wants what I have offered, Los said. Dora.

She's not for sale.

Now listen, Los said. They have the production side covered. The crops, the transportation, the distribution. But they're tired of selling wholesale. They want our fat-ass markups.

They want to be dealers, Vik said.

I'm calling it *vertical immigration*, Los said (emphasizing his own accent: *eemigration*). And I'm going to make it possible.

Just you? Vik thought, with a fear in his guts like he hadn't felt since he was a little boy, alone in bed late at night. The engineer in him coped with this fear by projecting it, speculating on what practical problems this ill-defined project would create for *him*.

This partnership, Vik said. Or whatever the fuck you think it is...it doesn't work when I'm not in the loop. I want no part of this. The code isn't even yours.

Careful, Los said—his tone chillingly sober all of a sudden. I'd say we have joint custody.

16

Statistically speaking, if you bought cocaine in America anywhere west of the Mississippi during the early twenty-first century, you bought Vicente Gamboa's cocaine. But from a human resources perspective, the Gamboa Cartel existed primarily south of the Rio Grande, from Mexico to Bolivia, in the jungles and warehouses where coke is cultivated, harvested, processed, bricked, and exported. The U.S. side of the river—the sales side—was 'understaffed,' from the cartel's perspective. It was a patchwork of geographically contiguous, yet fiercely independent fiefdoms. And in each one, a 'Los'—some enterprising motherfucker who knew the lay of his land and where the bodies had been buried, having put a few there himself.

We are in the drug business, Los told Vik. But really, we are in the territory business. This is our core competency.

Are you reading business books again? Vik asked

Territory, Vik. Do not forget this. And yes, I like business books. Also, history. Don't you?

Not those kinds.

Oh, but history is so important, don't you agree? *Especially* you. Trying to predict the future.

I see what you're saying, but no.

And why is this? Los asked. Why don't you like history?

I don't know, Vik said.

Yes you do.

I'm trying to be nice.

Don't.

Okay, Vik said. Well. For one thing, it's super skewed.

Written by the winners, you mean.

That's part of it.

That's *all* of it, Los said. Everyone knows that. It's the same with the business books. Who wants advice from some bankrupt piece of shit?

Maybe, Vik said, that'd be the best person to listen to.

Los peered crosswise at Vik. Vik hadn't been out to make an argument. Truly, this was not something he cared very much about; but, forced to take a position, he decided he preferred the rich guys who *didn't* write books, the hidden hedge fund managers, the guys behind The Guys. John Paulson had recently made $3 billion betting against the housing bubble; he could walk down most any street without drawing an eye.

Los told Vik, If *you* wrote a book, I'd read it.

Well, Vik said. Dora's up to twenty thousand lines now.

And all about history, Los said.

True, Vik said. And business.

Only, not in my language, Los said.

Mm.

Los at this point decided to tell Vik something he'd observed over the years but which had only recently struck him as a lucrative situation: each sales territory was unique, but only in the way that the root system of one tree differs from those of its neighbors. Roots are roots, Los argued. And distribution channels are distribution channels. While Dora had focused on a single tree, Los had the luxury of remove and from that vantage had glimpsed the forest.

Los was prescient, too, as men who become rich usually are. He'd been the first to notice Gamboa seizing control of various fiefdoms. Buying loyalty here, cutting up a middle man there. Optimizing. Moreover, Los realized that Dora would work in all of these sales territories—that there could be unification through standardization, through *software*. As soon as Vik saw this vision too, he jumped onboard, or more precisely, below decks. The ship sailed. Gamboa as captain, even if no one ever witnessed him at the helm, *per se*. And Los —that schemer, that silver-tongued maker or breaker of mutinies, that manipulator of meek and mighty alike—Los became Gamboa's new first mate.

From the outset, Gamboa demanded full exclusivity. This was the only project Vik was allowed to work on, and how Gamboa would know otherwise...well, Vik tried not to wonder about that. What he did instead—what he *could* do— was put his head down and work. There was a sea of new data to synthesize. New functions to devise, debug. Half a million dollars to be made.

The algorithm as it developed had no intermediate milestones, no places Vik could pause to show off partial functionality or give a sense of his progress. It either completely worked or it completely didn't. And after a month, it didn't (yet). From Gamboa's point of view, nothing was happening. So that's what he assumed. This, as communicated to Vik by Los. Neither Los nor Gamboa had any real sense of the magnitude of the project. Both lacked statistical literacy. So it was hard for them to appreciate what Vik was trying to pull off.

In a gesture to appease, Vik floated the idea of subcontracting out some of the work. He didn't want to. He knew it would only slow things down to have to explain the project to someone new. He also knew firsthand the kind of compromised shit that results from design by committee.

Thankfully, Los rejected the idea without even consulting Gamboa. Out of the question, he said. We have to protect the recipe, you know?

Okay good, Vik said. I'm glad you see that.

You're our man. No doubt. You have our trust. But go faster. Do you understand me?

Vik did. He worked another 15 days straight and cooked up code with spaghetti-bowl logic and lots of places for bugs to hide. But the damn thing compiled. It ran. *Shoot the engineer.* Gamboa was apparently of similar mind.

Ship it, Los ordered.

17

os had been right: Gamboa *was* doing some serious consolidating. He'd so far managed to bring 92 U.S. dealers and wholesalers into the fold. Now, with Gamboa's blessing, Los had convened them all for an unprecedented sit-down. Never before had these 85 men and 7 women been in the same room, but Los was convinced this was the only way to do it. So he'd carved out a precious window of time on a Tuesday in mid-May, and rented a massive house in Half Moon Bay with panoramic views of the Pacific. He'd paid for shuttle vans and plane tickets, and had ordered everyone to turn off their phones and leave their customer base hanging at least long enough to hear him out.

And now here they were, seated around a dozen rented party tables, having spent the first hour availing themselves of the sushi and fajita bars (though not the open bar, not yet), and wondering when someone was going to explain what the hell was going on. A smart bomb, guided down the chimney of the house, would have decimated the U.S. cocaine trade (for perhaps a year).

Vik had converted the massive main room into an audio/video presentation chamber, complete with a dais, surround sound, and a projection screen. He dimmed the lights. Taking his cue, Los jogged onstage to scattered whoops. He wore a black mock turtleneck, faded jeans, and rimless spectacles. He had purposefully neglected to shave for a few days.

Let's get started, he announced through a jaw microphone. *I*...am Steve Yobs.

This got laughs. Vik projected an image of a smart phone calculator onto the screen. Every button had the dollar sign on it. Los proceeded with the pitch he and Vik had prepared together.

It was Dora's *quinceañera.*

There was considerable airing of concerns during the subsequent Q&A. In Vik's view, Los did a masterful job keeping the tone non-combative. He allayed fears and instilled confidence. He redirected the technical questions Vik's way. And when things really heated up, Vik stepped onstage at Los' behest, and did his best to reinforce Los' rhetoric, the party line being: *this is the future motherfuckers; you're gonna make a ton of money.*

At one point, Vik invited a tableful of dealers onstage— an unscripted move that made Los wrap a hand over his jaw mike and whisper to him, *What are you doing?*

Vik ignored this. Once onstage, the dealers turned coy and monosyllabic. Lacking the bravado of their salesman selves, they came off as sincere. Vik pumped them for testimonials about how Dora was the real deal. He singled out a 35-year-old former college running back with massive diamond studs in both ears.

Tell me how *you* use Dora, Vik said.

I don't know, the man said. I don't even think about it anymore. I mean, you just get used to it. Like, how the numbers go in and all that shit. It's just like they're telling it, though—know what I'm saying? The thing'll get you prices you never expected.

That's true, Los said—now following Vik's lead. And tell us, how's the money been?

Good, man, said the dealer—almost laughing. It's been real good.

Yeah? Los said, pointing to the other dealers on stage for confirmation; all of them nodding.

Better than you've ever made? Los asked.

Oh, definitely, the dealer said. That salary—it's nice, man. Keeps shit stable. Then you hustle, you make commissions. Bought me a big-ass truck.

Laughter. The assemblage suddenly a bit more animated, the vibe in the room swinging positive. Perhaps feeling like he'd overstepped, the dealer dragged his palm down across his face, drawing his mouth back into a thuggish pout.

Thanks for sharing, Vik told him.

Definitely, Los said—looking not at the dealer, but at Vik. Thank you.

There would be more convincing necessary over the coming weeks, after the dealers returned to their territories and truly grappled with all the new implications of Dora. During that time, Los would come by Vik's place every day, only to spend hours on the phone driving home the message via Bluetooth headset, one dealer at a time, while he paced Vik's kitchen. Soothing the slow-to-see. Selling the dream.

But for now, with the Q&A running out of steam and the tide turning their way, Los invited everyone outside to join him for lines of coke off the edge of the infinity pool.

Within a year of its broader implementation, Dora was the Microsoft Windows of the west coast cocaine trade and Vik was five million dollars richer.

He kept his money in a sheltered account, opened for him by Gamboa at HSBC Switzerland. Gamboa held unholy sway at that bank. This account was in addition to the now-paltry $200k Vik kept in an account originally opened for him at Wells Fargo by his father, Mr. Singh, who held zero sway. Mr. Singh had served as co-signer on that account until Vik was in high school. Funny though: Vik felt the same lack of full ownership with his HSBC monies.

What few transactions he'd needed at that point had been handled via requests made through Los to Gamboa, without whom the shelter account would not exist. This left Vik feeling child-star rich, his new fortune not exactly *his*.

That's why, for palpability and sound sleep, there was nothing to compete with his water-heater vault.

Dora's interface had not changed from its original look —that of a calculator app. As with Google's home page, her computational muscle hid behind an unadorned veneer.

Some of the dealers told Vik they couldn't imagine how they'd worked without Dora before. And the program did *work*, as Microsoft Windows 'works': which is to say, Vik had to release weekly updates to keep it from crashing. Under the hood, Dora was hideous, a snarl of interdependencies, her outputs becoming increasingly incoherent and unpredictable, even to Vik. He was putting patches on patches.

Despite his intentions, he'd succumb to a stereotype— the time-honored Indian clusterfuck known as *jugaad*, a culture of creative workarounds, borne of inadequate resources. On Vik's sole visit to India as a child, he'd witnessed a woman pedaling a floating bike, propelled by ceiling fan blades, up a dingy river. His father had loved it. But for Vik it has always been the image that came to mind when he heard someone slandered as a hack. But Dora was *jugaad*.

Gamboa, meanwhile, was much pleased with Dora. At least that's what Los said; Vik still had not met the man, nor did he have any desire to. Like Los, Gamboa had needed to see the thing work before the new era of analytics fully dawned on him—to see the heretofore-mysterious circulatory system of his operation suddenly mapped and color coded; to see it pulse in real time, across three time zones, as it always had —before *El Luchador*, before *El Chapo*, before Escobar; before Pedro Avilés Pérez—except now the black box had become a diorama, with the giant face and greedy eyes of Gamboa peering in, his big hands reaching in to meddle.

When Vik first demanded permission to start fresh, Los had said, No. He'd been protective of his sporadic audiences with Gamboa. This exclusivity amounted to power, and Los knew how to wield power. He'd been hesitant to propose anything new for fear of tarnishing the relationship. It had taken Vik months to convince Los that Dora had gone as far as she was ever going to go. That her problems were no longer just tumors Vik could excise, but a cancer of her blood itself.

Vik's proposed solution? Simple. He told Los he merely needed to go somewhere quiet, and code. Somewhere like... Tahoe. For Vik had by then learned from the best—Los— about how to sell. To get *his*.

Finally Los made the call. And after that day never let Vik forget that it was only through his (Los') considerable gifts of persuasion that Vik had been allowed to convert some of his Swiss cash into Tahoe real estate—a transaction that, for Vik, had all the funny-money surrealism and impulsive greed of a turn in Monopoly. Gamboa had put his lawyers on it; Los said it was all very complicated; but for Vik it had been straightforward—coke became cash, and cash became cottage. A cartel boss paid off a junk-bond trader's wife, and a coder got to move to the mountains and rebuild.

They could blame Vik all they wanted for having to start over; he felt no guilt. Innovation, as he knew, was never a bulb over one's head, but a heap at one's feet. The bulb itself being all the proof you need: Edison had to first discover 1,600 materials *not* to use for the glowing filament. It had never been easy for Vik, staring into a blank terminal window. The cursor throbbing, waiting for instructions. Oddly (or not), it had been one of his writing teachers in high school whose advice had always stuck with him: *the way to start is to introduce the characters.* And so he once again played taxonomist, giving all the variables names like Adam with the animals. He preferred long, self-explanatory names, conjoined by underscores: stackAve_Counter, matrix_Mult. Next came the functions. Each element of the code coming to life as soon it was necessary, and no sooner.

Soon he had momentum. And whenever he looked up from his work, he saw Lake Tahoe. It was the best summer of his life, hands down. The work had been exhilarating, if exhausting.

He'd fallen half in love.

Before a month was up, though, Los started hounding him. Vik had kept him at bay.

The new code was going to be bulletproof. Functions were called out by colors, with comma-delimited arguments nested neatly within ()s, {}s, and []s. Everything in its place. Each function doing just one thing. Indented such that any developer from off the street could infer its hierarchy from halfway across the room. Comments, called out by strings of #'s, broke the code into paragraphs, reminders of what each cog did, what other cogs it engaged. The code would need to run on a processor, but more importantly, someone would need to read it: Vik would, at least, but maybe others. It would need to be understood, and interpreted, and improved. Its intent self-evident. Its eloquence derived from its brevity.

Whereas Dora had been a mess—a product—this new program would perhaps live up to the Sanskrit name he'd given it: *Kavi*—the 'seer,' the 'poet.'

But the summer was coming to an end. Los had now gone from irritated to irate. Three weeks ago, he'd given Vik two more weeks.

Good work takes time, Vik explained. You know that. Trust me.

You always ask for too much, though, Los said.

Time?

Trust, Los said.

And then Los went radio silent.

And then the particles of cocaine moved.

And life as Vik knew it was over.

PART III: CLOSE TO HOME

18

Vik treaded water. Unbuttoned his shirt with numbing fingers. Let it drift away. He tugged his phone out; it clung to the lining of his pocket like a creature being hauled from its den. By habit he pressed the home button. The screen was flickering, and he turned it facedown into the lake, lest it become a beacon. The water was frigid. A man was once discovered in that part of the lake still clad in his wetsuit, weight belt, and air tank, his gelid corpse having been preserved in anaerobic darkness for nearly twenty years.

Vik let go of the phone. Felt it glance against his foot as it sunk. He started to feel sorry for himself. But angry too. The anger took over. It churned the water.

He took off his shoes and held them tight while he peeled off his socks and let them go. He unfastened his belt and the Nalgene floated to the surface. He kicked out of his pants, then cinched the Nalgene and his shoes into a bundle which he then towed behind him as he swam, wearing only his black undershirt and boxers. He picked a heading and kept on it, resolute despite his slow pace, trying not to splash or draw attention, his limbs anesthetized, the lake black as ink. The shore was a quarter mile away, but the million stars above looked so close as to be touchable.

Vik knew he was in Rubicon Bay. The familiar, mile-long sandy beach was hemmed in by steep, forested slopes.

Docks necked out from the shoreline. Out in the bay, boats on buoys rocked gently on the wake of the boat Vik had just leapt from. The boats' ski platforms slapped the water. A pack of children were playing in a cone of light at the north end of the beach. Their carefree shrieks carried to Vik across the water.

When at last Vik could touch bottom he waded in, his shirt plastered to his chest, his head leaden. He put on the shoes and glanced at his watch. It had been just twenty minutes since he'd stepped from the boat, which had since rounded Rubicon Point and disappeared from sight.

He didn't know what to think about me, only that he couldn't *stop* thinking about me. He pictured me still sitting there, waiting for the drink that would surprise me. He knew it would be in my best interest to raise an alarm as soon as I caught on; otherwise my silence would only be seen as collusion to anyone keeping track, be they cop or cartel. Either way, hazards awaited me back onshore. Vik could only trust that I'd handle myself. I'd shown that I could bend circumstances to suit me, and he didn't exactly blame me for that: that's exactly what he'd just done after I let him in on my traitorous little secret. But for Vik there was no denying that, in my final calculation, I'd sided with him, at huge risk to myself.

Vik didn't know: maybe I'd already told someone he was missing. Were they looking for him, then? For the foreseeable future, he'd have to assume they were.

They.

All of them.

The foreseeable future.

It used to stretch out years. Now, minutes.

Love.

I'd used that word.

A gust of wind swept off the lake, shaking pine needles from the boughs. A pinecone loosed somewhere in the forest struck down with a crack. Vik had begun to shiver as violently as he ever had, and resolved to keep moving. He clambered up the forested hillside, eyes adjusting to the canopied gloom. He'd lost sensation in his feet, and stumbled over the rocks and roots and deadfall. He leaned against a tree to wait out a wave of dizziness. Each breath quick and shallow.

He traced a small creek upstream and emerged into a neighborhood: hillside garages, steep wooden staircases, homes tucked into the pines. He peeled off his shirt, hoping to pass for a man returning from a dip in the lake—an innocent man, if a strange one, in dress shoes.

A redwood bear stood at attention beside a mailbox; another lazed on a roof eave. Dozens of cars were parked along the street. A Toyota pickup had the hatch of its camper shell flipped open, a trio of wetsuits drying on its tailgate. One was gigantic, one was a child's, but one was close to Vik's size, and he did not hesitate to play Goldilocks. He ducked behind the truck. Stripped naked, stepped into the wetsuit, contorting to tug the zipper leash up his back. It had short sleeves and legs, with a roomy turquoise breast: *Momma Bear*. His core felt warmer already. Not his hands and feet.

A merry conversation was underway on a deck below the road, some couples sharing drinks around a copper fire pit. Vik crossed to the opposite shoulder. Headlights approached. He huddled in a ditch. The car came and went. A pair of Golden Retrievers loped across the road and swirled at his legs, sniffing. The sound of a far-off siren drifted in on the wind.

Vik started testing the door handles of parked cars as he went. The first four were locked, but a Subaru wagon opened up. He nearly got in: the cabin was so warm. There were two car seats in the back. Raisins and bits of cereal on the carpet. The siren's high/low wailings had grown faster, louder; a dog was barking back, prompting retorts from other dogs along the road. Vik nabbed a backpack from the front seat, then jogged on, rifling the contents as he went: school supplies, a can of soda, loose change, and—*yes*—a hooded sweatshirt. He pulled it on, cinched it up. *Tunnel vision.*

He was drawn toward the light of a gas station, but kept his distance, eyeing it from a stand of trees across the road. The pumps were empty. A pickup with a boat trailer was parked near the restroom. Three young men were inside the minimart.

Vik ran across the road to the boat—a Cobalt, with a

blue canvas cover stretched tautly over its entire length. Vik unsnapped two of the cover's buttons from the gunwale and shoved the backpack in through the opening. He looked around, then followed the backpack in, headlong.

A sharp pain shot the length of his shin, but he ignored it and re-snapped one of the buttons. In the meager light he had, he inspected his leg. Blood was dripping down his calf and ankle. He found a towel on one of the leather seats and pressed it against the wound.

The siren reached a crescendo. Peering out, Vik saw the tree trunks flickering red and blue. He couldn't see the squad car, only hear it roar through the empty intersection. Its high-low calls elongated into the night; the flashing lights faded. Soon Vik could hear the wind in the trees again.

He breathed out air he hadn't realized he was holding in. The cabin smelled of mildew and gasoline. He draped his injured leg on an upholstered engine compartment. Checked his watch. Its hands glowed faintly, and he squinted at them, trying to get a read, but what did it matter? He was living minute to minute. He'd leapt from one boat only to land in another.

19

Vik took inventory. He had the things he'd stolen—the wetsuit, sweatshirt, and backpack—and the things he'd stepped off the boat with—his soaked underclothes, dress shoes and watch; his keys; the Nalgene, and inside it, his wallet and thumb drive. The drive held 19 gigabytes of code and data; the wallet, $115, a credit card, an ATM card, a driver's license, and various membership cards.

Membership: something he'd need to forgo now. Like his computer, he would need to remain detached from any network. He wondered, then, when he might be able to rejoin the world, or if he'd just condemned himself to forever go sneaking through it.

He heard voices; the young men from the minimart were approaching the boat. He clutched the backpack and waited in the dark, breathing the stifled air. One of the men came over to the tow hitch. There came the sound of unsnapping, and suddenly the cover peeled back from the bow. Vik crouched behind the captain's chair. Light from the gas station spilled in over his hands, up his leg. More snaps, more light.

Vik tried to think of something clever, some distraction. He had so little to work with. He squinted in the light, his eyes having attuned to the darkness below the cover. He could make out a young man's face. A friendly face, freckled and round, with red hair. Twenty-something. He reached in for a duffel bag stowed in the bow.

What the fuck? he said.

Vik tensed, riding a knife edge of possibility, ready to leap out and flee into the forest. Let these young men give chase: Aesop's fox runs for its dinner, but the hare runs for its life, and so escapes...

What? came a response.

Your sunscreen got all over my shit! yelled Red Hair.

(Laughter from the truck.)

It's all over your shit, too, Pete. (Laughter from the bow.)

Red Hair hoisted the duffel out of the bow, then rejoined his friends at the truck. (Vik, not laughing, not breathing.) The truck's diesel engine burbled to life. Tires crackled against the asphalt. The trailer lurched. They were underway.

Vik felt a pang of failure. For he had not been able to think of a way out of his predicament when he needed to. He had only escaped detection by sheer luck.

The road traced the lakeshore, curving and dipping. Vik peered out through his little slit. Though it struck him as preposterous, cruel even, he could not pretend he didn't see her, out past the docks and buoys, her fake paddlewheel rotating as she cut a course back to port. The *Tahoe Gal*. He was magnetized. He caught himself repeating my phone number like a mantra, as if forgetting it would mean losing me, and maybe it would. The mantra morphed; Vik's fingers started tapping against his knee—a rhythm lodged in his mind decades earlier at a Sierra summer camp: three fast, three slow, three fast. Or was it the opposite? It doesn't matter: when repeated, it runs together: S.O.S.O.S... He recalled my imploring eyes and felt a stab of resentment, but more so he felt the urge to swim back out and lay hands on me. To hold me or to hurt me, he didn't know.

The road bent. The boat slipped from view, and Vik busied himself crawling around the galley, looting storage compartments. He cobbled together a rodent's nest of towels and lifejackets and then hunkered down—a stowaway, indifferent to destination. *Distance* was all he needed.

The truck turned away from the lake and headed to the town of Truckee, then up the mountain pass. The trailer's tires hummed on pavement pocked by snow chains. At Donner Summit Vik peered out at a serrated horizon and felt as powerless and unmoored as he ever had. Adrift.

Then down, down, into the lush Sierra foothills. The stench of overheated brakes wafting into the cabin. The air was warm and heavy, not like Tahoe. Vik could taste it. He'd grown up thirty miles from there, in the lowland sprawl of Sacramento. This was the suffocating air of home.

He found a pair of sweatpants in the back of the boat and used his house key to perforate the thighs and rip them into shorts. He drank the warm soda he'd stolen. When the can was empty, he took a piss in it.

The truck exited the highway in Rocklin. Vik crawled around the cabin, putting back the things he'd moved except the bloodied towel. He came to a neighborhood of single-story homes with big yards. Vines enwrapping power poles, moss tracing seams in the sidewalks. They pulled up in front of a yellow house and parked in the street. With the engine off, Vik could hear the crickets. The young men spilled into the yard, where they loitered, yawning and stretching and talking in groggy voices. Vik felt a warped kinship with them, as if they were knowingly abetting him. He also wanted them to go the hell inside.

Eventually they did. Still, Vik stayed put, waiting to be convinced beyond a doubt that they were not coming back out. He was going to be the Indian with a branch tied to his horse's tail. He would leave no tracks linking him to Tahoe.

He peeked out. The yard was empty, save for a threadbare cat crouched on the top rail of a fence. Its triangular ears pivoted to the incongruous, staccato sounds emanating from the previously inanimate boat cover. Vik pushed a hand out through the rend he'd created. The cat watched as this hand became an arm, a head, a man. Vik righted himself on the diamond-plated wheel well of the trailer. Looked up the street. Reached back into his canvas chrysalis and yanked out the backpack, the soda can full of piss.

Snap, snap.

Cat and fugitive slunk their separate ways.

Finally warm, Vik stuffed the wetsuit into a mound of grass clippings in a dumpster. Further on, he nabbed a pair of neon running shoes off a porch. They were caked in mud and two sizes too big, but preferable to his dress shoes. The sun wouldn't be up for hours. No one on earth knew where he was.

Money would have helped, but he had to make do with the $115 in his wallet. He couldn't risk using his credit card or withdrawing cash from an ATM. Both would put him on the map–turn him into a little pin, falling to earth from the cloud, for anyone to see. He refused to provide the world proof he was alive until he was sure the world wouldn't kill him.

He sidled through a hedgerow into the welcoming aura of a McDonald's drive-thru menu board. He stood pondering the mouth-watering verisimilitude. A disembodied voice squawked a greeting. Vik ordered, then walked around to the pickup window.

Cream, sugar? asked the female attendant, who showed no sign of surprise at Vik's general dishevelment or lack of a vehicle.

Both, Vik said. And ketchup.

He took the warm sack to a grassy embankment away from the streetlights and dug in. He considered looking for somewhere to bed down, but was too wired, buzzing on a cocktail of trauma and thrill, caffeine and corn syrup. How many desperate down-and-outers have we all passed over the years huddled on curbs just like this, staring into oblivion, spouting nonsense? An invisible multitude. A sea into which Vik now hoped to dissolve.

This was a different plane of existence. Vik had been on the wrong side of the law for some time by then, but had never felt quite like this: like an outlaw. Everything a bit more palpable, a bit more precious. The soft bun, the triangular protrusions of toy-yellow cheese, the greasy disk of beef. Vik remembered these things like he remembered this air. Despite the fact that his mother was a formidable cook—samosas with mango chutney! butter chicken!—as soon as report cards came out, Vik and his brothers always got to make the call as to how their straight A's be commemorated, and they invariably asked for McDonald's.

McDonald's conjured a sour memory, too, of the dealer Vik had assaulted while Los looked on with something like paternal pride. Perhaps, then, all those straight A's had put Vik on a path. As a boy he'd watched the evening news every night; he wanted to be a weather man. With their mustaches and flashy suits, guiding storm clouds around the Central Valley, weather men were prophets, mathematical and magic. And perhaps if he'd become a weather man, he would have been at home, asleep next to his mostly sunny wife, instead of hiding in the dark. Perhaps he'd ended up on this path instead because, while he was good at many things, he was best at getting away with them.

His body's basic needs met, Vik's mind drifted to the problem space, with its unalterable initial conditions. He'd been betrayed by those he trusted, himself included. No one was coming to his aid. Not with this. I didn't know the full scope of his situation. I had problems of my own now.

Vik found a phonebook dangling from a payphone and tore out the rudimentary city map. It showed a Greyhound bus station in Roseville. The length of his fingernail equated to three miles, and Roseville was only an index finger away. He folded the map into the kangaroo pocket of his backpack and started walking.

He walked for hours, under streetlights, under starlight. Walking was something else he remembered. He hadn't realized how much he'd missed it. In grad school and later at various jobs, he'd come to a crux in his code and get up and go wandering, not really seeing the streets or campus pathways or the people he passed, his mind and body navigating separate spaces. Forward momentum, fresh blood. Invariably he'd arrive back at his computer with a next move, if not an outright solution. But he'd all but stopped walking when he moved to Tahoe. Why?

Vik thought about that, and about the roads near his cottage. How the separation of the homes and the rarity of pedestrians always made him feel conspicuous. Discrete. *Personal space is the worst thing about America*, Vik's father used to say when he got nostalgic for the communal density of Bombay. Perhaps Vik had been misguided, then: one moves to Incline to be *someone*, but what he'd wanted all along—and needed now—was to be *anyone*. A drop in the ocean. His father's kind of Indian.

He passed a woman on a jog; he sliced through an oncoming trio of teenagers; he passed a man leaning against a telephone pole. Everyone, at that hour, seemed up to no good. Still, with each encounter, some deep-seated decency—his father's, probably—compelled him to catch the eye of his fellow nightcrawlers. To nod. The looks Vik received in return made it clear that all suspicions were mutual.

Eventually birds began to shriek. Light bled into the sky behind him. Vik continued west, where the horizon was still black and would be for a while yet.

20

F riday morning, the sun fully up. Vik stood outside a converted railway depot, now a Greyhound bus station, and stared up at a sign reading simply: ROSEV-ILLE. Which seemed at that moment like a made-up place, a square one might hope to land on in a board game.

The ticket window didn't open for two hours. Vik availed himself of the drinking fountain, sucking greedily at the arc of metal-tinged water, then slumped down on a bench. He was beat. He removed from the backpack a mechanical pencil and the binder of one 'Jolene Anderson.' He'd arrived, after his long walk, at a couple of ideas for his code. On a fresh notebook page, opposite drawings of pulleys and other things for which there have long existed governing equations, he jotted notes about things for which there haven't. Cryptic prompts only he could ever make sense of. If he ever got to.

A crow perched on a nearby garbage can. It cocked its head at Vik as if fretful about what he might try: a bird needs to eat, but first it needs not to be eaten.

Traffic on the road was picking up. People commuting, starting normal days. *What is Remi doing, right now?* he wondered. *How normal will* her *day be?* The same sun had risen on me—true—but Vik and I existed for the time being in separate worlds.

Vik had considered retreating to San Francisco. He

knew the city, and where to get the things he would need. But the possibility of being recognized was too high. He needed a place he knew well enough to be efficient but was otherwise a stranger.

The first bus of the morning rumbled into the turn-around, disgorging diesel fumes and weary passengers. They towed their luggage across the parking lot to the station. The driver stepped down to smoke a cigarette. A woman came up the sidewalk to the bus station. She carried a thermos. She passed Vik without so much as a glance, then unlocked a side door to the ticket office. A few minutes later the customer window slid open. Vik approached the counter, still wearing his cut-off dress pants and stolen hoodie. She lifted her chin.

Help you? she asked.

Vik's voice had gone unused long enough that it cracked when he spoke: Is there a bus to Santa Cruz?

There is. It leaves at...(she keyed a few strokes into her computer)...5:40.

Oh. Tonight, then.

Correct.

That's the earliest one?

You in hurry, sir? she asked—looking quite the skeptic.

Vik turned around. A small line had formed behind him. How much? he asked.

One way or round trip?

One way.

Refundable or Non?

Non.

The agent clicked her mouse a few times. Thirty-two even, she said.

Vik peeled off a third of his remaining cash and handed it through the window.

Photo ID, she said.

Sorry, don't have it on me, Vik lied.

I can't sell you a ticket without ID, sir.

Vik smiled. Chuckled. I'm sure there's some exception you can make, he said.

She smiled back. Did not chuckle. I'm sure there isn't, she said.

The agent handed the cash back through the window.
Next, she said.

The day soon buzzed with heat. Anvil-shaped thunderclouds amassed above the flatlands to the west. Vik considered hitchhiking, or paying a trucker for a lift. He could get to Santa Cruz some way—that wasn't the question. But nor was Santa Cruz the answer, he realized. It was just a place he used to go to get away from San Francisco. And in the middle of the night, feeling hounded, it had seemed like salvation. *Santa Cruz* was ROSEVILLE.

He walked down a busy road. A daylight somnambulist, a faceless pedestrian. Stumbling down the shoulder, the traffic at arm's length. He turned and came to a concrete roadblock with a sign proclaiming simply: END. Beyond it, a small but steep ravine choked with trees. He clambered down. Kicked a hole into the hillside and shit in it. Used the phone-book map as toilet paper. Rested for a while in the shade of a live oak.

Went back to the road. The air humid, charging up. The heat from the asphalt coming through the soles of his stolen shoes. He walked until midday, then ate a gas-station sandwich. Refilled his Nalgene with sink water. He'd slept one hour of the last 36, but the only thing he truly craved was information.

He stopped into a pawn shop, setting off an electronic ding. The door closed and he lingered a moment, letting the air conditioning cool him. A fat man with a shaved head set down a catalogue and rose from his stool. His reading glasses dangled on a chain that disappeared into the meat of his neck. He asked how he could help. Vik unhooked the clasp of his Rolex. Its steel band clacked as he lay it on the glass display case. The man picked it up and studied it.

It's real, Vik said.

Yep, agreed the man.

It cost me six grand. The man grinned. He set the watch back down and pointed past Vik to a case full of watches, saying, I'm not exactly in need, pal.

Vik said, Just make me an offer.

The man excused himself to confer with an obese woman hunched over a computer in a side office. Vik pretended interest in some classic movie posters. The broker pointed over the woman's shoulder at her monitor. His face soured.

Best we can do is nine-fifty, he said when he came back.

Wow, Vik said. He looked down at the watch, feeling sorry for it. He strapped it back on.

Back on the street, Vik continued west, but was interrupted in his retreat by a stoplight. He leaned his head against a power pole, too exhausted to think straight, but trying. Cars and buses blurring past. The light changed. The crosswalk was his. But he turned around and went back into the pawn shop, lay the watch back down on the counter. The broker came over, left his glasses off.

Twelve hundred, Vik said.

The broker frowned. Vik could see now that the Rolex was just a constant in this calculation. *Vik* was the only variable. It had been a small risk to expose himself this way: a zealous investigator might make a routine check of all such shops in the region. But Vik needed money. The broker pursed his lips.

Eleven, he said.

Vik crossed the American River on a converted railroad bridge. Persistent drought had left the river running low, reminding Vik of the joke about the statistician who drowns crossing a river that's only three feet deep *on average*. It was mid-afternoon, but darker than the hour deserved on account of the thunderclouds. Vik followed a meandering bike path. Fit young parents shot past, mushing jogging strollers; drunks lay prostrate on the grassy banks. The buildings of downtown Sacramento had served as his beacon all morning. Now he'd come under their looming shadows. Vik had left Sacramento right after high school. He couldn't think of anyone he still knew there, except his mother, Mrs. Kumari Singh, whom he hadn't seen in almost a year. The last time he'd talked to her was over the phone, on her birthday, two months ago. Every time he'd seen her over the last few years she'd looked even less like his mother. Maybe that's what had made it easier to stay away. She'd reacted to Vik's father's cancer and rapid decline in much the way Vik had. It had completely changed her. As a widow, propriety had dictated that she stop wearing the red *bindi* on her forehead. Perhaps to compensate, she'd started donning saris—loudly colored and silky, the type Vik's father had forever begged her to wear, to no avail. (She'd favored designer sweat suits and gaudy jewelry ever since setting foot on U.S. soil.) This fashion shift had proved as much a way of mourning as a way to conceal the weight she soon packed on. When Vik visited, she'd seemed only to *want* to believe, but not *actually* believe, the lies he fed her to explain his Rolex, or the red in his eyes, or his new place in Tahoe. Once, she'd asked him why he didn't come back to live in Sacramento. He'd equivocated. And she'd come right out with it: You never really belonged here, did you, Vik?

What a perfect place for him to go now.

He stopped at a drug store. With the cash he'd fetched for his watch he bought a burner phone, a 60-minute prepaid card, a toothbrush, and toothpaste. Further on, at a department store, he bought shorts, Levis, underwear, socks, and a polo shirt. He asked the clerk for directions to the nearest public library. She had no idea. He asked her where the bathroom was. She pointed.

Vik changed.

He tracked down a library branch on the north end of McKinley Park, open until 8 o'clock. It was housed in an historic brick building. He followed a musty, flyer-laden corridor into a vaulted main room, where he zeroed in on a pair of outdated Dell workstations designated 'PUBLIC ACCESS.' One was already occupied by a bookish young boy whose chapped lips and impenetrable focus brought to mind a young Vik

Singh.

The fugitive Vik Singh opened the one available browser—Internet Explorer, which he hadn't used in years—and searched out the webpage of *Ignatian Literary Magazine*. The magazine's editorial office had been down the hall from his office at USF; he'd read the nameplate so many times that the word *ignatian* was forever etched in his mind. The email address listed on the submissions page was *IgnatianLitMag-@gmail.com*. So Vik created a new email account—*Ignatian-Magazine@gmail.com*—slightly different than the official one, and wrote an email structured like a letter he'd received in sixth grade, and never forgotten, from the selection committee of a code-writing contest:

> *Dear Remi,*
>
> *Congratulations! We are excited to inform you that we have decided to publish your short story, 'How to Cut a Mango,' in our upcoming issue. There's much to admire in the story's physical details, the descriptions of the relationship, and the inner conflicts of your heroine. Strong writing from start to finish!*
>
> *Please respond at your earliest convenience...*

Vik signed off as 'Marla Ett,' feeling sure I would recognize the name of the lake at which said mango had been cut. As contact information, he gave the newly created email account and the number to his burner phone. He sat for a moment before pressing Send. He knew me to be duplicitous, and yet I was the only person he trusted. He wondered if that was something like love.

Through an open window, he could see the crown of a willow tree swaying in the wind. The scent of rain stole into the library. Loose papers blew off a desk. A librarian got up from his desk and hustled away, presumably to go handle the situation. Vik clicked 'Send,' and handled his.

He had every confidence I would recognize his email for the secret communiqué it was. Still, he feared that I wouldn't take the necessary precautions when getting back in touch—that I'd underestimate the stakes, do something sloppy like call him from my personal phone. But he was dying to know what had become of me once he'd slipped off the grid.

I never saw the email.

21

While the librarian closed windows Vik scoured the websites of the *Tahoe Daily Tribune* and the *Reno Gazette Journal* for news of his disappearance. Nothing.

He nabbed a picture off the internet of a young man in ski goggles and a helmet; another picture of a similar young man—this one shirtless, cliff jumping; another in full Burning Man attire. These he combined to create a single Facebook page for one 'Justin York,' from San Francisco, where he'd attended Stuart Hall, a private high school. Vik disliked 'Justin' for his predictability, but had neither the time nor the need to tie a fancier fly. Powerbait catches fish. Justin was busy sending out friend requests to me and all my friends when the librarian tapped Vik's shoulder. He minimized his browser window with a reflexive keystroke and turned around.

Didn't mean to startle you, the librarian said. We're closing up.

Vik refreshed his new email account one last time. It had not yet received a message, nor his new phone a call. He packed up his things and left. Street signs were swaying on their lines. A few miles off, tentacles of rain reached down from a thundercloud's gray underbelly. He took shelter in the alcove of a shoe store as plump drops began to splatter the hot sidewalk. A man hurried across the street holding a newspaper over his head. It poured. Wind striated the wet asphalt. Vik lay a bead of toothpaste on his new toothbrush, held it out into the onslaught, and then proceeded to brush. He brushed for a long time, listening as he did to the thrum of the rain on the metal awning above, a noise both soothing and complex. He felt a little better.

He stopped at a minimart for a bottle of water. The clerk was an Indian man. Vik watched the man's long, dark fingers counting the bills into his own long, dark fingers. The man smiled at Vik in a strange and prolonged way that Vik took for kinship. Vik returned the smile, thinking all the while: *I may have fallen, but at least I leapt; whereas, you—you have probably never truly risked; or, if you have, is this small-change existence your reward?* At which point Vik caught his own reflection in a sunglass display—his bloodshot eyes and dirty, unshaven face—and the clerk's expression became clear. It was not kinship, but disgust. The clerk was looking across his hard-worn, hard-won counter at a fuckup, a disgrace to the race. He was forcing a smile out of common courtesy. The customer is always right.

That all, sir? he asked.

Vik peered up at the smorgasbord of high-margin items shelved out of customers' reach: Marlboro and Copenhagen and Trojan and Tylenol and Smirnoff. The customer is always human. Humans get high. Humans fuck. Humans steal.

Bottle of Jack, Vik said. Please.

The man smiled.

Vik found an empty picnic table in McKinley Park. Nearby, a group of Hispanic men and children were playing short-field soccer on wet grass in the last of the twilight. Vik cracked into the whiskey. He didn't savor the taste, just wanted it in his blood. He closed his eyes and listened to the shouted Spanish, punctuated by thumps of the ball. He fantasized about escaping south, somewhere warm, with me. He wondered what it would feel like to live like an animal, beholden only to his stomach and his balls. He was tired of being beholden to his head.

Here are the five traits of a scholar: far-seeing as the crow, concentrated as the stalking crane, light-sleeping as the hound, in control of the appetites, unencumbered by desires or household. These according to the Neeti Saara, a collection of morals set down by a Telugu poet in the thirteenth century and, in 1994, snipped by Mrs. Singh from a book found at a garage sale, then laminated and taped to the yellow refrigerator of a modest suburban home in Sacramento, California. Vik had eventually come to correlate these five traits with hunger itself, the hunger that drove him so often to the refrigerator when he should have been studying.

Always studying.

He had not become 'far-seeing as the crow.' Not far-seeing enough, at least. If he had, he wouldn't have landed in that particular park, medicating with whiskey. But he decided at that moment that he didn't *want* to see far. He wanted to keep his eyes on the ground. And actually, what was more *far-seeing* than that? The ground *is* the ultimate destination, for crow and crane, alike. For dog and for man. What better to keep one's eyes on? What better pose to assume than the downward-facing dog?

Late that night, a fog settled into the park. Blurry coronas enshrouded the lights along the paths. Drunk, Vik relieved himself into a metal urinal clogged with chew spit and gum. He scanned the doggerel on the restroom wall. In his stupor, he assigned profundity to things. He found himself empathizing with all those unseen defacers, like a prisoner does with the prior occupants of his cell. Here were men cutting to the core of things. Cartoonish cocks and pot leaves and buxom women in compromised positions. The wall was open source; it debugged itself: the word 'bigot' had an arrow pointing at the word 'fag,' which itself had an arrow pointing at an invitation to this very bathroom at an appointed hour. Vik felt *membership*.

Re-emerging to the ghostly park, Vik spotted a man stealing his backpack. He ran across the grass and, without thinking, took hold of the pack. A bizarre tug-o-war commenced. Vik could smell the man's sour breath and clothes; his eyes were sunk so deep in their sockets as to be unreadable, just holes. Without letting go of the bag, the man reached into his coat. Vik caught a glimpse of a switch-blade as it whipped past his face. He let go of the bag, stumbling backward. The man was making horrible, hacking noises, something akin to laughter, rattling some sickness in his chest. Then Vik noticed the silhouette of a second man under the trees, beside a pair of junk-laden bikes. A pipe wrench dangled from the second man's hand.

Vik turned and ran.

He ran, cursing the men, cursing himself. He still had the thumb drive jangling around his neck, and his wallet, with its useless cards and its cash, but he'd lost his extra clothes and the burner phone that had yet to ring. His mind raced. *Maybe Remi didn't decipher my email. Maybe she doesn't want to talk to me. Maybe she* can't.

Pigeons had congregated with impunity in the vacant streets. Shifting mists drifted among the buildings, blocking out the stars. Vik's adrenaline wore off. He found himself halfway between drunk and sober, as afraid for his sanity as his safety. He came to an intersection. A solitary white pickup rolled up to the red light. The driver had his arm out the window, his old skin tattooed with eagles, rifles, dates.

Vik lifted a palm. Know anywhere to eat around here? he asked.

The man pondered him. The truck's engine gurgled. You mean, like a shelter? he asked.

Vik lay his head down upon crossed arms. Probably he slept: his meal materialized too quickly otherwise. The lone waitress doted on him, her lone customer at that early hour. She had a kind, round face, like another waitress Vik had known, and he felt only further disgust with himself.

He ate. The waitress and the cook stood on either side of the counter, chatting in low voices. It was still dark outside. The view in the window was merely a reflection of the empty restaurant, all Naugahyde and Formica. Less than 48 hours had passed since Vik had stepped off the boat into oblivion, but already he could feel the toll of that decision. His body ached from sleeping on the ground and from the miles covered. He smelled of whiskey. He longed for me, as if I might magically appear, slide into the booth across from him, and smile. He believed that was all he needed. My body, my *self*. The plain, physical fact of me—that was all the assurance he was asking for. The only real currency was time; he'd convinced himself of that. And presence trumps promise.

But no. He'd left me behind.

Eventually other customers filtered in: an elderly couple in sensible shoes, a trio of men in spattered Carhartts. A teenaged girl took a stool at the counter and was soon arguing in exasperated tones with the waitress, who listened as she buttered toast. The girl rose in a huff, shouldered a large bag, and left. The waitress came and freshened Vik's cup of coffee. There was light in the sky now. The windows were regaining their transparency. Together the waitress and Vik watched the girl recede down the street.

Yours? he asked.

Unfortunately, the waitress muttered—though the longing on her face betrayed her: that girl was the most precious thing in her life. Can I get you anything else, young man?

I'm okay, he said.

She patted Vik's shoulder. For she, of course, was not the same waitress who'd bared her breasts to thugs while he looked on, saying nothing. She set his check on the table. Facedown like a graded exam. The cost of things being a private matter. Concealment a courtesy.

Vik tucked a pair of twenties under his coffee cup.

He was right back on the street.

What day was it? he wondered. Monday he'd sprawled half naked beside a lake with me, Tuesday I'd stolen his bike, Wednesday I'd brought him take-out, and Thursday he'd fled. Yesterday he'd returned home—his whole life in upheaval, his father in the ground, his mother in the dark. *It was Saturday.* The morning light harsh. Vik hungover. He walked back to the public library. It didn't open for thirty minutes. He waited outside, amidst the small-engine noise and hollered Spanish of a platoon of landscapers, until the big metal front door swung open and a fragile man in khakis propped it open with a rock. Vik followed him inside. The computers were not booted up, so he took the liberty. The librarian came over, unbidden, and logged Vik into a public account, then disappeared into the stacks.

Vik had received two emails, both regarding the terms and features of his new email account. He compulsively clicked the inbox refresh button, summoning nothing. He typed his own name into a search engine, filtering the results to recent postings. A link appeared to the *Tahoe Daily Tribune*. A click later he was staring at the mug shot from his old university ID, and beside it, a far more flattering picture of me. The headline: LOCAL COUPLE MISSING, FEARED DROWNED.

22

Vik slipped outside of himself; he felt like he was reading over his own shoulder. It was such a morbid and prurient story, about the type of people such tragedies always befell—*other* people. He scrolled through the story in too much of a panic to properly digest it, taking in only phrases: 'last seen aboard', 'authorities,' 'Singh's mother'. He returned to the top and started again, reading it all the way through as slowly as he could manage, trying to get a sense of what the authorities knew, or were saying. It was known that he and I had boarded the *Tahoe Gal* together. Neither of us had been seen since.

According to the story, when I didn't come home, my roommate tried in vain to contact me, then called the police, who'd kicked into high gear. The lake and shoreline had been searched.

Vik's heart was in freefall.

He couldn't tell if the article's aggravatingly thin detail was a sign that the authorities were playing close to the vest. *If so, what did they know that they weren't saying?* The article was mostly filler, and went on much longer than the meager facts it conveyed seemed to justify. Vik stared at the two pictures; he saw what everyone else must surely being seeing, too: *the girl next door and the dead-eyed foreigner; she has worried friends, he is a complete mystery. Assume away. No matter what fate has befallen these two, how could she be the one to blame?*

The article mentioned that Vik's mother had been contacted, but that was all. Vik pictured her now: sitting, fretting, in one of the matching recliners in her empty nest, just a few miles away.

He felt wretched for putting her through this. But he also knew that whatever story she'd cooked up to explain her missing son was probably less horrifying than the truth. And contacting her would only put her at risk.

The article mentioned that my parents and younger brother were flying out, from Iowa.

What have I done? Vik thought. Though he knew full well. Fight and flight had become equally futile, the flailing of a fish being carried off in talons. He'd made a living solving complex problems, but didn't know where to begin with this one. He felt powerless.

Have I gotten her killed? Has she killed herself?

He checked in on 'Justin,' who'd so far lured five of my friends. Their Facebook pages were abuzz about my disappearance. Postage-stamp-sized profile pics—a swim-suit selfie, a corporate logo, a hamster—were juxtaposed with links to the article, exclamation-point-ridden pleas for info, calls for prayer. Nobody actually *knew* anything, though.

Vik had to go outside for air. The sky was pale and cloudless. A man and woman rode past on their bikes, chatting. A bird let loose a riot of chirps. Vik started down the stairs. The bird reiterated its urgent, unintelligible message.

Vik did the only thing he could do. He walked. He was free-falling through an information vacuum. But he understood well that hard data comes at a price. It must be beat out of skimming dealers, or milked from imperfect sample sizes, sometimes at the expense of one's principles. For him to find out about the state of affairs in Tahoe or Tijuana or anywhere else would upset the delicate *im*balance he'd created in his favor the moment he slipped off the map. Putting up one's periscope means the enemy can spot you, too.

By Vik's reckoning, he held only two cards. First, they did not know where he was, let alone *if* he was. There would be a price to find out. Who would pay it, though? His girlfriend? His mother? He tried not to prognosticate. Second, he knew everywhere they were, or at least their operations— their soldiers, their stockpiles. He could not know about the very latest transactions. Nor did he know where Los was. And no one knew where Vicente Gamboa was, except maybe Los.

What do they want from me? Vik knew that the answer to that question depended on who *they* were. The FBI wanted the cartel. The cartel wanted the code. The code— and the data upon which it had been built—*was* the cartel. So maybe this incestuous equation reduced to a simple, transitive truth: everyone wanted the same thing = Vik.

Worse, if the cartel had already replaced Vik with some hired hack, then Vik might already be on the hazardous side of their balance sheet: no longer an asset, but a liability, a defector, privy to the ins and outs of their sprawling criminal enterprise, while owed nearly a quarter million dollars for something he hadn't technically delivered.

Patience, Vik told himself. *It's all you have.* His only play was to hold out long enough for his pursuers to show their cards. Then react. He was stuck in purgatory, somewhere between the Eden we'd discovered at the lake and whatever hell might soon await us.

No.

He changed his mind. He'd walked far enough to see a better way.

He found a phonebook and looked up the address of a law firm near the capital building that was home to nearly a hundred lawyers and lobbyists. This firm was also one of the bigger pins on Dora's map of the Central Valley. Half an hour later Vik was standing across the street from the firm. He made a call from his new phone.

Ronaldo's Brick Oven Pizza, how can I help you?

Yes, I'm calling from York & Dupree, Vik said.

Hey. You guys want the regular order?

Actually, I was wondering—what's the delivery guy's name again? Our usual guy...

Sean?

Maybe, Vik said.

It's probably Sean. He's the one who usually delivers over by the capital.

Is he around?

He don't come in 'til later.

When exactly?

Dude, I don't know. I think he starts at like three. Who's this?

Vik hung up. At 3:30, he called back. Got a different employee—a young woman. Ordered three large margarita pizzas for delivery to the law firm.

You guys workin' the weekend? she asked.

You know us, Vik said. Big case. Thing is, the lobby's locked up today. So could you tell Sean to wait out on the sidewalk, and I'll just come down and meet him? I've got to come out through a side door—has to do with the alarm. Long story.

No worries, she said. I'll let him know. Give us about forty-five minutes.

Vik checked the time, started working out logistics, contingencies. Let's make it 4:30, he said.

He used more of his cash to buy new clothes—expensive-looking loafers, dark jeans, a white Ralph Lauren polo. He didn't bother buying socks. In a department store restroom he transformed into a working-on-the-weekend lawyer, taking his sartorial inspiration from Los.

The stiff shoes raised a blister on his heel as he walked the eight blocks to York & Dupree. He stationed himself in the alcove of an adjoining parking garage. From the bottom of the entrance ramp he could see up to the sunlit street. The workday district was a ghost town.

At the appointed time, he ascended the ramp to the sidewalk and peeked around the corner to the front of the building. There, leaning against a pearl-white Lexus with chrome rims, was a man in a Ronaldo's baseball hat and matching t-shirt. He had his phone out. Vik approached, all smiles. The dealer was tall; he looked Vik over, then opened the back door of the Lexus and tugged out a large red thermal bag. He handed over three pizzas.

Vik played up the goofy charm, buckling slightly at the knees. Whoa, he said. Heavy!

You new? the dealer asked, looking up and down the street.

Just started, Vik said.

Cool, cool. And ya'll just wanted pizza this time, then? No calzones or anything?

As he said this, the dealer's tone changed. They'd dipped momentarily into doublespeak. Vik continued to play naïve.

That'll do it! he said. So, what's the damage?

The dealer handed Vik a bill, folded in half. Vik made a show of searching his pockets. *Damn*, he said. I grabbed my wallet but not my phone. I always use it to figure out tips...

The dealer said nothing.

Vik went on: This might sound kinda weird, but—mind if I borrow yours? Just for a sec...

The dealer looked at Vik sideways, then shrugged. He keyed in his passcode and handed the thing over.

Vik thanked him, then turned away slightly—as if wanting privacy for his calculation. The dealer pretended interest in a street sweeper a few blocks down. Vik opened the calculator app and casually rotated the phone, engaging the full scientific calculator, then tapped the 'pi' key, spilling the constant in all its seventeen-digit glory across the display. The first fifteen decimals were truly the ratio of any circle's circumference to its diameter, but the last two represented the version of Dora currently running on that particular device: 23, meaning the second major release, third update.

Therefore: not only had the cartel found a way to tie together the loose ends of his code, they'd actually *released* it. Vik's masterpiece had been finished by a forger. Also: already *three* updates? Had there been that many bugs? *Jesus—is that even the point here?* Vik chided himself. But he didn't know how else to feel. Kavi was out in the world now, on her own. In Vik's former life, reaching a milestone like this would have meant champagne in the conference room, cocaine at the after-party, a week off in Mexico...

The dealer was staring at him.

Vik apologized. He handed back the phone, and tried making a defusing joke about having gone to law school because he sucked at math. The dealer checked his watch.

We good? he muttered.

Yeah, Vik said. Thanks.

...*for the pi.* The dealer took the four twenties Vik gave him, ducked back into his Lexus, and sped off, leaving Vik on an empty sidewalk with more than he could eat or comprehend. Exactly what he'd paid for.

23

Vik's masterpiece (in its near-complete state) represented 217 kilobytes on disk, but it was the 19 gigabytes of raw data with which it shared silicon on the thumb drive that had the real worth. (What I hadn't known when I swiped it and listened to the songs saved on it was that Vik encrypted all his work within audio files, which looked and played like normal music despite their hidden payloads.) The data were Vik's greatest asset, perhaps his only. He who lorded over the data *was* lord.

As such, the thumb drive came to feel to him like it had inordinate physical weight; he could actually feel it tugging at his neck; its gravity warped the world around him. Absurd, he knew. It was purely psychological. But that didn't mean it couldn't be physical, too: we feel what we feel. So what if it was a lie his mind was telling his body. Did that make it any less true to him?

This is how people go crazy, Vik thought.

There's a joke he'd seen once on a popsicle stick.

Q: Which way did the computer programmer go?

A: Data way.

Were he so inclined, he could have walked to the nearest police station and politely requested an audience with the FBI. Lifted the lanyard off his neck and dangled the entire Gamboa cartel before their eyes. He could have gone data way. Were he so inclined, he could have started making some pretty heavy demands.

Were he so insane.

He gave one of the pizzas to a prostrate homeless woman. She looked up at him like he was glowing. He gave another to a teenaged couple with punk hair and gauged earlobes. Then he plunked down on a curb and steadily consumed the remaining pizza himself, then spent the night in a park by the river. It took a long time for him to fall asleep. Mind and body both struggling to digest it all. He was awoken by a ratchet-like sound, something metal dragging across the aluminum picnic table that comprised his roof. The sun was up, and far too bright. Vik peered out at a pair of polished boots.

This ain't a campground, pal, a voice said.

Vik wriggled out from under the table and stood up to face a cop. He was slapping a Maglite against his palm, his partner standing off to the side. Vik was coated in sweat. Groggy. He rubbed his eyes and made a compulsive little touch of the lanyard through his shirtfront. There were children on the playground now, their mothers pretending not to look over. Vik fetched his things out from under the table while the officers watched. He turned to go.

Hold on, said the first cop.

Fuck fuck fuck. Vik assessed the cops' physiques, the intensity in their eyes. The partner seemed the one he'd have to outrun.

You got some ID?

Vik shook his head, no. The cop seemed unsurprised. He asked where Vik was from.

Roseville, he said—that fakest of places.

And, how'd we end up under this table last night?

Vik shrugged.

The officer reached into the breast pocket of his uniform for a stack of cards. He peeled one off and handed it to Vik. It featured a clip-art sun alongside a phone number for the 'Homeless Outreach Team,' or 'HOTline.' Vik almost laughed. *I have a house in Incline Village and a ten-thousand-dollar espresso machine,* he thought. And yet to set the record straight would only make the cop's question more valid: *How did we end up under this table last night?*

Thank you, Vik said. He held up the card and pursed his cracked lips in speechless gratitude. The officer nodded sadly, which Vik took as permission to go—to waddle off to whatever private ruin he clearly preferred for himself. The second cop spoke up: *Hold on.*

Vik tautened, still not out of the woods.

That your pizza box under there, bud?

Vik peered under the table as if for confirmation there existed such a box, such a past. The officers watched with satisfied expressions as he fished it out.

He went straight to the library. The same librarian—a balding man in a navy sweater-vest—was back on shift; his face softened when he glanced up from his monitor at Vik. Welcome back, he said, and Vik felt his anonymity slip off like a towel. This was the first person to recognize Vik since he'd fled. Vik chided himself. People had patterns; he couldn't. Habit would render him vulnerable. He took a seat, resolved to find a new library just as soon as he re-made his searches.

He didn't have far to look. On the *Tahoe Daily Tribune* site, below a banner ad for prime rib at the Crystal Bay Club, was his picture again, this time as part of an altogether different news item. Atop the article was a still-frame link to an accompanying video. And there, lurking behind a triangular 'play' button, was a startlingly familiar façade, even if the contrast of flame against darkness had been nearly too much for the camera.

What?!...

Vik turned down the volume on the computer and leaned close to the monitor. Pressed play. A reporter with good hair began narrating the obvious from the safe remove of Vik's cul-de-sac, her Channel 11 fleece bathed in tungsten spotlight, her backdrop Vik's steadily collapsing cottage. The camera zoomed in over the reporter's shoulder to capture the smoke surging out though a hole in the roof. The flag smoldered on the crumpling front wall. Firefighters were directing their streams out over the blaze, suppressing the flames, but long past fighting them. Sparks drifted into the night sky.

Oh. My. God.

The reporter had precious little to say: a house was burning—see it? No one was believed to be inside. *Firefighters are working to prevent the blaze from spreading to nearby forest service land and neighboring homes*, she said, glancing at a notepad. *Authorities have yet to comment on a possible cause.*

Behind her, a man in slippers and sweats led his Labrador across the cul-de-sac. The reporter interviewed the woman who'd called 911, and was therefore the closest thing the story had to a hero. A pair of teenaged boys slipped into the frame behind her and flashed peace signs.

The full written article had been posted later, at 7:45 AM, and had slightly more to tell. By then, the paper had linked the address of the cottage to Vik, *the missing man, Vik Singh of Sacramento by way of San Francisco,* a *recent transplant to the Tahoe area* (as in *not indigenous*; as in, *invasive*). Authorities could not (would not?) comment on any link between the couple's disappearance and what was now being investigated as an arson. *It certainly raises new questions*, was all the police spokesperson offered.

A gallery of photos was posted further down the page. They seemed to have been taken just after dawn. The rich morning light endowed the scene with a sickening, artistic look. Vik recognized that light, the colors it painted on the pines. He no longer recognized the cottage. More than half of it was gone. Some of the carbonized surfaces had turned matte, others glassy. No longer was the unfinished main house the eyesore of the property.

Vik played the video again on mute. That wasn't his place. It couldn't be: all his things were still in his place. His books. His picture of a placer miner. His sun-warmed rug. His computers, with their memories full of music, photos, ideas—some of which had been backed up; some of which hadn't. It was *him* in there, in that cottage. It was there he was going to return when all of this was over; hence, *impossible.* Hence, Vik again felt more like a voyeur than a victim.

Odd things had been spared by the flames: a chair from the kitchen table; much of the kitchen. In the southeast corner, the two big window frames were still standing, though they now lacked glass. It looked as though the front room had burned first, and most, as if someone had thrown Molotov cocktails through the front window, and maybe someone had. The west side of the cottage had suffered too, but the storage closet off the front deck looked intact, its door still shut, presumably still dead-bolted. How quaint. And inside (presumably? or no possible way?), the water heater, like the fuselage of a dud rocket, with two-hundred-thousand-dollars in uncombusted fuel in its belly. The stone hearth and chimney still stood, as Vik would have were he there now himself. For it was clear to him that he had now survived something, even if he wasn't there to inhale the smoke or feel the remnants of his favorite place on earth crunch underfoot.

The sheer injustice of it was overwhelming. Vik felt an urge to yell for someone, anyone. To stand up from the computer and motion for the librarian to come over and bear witness. To call the newspaper, the National Guard, Customs and Border Patrol. Get the goddamn governor on the line, safe in the capital building overlooking the park where Vik had slept the night before and say: *Look: do you see?* Vik wanted someone to say to him, *Yes, your world burned while we stood by. But you have built your share of this empire, this California; you are enterprising, entrepreneurial, and innocent until proven otherwise. So, please. The floor is yours, Vik Singh. State your case...*

Vik had never felt so *wronged*. They were coming over him again, those same throes of righteous indignation he'd felt watching the traitorous dealer eat garbage. He felt: *Fuck This. Fuck Them.* Feeling was all he could do as he glared at the screen. He laced his hands together and rested them against his chin, as if in supplication, but truly the opposite. It wasn't a prayer, it was a curse.

He was halfway to the door when he thought to go back and close out the webpage, lest the nosey librarian catch a peek of Vik's picture in the article and end up on the news, praised for his vigilance. *If You See Something, Say Something.*

Vik had seen enough.

24

Vik had committed me to memory on the boat—my face, my voice, my number. And now, standing beneath a sprawling live oak on the California capital grounds, he keyed me into his second burner phone in as many days and watched a low-resolution phone icon twirl about on the tiny display. He contemplated the vow of silence he'd made just days earlier, out of self-preservation. A vow he was about to break. Someone answered.

Remi? he said. Is that you?

Vik..., said a voice. No elation in it. The acoustics were strange; possibly speakerphone. But the voice sounded like mine. Hearing it, Vik became instantly willing to consider all manner of compromises.

You're there..., he said.

You left me.

Are you okay?

Why didn't you come, Vik? They're—

He heard a single, truncated shout, then a garbled exchange.

Remi? he said.

More shuffling. Multiple voices. English. Spanish.

Remi, what's going on? ... *Remi!*

Vik tried to stay tuned to my voice, though it grew distant, a signal fading to static. He pressed the phone's flip-up speaker to his ear and covered his other ear with his hand. He spoke my name yet again into the void. He heard a binging sound; the thump of a car door. Rustling. A familiar voice.

Veek, it said. Hello, old friend.

Vik's heart stopped. He closed his eyes and held the phone against his leg for a moment. He could hear Los talking, the lilt of his steady banter. *The two loose wires of my life have crossed,* Vik thought. *And shorted.* He brought the phone back to his ear.

...know you're there, Los was saying. I can hear you breathing. It's nice to hear. We had a pool going. People thought you were dead. Not me, though... C'mon... Say something. *Veek*.

I hate you.

Ha! No you don't.

This has nothing to do with her.

Oh, don't worry. We're being nice. Nicer than *you*. You just leave her to the wolves.

Vik refused to be baited. He forced a deep breath. Nearby, a triangle of girls was tossing a Frisbee; a toddler ambled across the grass, pursuing a squirrel. What world did everyone else even live in? For so long he had lived in it, too. It was a nice place. Just, not a real one.

You broke into my house, Vik said—not yet wanting to reveal all he'd seen: he didn't want to give Los the satisfaction.

This is true, Los said.

You stole my work.

It's not stealing if it belongs to you, Los said. But no matter. Your program doesn't run.

It does run, Vik said. You already *updated* it, asshole! So don't lie to me.

I don't know what you're talking about, Los said.

I saw it on a dealer's phone, Vik said Last night! So, you found some hack to finish it off, fine. But it's mine. I made it.

I have no idea what you saw, Vik. What I know is, the cops are trying to tunnel in. And if they crack this thing, if they use it against us... At this, Los let loose a discomforted laugh. From the start, the possibility of the program backfiring on Gamboa frightened Los to death.

My people, they finish what they start, Los went on. I

see to that. And this thing you're building needs to have walls, moats. Keep our kingdom secure. You hear me?

Vik, meanwhile, was stuck second-guessing himself. Blame turning itself inside out. A horrible feeling.

I have to call you back, he said, hanging up before there could be debate.

He started running.

The library was a few blocks away. He took the front steps three at a time, then slowed, calming himself as he passed the main desk. The librarian looked up. Vik raised a hand. *Here I am again! Take a good look!* The librarian smiled and waved.

Vik proceeded to his usual computer, looked up *pi*, and was forced to confront his mistake. The dealer's calculator had been merely that: it had output *pi*, same as it ever was. The 2 and the 3 had not been version and release numbers, but the actual sixteenth and seventeenth digits past the decimal. An obnoxious, chirping ringtone disrupted the room. Vik glanced around, only to realize his own pocket was vibrating. He'd never heard the phone ring. He unfolded it.

Hold on, he whispered.

Yoo-hoo, said the librarian, who'd now risen from his seat at the counter. No calls, please?

Vik stood up and headed for the exit, the phone cupped in his hands like the lizards he'd caught as a boy, their little bodies like electricity. A life in his hands.

Okay, Vik said when he was outside again.

We're going to figure this out, Los said. *Together.*

Let Remi go, Vik said. Right now.

You sound like you're in a hurry, Los said. But when we ask you to finish your job, you are never in a hurry.

Los. C'mon. These things take time. You know that.

Yes. And this is an arms race, Los said. *You* know that. With the FBI, the DEA, the fucking USA. And you were our secret weapon—at least I thought so—until your little *novia* started meeting up with cops...

She got arrested, Los. That's completely unrelated.

Vik, *please.* You are very good at what you do. I respect what you do. But I think maybe you do not respect what I do.

How long have you had her?

Since you abandoned her.

I didn't *abandon* her.

She got off the boat alone, no?

That was your man following us, then? On the dock.

Los said nothing. Vik knew it was as near an answer as he was going to get, and could only shake his head, standing there alone outside that library in the Central Valley of California, the sky blue overhead, the eye of a hurricane of his own creation.

Los said: You should know that she's been trying really hard to get in touch with you. Calling, texting, emailing. It's killing her.

Vik said, I emailed her.

No you didn't, Los replied.

And how would you know that, Los?

Because I read the fucking emails.

Yeah, Vik allowed—roiling on the inside to remain so outwardly patient. But did *she*?

Los didn't answer this, and Vik could stand it no longer. He snapped. *There's no use holding your cards close to the vest if you're the only one playing.* This wasn't a game of wits. It wasn't a game at all. Vik had been wrong about pi. He needed to know what, if anything, he was right about.

You burned my house down, he said.

Ah, Los said, and he paused. The conversation seemed to pivot on this pause. Forgive us our trespasses, he said.

Vik stayed silent.

When my son acts up, Los said, I ask him nicely to behave. I ask him one time. After that, I spank him.

Vik could only seethe.

It's interesting, Los went on. My daughter, she listens the first time. She prefers to avoid violence. But Angelo. Dude. Violence is that boy's second language. It's better than his Spanish.

I have nothing left, Vik said. *Nothing!* Do you realize that?

Los laughed.

This is funny to you? This is *insanity*.

It's *not* insanity, Vik! Los said—raising his voice for the first time. It is the complete opposite of insanity. It is logical. You go down a rat hole, I smoke you out.

What the hell do you want from me?

Loyalty, Los said.

You have it.

Si? So, *show* it.

How?

Stop running.

I'm not running, Vik said.

You're hiding.

I'm right here!

Yes, and where is that, Vik? Where are you?

Where are *you,* Los?

Me? I'm sitting in my truck, watching a pretty girl squirming in the dirt. Tight little ass. But *you* put her in that position. You put all of us in it. *You* decided to go off the grid. What are we supposed to think when you do that?

Think whatever paranoid shit you always do, Vik said.

I do, Vik. I lie in bed every night and think paranoid shit. And it's made me rich. And what I think right now is, if you're not talking to me, you're talking to somebody else.

I'm talking to myself.

But you call *me* insane...

Crazy people burn shit down when things don't go their way.

I speak the same language as my son, Los said. But I waited on you. There were those who wanted to move that night you took off, but I told them: *Vik will pop up. I know him. Trust him.* So we waited. All day Friday. All day Saturday. But I am only so influential.

Put Remi back on the phone.

I'm sorry. She's unavailable at the moment.

I talk to her or nothing happens.

Come see her. You can kiss her boo-boos.

She doesn't know anything, Los. You realize that?

Oh, but she does, Vik. *Now* she does. She knows *us.*

She's done nothing wrong, Los! *I've* done nothing wrong.

What a beautiful thing, Los said. A man with a clear conscience.

And something in Los sarcasm struck a chord in Vik. For it was a sore subject, denial. He'd let himself believe that his access to the cartel's upper echelon made him exempt from their suspicion, when of course it had been just the opposite. Vik was the sorcerer whose black magic had won a king his throne. And for this Vik had earned the king's gratitude, but not his trust.

Please, Los said. Let's not go in circles. All your stalling, all your fine tuning, it put us in a bad position. A position of weakness.

You want the new version.

I want assurances. I want to know beyond a shadow of a doubt that Vik Singh is who he says he is. That he's still a bad guy.

Vik considered that.

There is only one way this works, Los went on. You come in. You work with us. *Among* us.

When Remi's safe.

She's never going to be, Vik.

She can be away from *you*.

We are everywhere, Vik. You know this.

I do, Vik said, sadly. We are.

Neither man spoke.

Me for her, Vik said. I come in, you let her go.

If that's what you want.

I'll call back in an hour, Vik said. I'll give you a location.

We'll be right here, Los said, playing in the dirt.

25

Vik stood at Pier 48, looking across McCovey Cove at the looming stadium. Giants fans donned their oranges and blacks as they funneled out of downtown offices toward the waterfront for the 5:15 game. It was a beautiful summer evening in San Francisco, and a baseball game seemed cause enough for celebration— the pennant still up for grabs, though it was getting late. September had begun.

Vik had his game face on. A ticket in his pocket. Like many of the fans, he wore a backpack. He'd bought a new one to replace the one he'd stolen, which had then been stolen from him. It had a blonde female wig in it, plus an assortment of women's clothes, a pair of running shoes, sunglasses, $600 in cash, energy bars, and bottled water. A mango. A keychain with a spray can of mace. A new burner phone. A map of San Francisco. A note card with the name and contact info of T.J. Lawrence, the chemist-stoner from USF he'd partnered with in the Red Dot days.

He had just called T.J. out of the blue a few hours ago. Told him there was a girl who might need a place to lay low for a few days, if he'd be so kind. It had been a risk to call: there was a chance T.J. had heard through the grapevine about Vik's disappearance. But from what Vik had heard, T.J. didn't run with that crowd anymore. He'd moved to Hayes Valley with the hipsters. Had a fiancé.

I don't know, Vik, T.J. had said. Sounds kind of sideways. I'm not really in a position...

To what? Vik had asked, trying to laugh. Help a friend?

Dude. We haven't talked in a while. I've moved on. Sounds like maybe you haven't.

I should be better about keeping in touch.

T.J. asked, You see Los anymore?

Not really, Vik said. Not if I don't have to.

Man, T.J. said. *That* guy was a complete psycho.

Yeah, Vik said, staring blankly at a mussel-encrusted bulkhead.

I always felt like we were getting taken, T.J. said. We were taking all those risks, but it felt like he didn't give a shit if we lived or died, you know?

I'm not sure I felt *quite* that way, Vik said. I know what you mean, though.

T.J. muttered Los' name again to himself nostalgically.

Vik was through reminiscing. I've got to go, he said. Will you do this for me?

Nothing illegal, T.J. said.

No, Vik said. I just want to make sure she's got, you know, someone to call. She's my, um...

Partner in crime?

Girlfriend, Vik said. (Vik felt good revealing this to someone. Giving the relationship a witness.) He added, She probably won't even call you, but if she does...

I'll answer.

Thank you, Vik said, relieved. You're a good man.

You're welcome, T.J. said, in a way that made it clear Vik should never ask for anything again.

Let's get some beers some time soon, Vik offered.

Take care, Vik.

You too, Vik said. Stay out of trouble.

I'm trying, asshole.

I know, I know, Vik said. I'll try too.

You're the math guy. You know you can go halfway forever and still never get somewhere.

Theoretically, Vik said.

There was a letter in Vik's backpack, too. A third draft.

The first draft had served to get certain things out of his system, but he didn't think it fair to obscure matters with strong feelings; it had been, for him, like the line-priming rush of blood discarded for fear of contamination. In the second draft he'd wished me luck, then stated the obvious: saying I should be very afraid of the people who'd taken me. *She knows that already.* The third draft stated only that, were he in my position, he wouldn't think twice; he'd go straight to the authorities and tell them what little he knew in exchange for protection. He told me to act as though I were out only for myself. It went without saying, in his letter or otherwise, that he was not in my position. In closing, he'd allowed himself to use the word. *Love, Vik.*

He'd stationed himself near the stadium's main entrance, shaded from the late-afternoon sun by a corporate copse of palm trees. The plaza was bordered on two sides by busy boulevards. Near the intersection, a bronze Willie Mays was crouched forever in his signature follow-through, bat dangling as he watched an invisible ball soar over the modern offices and bars of King Street, invisible fans holding their collective breath, crossing invisible fingers. A tall man in a Giants visor hawked programs. A pair of policemen sat their panniered mountain bikes, eyeing the throngs through wraparound sunglasses. Queues had formed at the security checkpoints. People hooted and jostled for position in a communal way. The first pitch imminent. Home-field advantage. Life could be good.

Vik didn't even know who the Giants were playing. Still, he could sense the crowd's energy, expectation like static in the air. He felt charged up too, except with the wrong polarity. Somehow, this was apparent. A boy on his father's shoulders peered down at Vik, the smile on his little face becoming a stare of concern. A couple in matching jerseys let go of each other's hands to skirt Vik.

He'd specified the location, the time. He planned to hand me the backpack and the ticket and let me disappear into the stadium, where I could slip into disguise and dissolve into the crowd when it ebbed back into the city; or duck through a service door, or go straight to the stadium police.

Whatever it took. Whatever I wanted.

He was scanning the sea of faces when he felt a tap on his elbow and turned and suddenly we were standing right in front of each other.

The last time I'd seen him he'd offered to get me a drink. When he didn't return, I'd gone looking for him. I'd walked every inch of the boat. I'd called him. No response. I'd gone back to my seat on the upper deck and stared out at the moonlit lake, trying to understand. *Vik must have gone into the lake. By choice, though? Had someone harmed him?* I had no idea. When the ride was over, I'd disembarked with everyone else and sat for a little while on a bench overlooking the wharf, watching to see if he'd emerge from the boat. Vik's car was still in the parking lot, but I didn't have the key. I walked up to the main road and sat alone, waiting for the bus that loops the lake. An SUV pulled up alongside the bus stop; two men hopped out. They walked up to me slowly, and before I knew what was happening I was in their clutches, held off the ground, stuffed into the backseat. I was blindfolded and ziptied and driven for hours. I was put in a basement bedroom with a single mattress and a TV. I stared at game shows and came to the conclusion that I was going to be raped, and then killed. Unless Vik saved me. He'd gotten me into this. Only he could get me out.

There were men upstairs. The next day, they brought me food, and to my surprise and suspicion generally treated me okay. I felt like an animal being fattened for slaughter. They asked me lots of questions about Vik I couldn't answer. They kept my phone. Days later, I was being loaded into another SUV when my phone rang in Los' pocket, and he handed it to me, and Vik spoke my name...

Vik's first thought was to embrace me. That had been the way he'd envisioned this. Instead, he hesitated. Perhaps if I'd looked disheveled, or abused—if I'd looked the part of the hostage I'd become—embracing me might have felt natural. But I looked...*pretty*, though overdone. They'd dolled me up: make-up, hair, sexy dress, heels. A damn crucifix dangling between my tits.

Vik said my name. I could only look at the ground. I

wasn't the person he thought he was looking at. He looked like the groom at an arranged marriage, first laying eyes on his bride.

He managed to lock eyes with me; we compressed an entire conversation into a look. His eyes pleaded, mine held back. For there was simply too much; it would take years to get it all out. A lifetime.

I looked over Vik's shoulder. He turned. There stood Los. And behind him, a huge Latino man in a thin leather jacket. Vik didn't recognize this man's face, only his bearing —yet another of the interchangeable thugs in Los' employ. He had to assume there were others nearby he could not see. He'd chosen the location for the relative safety in numbers it provided, but that had been delusional: Vik had the data, but Los would always have the numbers.

Los stood studying Vik; he was being re-appraised. Having known Vik for years, Los was taking a fresh look.

Parking was a bitch, Los said.

Vik didn't so much as blink at this; he knew Los' tendency to downplay high stakes, to make everything a joke.

I was blank as a doll.

Everybody's looking for you at the bottom of a lake, Los said. But here you are, at a *béisbol* game!

Los went heavy on the Mexican accent—base-*bowl*—as if the word didn't deserve the effort of American articulation. He did the same with *fooot-bowl*—a passive-aggressive pronunciation. Los had maintained a love/hate relationship with America ever since his father and pregnant mother smuggled themselves across the border inside a crate of bananas, forcing American citizenship on him.

Base-*ball*, Vik said.

Los Gigantes de San Francicso, Los replied.

T.J. was right: Los was psychotic. This *was* funny to him.

Shut the fuck up, I muttered. Both of you. Just get this over with.

Los lifted his brow, explaining: Ever since you called, she is feisty.

I'd say she has a right, Vik said.

Los nodded in a way that said he understood why Vik

would say this, but that he completely disagreed. I don't put up with this type of shit, Los said.

That's because you're a pig, I said.

It shocked Vik to hear me talking this way. Los' man muttered something, and Los turned aside for a quick exchange in Spanish that left both men chuckling. Los turned back to Vik. What can I tell you? he said. She was nice when we picked her up. Very quiet.

A gag will do that, I said.

Do *you* put up with this shit, Vik? Los asked—the officiant at this bizarre wedding. (*Do you, Vik, take shit from this woman?*)

Vik stared at me and I could see he was dying to slip away to someplace we could walk and talk and cry and howl and lay beside each other for days on end, and afterwards decide how best to rejoin the world. Or whether to rejoin it at all. *Pure fantasy.*

I'd say she's putting up with *us*, Vik said. She shouldn't even be here.

But Los was still addressing his own question. Me, he said. I don't put up with bitches, men *or* women.

I muttered a curse under my breath and stared off into the crowd.

Well, I'm right here, Vik said. It's over. Remi can go.

Los nodded at the simple truth of this. A moment passed during which no one spoke. A woman approached with a cardboard sign: 'NEED TIX.' Los' man shooed her.

Yes, Los said. We could do it that way.

We *are* doing it that way, Vik said. That's the arrangement.

Los nodded. It is, he said.

Vik handed me the backpack, then pressed against me to slip the ticket in my hand. Los took a ceremonious step back and averted his gaze. (*You may now kiss the bride goodbye.*)

There's things you're gonna need in here, he whispered to me. To get you started at least...

I clenched my jaw. Tears came. The well was so deep.

This is all my fault, Vik said—though the letter said

otherwise: it had been drafted in the dark of night, but refined in the light of day, without having to look at me, and so all it contained were facts. It rested the blame on both of us. Seeing each other had made it all irrelevant.

I wanted so badly to lean my body into his. Plant a single kiss of absolution on his cheek. I couldn't.

Los and his man remained off to the side, eavesdropping on the most intimate and desperate conversation Vik and I had ever had. Every word bearing the weight of a hundred.

I'm doing what I can to fix this, Vik said.

Fix, I said—the word sounding just as counterfeit on my lips as it'd been on his, and Vik knew at that moment that he had nothing, really, to offer. No real allies. No resources. We had become puppets. This would go down however Vicente Gamboa wanted it to. And what Gamboa wanted was for Vik to enslave himself. To code himself into the cartel.

We don't have a whole lot of choice here, Vik said. Neither of us. I hope you see that.

I shook my head *no*, meaning, *of course*: I understood all of it, having consented to none of it. Something bright and hot inside me had been extinguished. I felt only resignation.

She's ready, Vik said. Let her go.

I looked at Vik, hoping he'd see that I wasn't ready. We both felt hesitant. We'd both gotten what we'd been yearning for since he stepped off the boat. We could see each other. Touch. And strangely, we felt a semblance of safety in this meet-up. No doubt these were bloodthirsty men around us, but it seemed they found no sport in sitting ducks; they would hold their fire until the birds took to the air.

Los said, You two done?

I was dabbing at my eyes with a fist. I leaned forward and rested my head against Vik's, the way I had on the boat. Then I stepped away and shouldered the backpack. My innocence on full display, all three men staring at me, my future in the balance.

All right, young lady, Los said. Have a good first day of school.

I hope someone kills you, I said.

I turned back to Vik. We locked eyes again; it was the only place left for us to hide. Organ music echoed inside the stadium. The crowd started chanting. Los stepped over and patted me on the head. It was a strange gesture—certainly a belittling one—but the way he'd had to maneuver around his man and squeeze between me and Vik gave the whole thing an artificial feel, like a play with bad stage direction.

That's when Vik noticed it. A dot of red light quivering on my forehead. I had no idea. Los put his arm around me; the other man grabbed Vik. Neither man had a gun that we could see. Vik struggled. His eyes scanning the crowd, the buildings across the street, the passing cars. *Wait*, he said.

Okay, Remi, honey, Los said. Run along now. You're out of my hands...

Remi, no, Vik said. You can't leave.

I turned to him. Yes I can, I said. That's how this works.

No, Vik managed. It's not. I was wrong.

I stared back at him, confused. Oblivious to the menacing *bindi* I wore. Unaware of our arranged marriage.

PART IV: *LA CASA DE HUÉSPEDES*

26

Vik and I stared out our respective rear windows. Neither of us had spoken since we were led against the flow of humanity to Los' Suburban, idling in an alley a few blocks from the stadium with a man at the wheel. Nor were we speaking now, as we were driven out of the city, restrained with luggage straps to leather captains' chairs. Zip-ties bound our wrists and ankles, tight enough to affect circulation. Vik's backpack, wallet, and thumb drive had been confiscated.

Los rode shotgun. The man from the exchange rode in the third-row. His cowboy boots extended into the carpeted no-man's land dividing us, the captive couple. Branded into his boot's lizard-skin was a skeleton in a hooded robe.

My silence was meant to be as much a suggestion as a shunning, and directed at every single man in the car. Mere minutes ago I'd wanted to kiss Vik. And though it was Los who'd reneged on Vik's deal, there was too much blame to go around. I was not in that moment capable of fairly divvying it out. My resentment landed wherever my eyes did. Vik. Los. Men. California.

And the men kept to themselves, with the exception of a few curt exchanges in Spanish between Los and the driver. Girder shadows contoured over the Suburban's buffed hood as we crossed the Bay Bridge. A new, multi-billion-dollar Bay Bridge was under construction alongside it; the old one was set to be scrapped, relegated to history, infrastructure reverted back to information. The sun looked dark orange through the illegally tinted windows. The driver flipped on the radio, pre-set to a ranchera station at high volume; he promptly lowered it to a more polite register. We looked out at Alcatraz.

Vik couldn't tell yet what he felt. It wasn't satisfaction, but nor was it fury, or even resentment. Those feelings had flared, yes, but they were already fading. Strangely, something about the surety of his new situation, fucked as it was, felt preferable to purgatory.

He couldn't tell what I felt. I sat facing away from him, my body a knot that would not be untied. I wasn't ready to give him the satisfaction of sympathy, as much as I wanted it. I was already hardening myself for another round of whatever this was. Vik didn't know where he was yet.

Welcome to hell, I wanted to tell him. *I'm already used to it.*

A punchy lilt of horns and strings filled the cabin. Ranchera music. For me, the music of unbidden tableside serenades by men in sombreros and ornamented pants. A sound to spell the awkwardness of a date gone horribly wrong.

We drove south through Alameda, San Antonio, San Leandro, San Lorenzo, Milpitas—American towns with names Los loved. Then east through yellowed hills to the I-5, aorta of the Central Valley, where we joined the flow of lettuce and asparagus, tomatoes and melons, cocaine and heroin, livestock and people—parallel rivers of white headlights and red taillights in the gathering dusk. We could only guess at our destination. There were only a few small duffels in back.

I was still done up in my dress and crucifix. I wriggled my foot until a high heel plunked to the floor, followed by the other. Like a toddler harnessed in a car seat, I exercised my limited means of protest. I did not, however, scream. I am not a screamer.

The fuck is this? Los asked, meaning the music that had now been playing for half an hour. He turned it off, put his window down. The stuffy air of the cabin swirled with the stench of nearby feedlots.

I started to speak; my voice cracked. Los turned around as if to confirm I had indeed broken my silence. I started again: Where are we going?

Los stared at me, most pleased. El Paso, he said.

All of the men ogled me, but the other men stared at my body. Los looked me in the eyes. I felt naked when he stared at me. Via the rearview mirror, I caught the driver smiling. I went back to staring out the window. I'd been with these men for days; their methods no longer surprised me.

We're driving to Texas? Vik asked.

Well, there *is* a plane, Los said. But I've been told it's too *conspicuous*. And so it sits in a hangar in Phoenix, collecting dust.

I rode it once, the driver said, earning a look from Los.

How far then? Vik asked.

El Paso? Los said. Oh, it's a ways.

The man in the back held his phone forward, between the captain's chairs, for Vik and I to see. It glowed with a map upon which a blue route, dictated by optimization software, snaked from the Pacific Ocean to the southern border of Texas. 'New Mexico,' as Los called it. He was forever reminding people that California used to be Mexico; Arizona, too, and Utah, and Texas, and Colorado; and of course New Mexico itself. A disembodied female voice from the backseat pronounced the sentence: One-thousand, one-hundred, and eighty-five miles...

Thanks, Vik muttered.

Oh yes, Los said. Thank you, Chavi.

Chavi nodded.

Los unbuckled and crawled back into the middle of the Suburban, where he wordlessly removed the luggage straps binding Vik and me. He left our ankles and wrists tied.

Relax, he said to Vik. Think of this as a business trip. All expenses paid. And you get to bring your girlfriend.

Vik was succumbing, as I had, days ago. There was no choice but to inhale, exhale, repeat. With each breath, in spite of himself, he was granting himself permission—as if it was his to give—to be taken for a ride. In fact, he'd begun to recognize the feeling in his heart: it was gratitude. For he'd been lucky. The exchange had gone south, but he could see that his failure to save me was probably the only reason I was still alive. The backpack he'd given me had been a suicide vest. Sure, I was clever, but taking on a cartel requires the type of brute-force resources only nations possess: intel; infantry. Gamboa was a country all his own, more powerful in some ways than Mexico, or even America. No amount of ingenuity would have protected me. Rock beats scissors every time.

We drove all night. At gas stations the men would climb out of the Suburban to stretch or take a piss while Los went inside to re-provision them with junk food and tall-boy energy drinks. Los rode shotgun the whole time, having synced his phone with the stereo to play an audio book, *The 7 Habits of Highly Effective People.* The dashed white lines slipped under the hood in an endless procession. Moonlit farmlands, strip malls, desert. The meditative look on Los' face was reflected in his darkened window for Vik and I to stare at, and hate.

The zip ties kept us bound only to a degree; a desperate man would not have been deterred by such restraints. A deranged man. Vik was neither. When I awoke, agitated, from a nap, and squirmed in my chair, Vik wondered about the length of my fuse. I'd been a hostage for four days by then. He'd only been one for a few hours.

It's freezing, I muttered to no one in particular.

Vik reached across the aisle and lay his bound hands on my knee. I curled into myself again and stared out into the night.

Where are we? I whispered.

Arizona, Vik said.

I have to pee...

Los heard this, and pointed out the windshield; the driver eased the Suburban across a rumble strip to the shoulder of the divided highway. Chalky dust swirled in the headlights. Los retrieved a pair of wire snips from the glove box, then climbed out of the Suburban and stood leaning against the fender for a minute, watching a pair of semi trucks go by —the only other traffic on the road. He pried open my door. I swung out my legs, presenting him with my conjoined ankles in much the same way a broken horse lowers its head to be unbridled. With a snip I was off, carefully picking my way out into the brush beyond the aura of the headlights. I could feel all the men watching, and lumped Vik in with them. This was all of men's doing.

I was already getting gaunt. Malnourished. Of my own volition. I had been offered plenty of food.

Rapidly, Los said.

I jogged a few conciliatory steps before reverting back to a walk. I ducked behind a creosote bush and squatted. My piss pooling on the parched ground. A semi roared by. When I was done I returned without incident. Los put fresh zip ties on my ankles, then looked across at Vik.

You now, he said, nodding toward the desert.

So Vik went shuffling out into the night. He, too, had no designs on escape.

Since Vik joined us, it seemed Los was having trouble deciding whether to treat us as hostages or as company, and had settled on treating us like children. Technically, Vik was still an employee.

Back on the highway, Vik took a cue from me and escaped into a nap—a self-indulgent hit from a hoarded stash of exhaustion.

When he awoke, we were at a gas station. Los returned from a brightly lit super-station carrying a powder blue XXL sweatshirt, screen-printed with saguaro cacti silhouetted against the sun, '*Arizona*' in stylized cursive. He tossed it in my lap, then snipped my wrists free. I dutifully pulled it on. It smelled of cheap polyester.

I left the sweatshirt's hood up. Pushed my wrists back out of the sleeves. *Ziiip.*

Eventually the sun rose to reveal beige and treeless mountains, a landscape both stark and beautiful, and only slightly easier to stare into than darkness.

Near midday we pulled off the freeway on the outskirts of El Paso, following a desolate road into sun-blanched hills. A few miles in we rounded a bend at the mouth of a canyon. A white van was parked anachronistically along the shoulder, aluminum ladders strapped to its roof. A faded placard on its side read: *Tony's Painting Service & Supply*. We pulled off the road and parked behind it. Los came around and opened my door. A hot breeze stole in. I took a breath as if preparing to dive.

We were shuffled toward the waiting van, the driver of which emerged to open the sliding door. Vik and I crawled together across the threshold. The corrugated metal floor was hot against our palms. Los and one of his men climbed in after us; they sat along narrow benches affixed to the sides of the cabin. The sliding door squealed on its track and slammed home. What light there was came through a curtain separating the back of the van from the front.

Sorry, friend, Los said to Vik, the sympathy in his eyes almost authentic, and the last thing Vik saw before he was blindfolded.

Y para ti, Los said, putting one me. It reeked of marijuana and body odor.

Vik and I tried to settle into the meager floor space we'd been allotted. The van began to move. I felt a hand on my head, forcing me down. My face pressed into what felt like a groin. *Sorry*, Vik said, attempting to rearrange himself, but there wasn't room; I had to be at least partly atop him. Los' man muttered something; Los laughed. I could feel Vik probing for me tentatively his bound hand. He gave my leg a gentle squeeze. *Ping?* I made my muscle tense, relax. *Ping.*

27

The thrum of the highway again. I sensed we'd continued on toward El Paso. We exited onto what felt like squared-off city blocks, all the turns right angles. I tried to sketch a mental map. Los reminded us to stay down, then called out some instructions to the driver. The van rattled over bad pavement. My skull butting against Vik's hipbone.

The van slowed and veered onto what felt like a sidewalk apron, then the incline of a driveway. We heard a garage door scrolling. Then everything went completely black.

The van door squealed. Someone cut away my ankle ties. There was a stench of exhaust and something else I couldn't place. Something human, yet unnatural.

There's a step here, Los said. He led us away from the van, Vik's wrists on my shoulder. The men followed. We heard a Spanish-language game show on a television in another room. Los spoke to someone. I felt hands on the back of my head, the blindfold loosening; strangely, my instinct was to resist, to keep my face pressed against the silk. To stay as long as possible in the dark.

With my sight restored, I looked first for Vik. His blindfold wasn't off yet. His breath had created a wet spot on the scarf over his mouth. His eyelashes flitted against the silk. Soon he could see again too, and he looked first at me, studying my face for clues about my state of mind, my level of fear.

I studied him back. It was not unlike waking up together.

We found ourselves in the entryway of a cramped and outdated home. Dead bolts on the front door; modest kitchen; linoleum throughout. Three men were watching TV on a massive leather couch in the living room. They glanced up from the show long enough to take us in, no longer. The two men from the Suburban took up spots on the couch. An industrial-looking AC unit droned in the corner; it was braced with nude lumber into a jagged hole in the sheetrock.

Los went to the kitchen and grabbed a bottle out of the fridge.

Cervezas? he asked—nodding at us. *Mi casa su casa*, he said.

Vik held up his zip-tied wrists as counterpoint to any insinuation of hospitality.

Los took a pensive pull on his beer, then started riffling kitchen drawers. Pausing, he looked at the ceiling and yelled: *Tenemos tijeras?*

Tal vez, came the reply from the main room.

Los shook his head. He took a rusty serrated knife from the sink and approached me with it. I offered out my wrists. He sawed away. When he had freed us both, he lobbed the knife back across the kitchen into the sink; it clattered in and out again, onto the floor. The men in the main room glanced over. Los left the knife and took out his phone.

Be good, he said to us.

I used my arms' newfound freedom to cross them over my breast. Can I go outside? I asked.

Los had his phone to his ear, a concerned look on his face. He shook his head, *no*.

I looked around: to the TV room, where there were no remaining places to sit; down the hallway, to unlit and seemingly off-limit bedrooms. Vik seemed to sense my indecision. He took a seat at one of the kitchen stools, a look on his face like this was a real home, *his home*, and not some outpost on the fringe of the first world. False as this nonchalance may have been, he was hoping it might buoy me, or at the very least entertain me. I looked down at my own dirty feet. I had not put the heels back on. Vik patted the empty stool beside his. Looking back, it was a lovely gesture: it made the simple act of sitting down seem like a choice I got to make, among alternatives.

The kitchen window had gauzy drapes through which we could see neighboring tract houses—the scabby dirt yards; the cinderblock walls; the small satellite dishes, aimed collectively at a common patch of blank south-Texas sky. Vik rubbed a hand on the counter as if cleaning crumbs. I stuffed my hands into the kangaroo pocket of my new sweatshirt.

Where does this end? I asked him.

Vik, of course, didn't have an answer chambered. There had been an error in his calculations, he knew that now—the equation would not balance; we could only end up with less than we'd started with. Through the window, we watched a rangy dog go trotting up the middle of the deserted *calle*. A street sign at the corner was too far away to read, and this almost came as a relief. For it was not lost on me that blindfolds can work both ways, that perhaps Los had been sparing us the burden of information. As if blind and blameless are ever the same thing.

I don't know, Vik said.

I was momentarily confused. The moment to have answered my question had already come and gone; he had missed it.

Vik got up. Started opening cupboards. None of the men seemed to care. The cupboards were mostly empty, though some of them—on the opposite side of the counter from me, out of my view—were packed top-to-bottom with bricks of cocaine. Vik gave no reaction to this, however. He carried on with his search, eventually finding a drawer of assorted plastic cups. He filled one with water from the sink and drank.

Want one? he asked.

Just fill yours again, I said.

I held the cup in both hands and sat nursing it like tea. One of the men came into the kitchen and grabbed beers from the fridge. He stared at me. Vik made a point of sitting back down beside me. The man winked at us and went back to the main room.

I upheld my end of the silence Vik and I seemed to have settled on. Small talk would have been just that—out of proportion with the scope of things. Real conversation—*honesty* —was impossible under the circumstances. Not speaking felt like fasting. It was harder, actually. I didn't know how much longer I could hold out.

One of the men left and came back with bags of fast food, one of which was left on the kitchen counter. Vik reached in, took a cheeseburger. I abstained at first, then began picking out French fries, one by one. Los went outside. He spent the next hour wandering the cracked concrete patio and dead grass of the backyard, his phone plastered to his ear. The men spoke in low tones.

I ventured down the hallway to the bathroom, passing a bedroom where one of the men was asleep on a bare mattress. The back of the toilet was stacked with porno magazines. Black mold speckled the ceiling above a dusty shower. The hot-water tap didn't work. On my way back I went into the kitchen and hunted down a piece of paper and a pen.

What are you doing? Vik whispered.

I'm going to write a letter, I said. To my family.

You don't need to do that, he said.

No? I said. And what reason do I have to believe that?

You have every reason.

I returned to my letter.

This is all a stupid game, he went on. A bullshit, machismo game. They wanna see me cave. So—*fine.* I'll give them what they want.

Now you will, I said.

Vik took that blow without refuting it. I glanced over Vik's shoulder at the men in the next room. You're not afraid, then? I asked.

No, he said.

Then why are you whispering? I asked.

Vik smiled at me, thinking, *Because I'm trying to walk a line between sanity and surety, Remi. For us. To protect what's left of us from them.* But whatever protection he thought he could provide us was needless. The nonchalance of Los' men was no act. They had lazed away the afternoon like a pride of lions, with a discomforting lack of concern for the couple in the kitchen—who, it seemed, could huddle and scheme all day. We were free to arm ourselves with rusty cutlery. Mount an attack. Make a break. Who knows: maybe we'd even manage to *kill* one of Los' men. *But what then?* All lions are born knowing the answer to that question. They take comfort in the answer. They take naps in it.

Los came back inside, sweating. *Un hora*, he said. The men nodded their acknowledgement and began to stir—yawning, stretching. Los headed toward the bathroom. He saw us and smiled.

For Vik, it was a smile he'd seen before on his father's face, when he drove Vik and his brothers into San Francisco to watch their first-ever professional cricket match. The boys jabbering away in the backseat, wrongly describing things they would soon see, but had never seen. Vik's father at the wheel, his lips sealed, but curled. The smile of a man content to let time do the telling.

28

The 12 men climbed out of the bathroom just after dark, the dusty shower basin having pivoted on concealed hinges to reveal a wood stairwell that led to a tunnel conjoining the twin cities of El Paso and Juarez. One twin spoke English, the other spoke Spanish. One had lately become a mass murderer.

The men looked frightened and filthy. They held tight to small duffels and hats. Los took obvious joy in our reaction to the tunnel. This reaction was awe. The tunnel was a hack, of course, but it transcended *jugaad*. Legitimate resources had been brought to bear. Legitimate design. It was a work not only of engineering, but of geopolitics, and art, and commerce, in the way that a multi-billion-dollar bridge can be, or a Banksy. The three women came out next—two quite pretty and seemingly aware of this, the third less pretty, and less aware in general, it seemed. Each woman clutched a bag of some kind.

The two groupings were under the direction of four Hispanic teenagers. I am left to dub them Polo, Tommy Hilfiger, Nike, and American Eagle Outfitters, on account of their apparel. As they emerged into the bathroom, each of these boys, in turn, adroitly slid aside a shoulder-strapped automatic rifle so as to embrace Los.

The eyes of the newly arrived men and women darted about, taking impressions. They quickly obeyed each of Los' instructions, all authority having somehow transferred to him here, aboveground. And perhaps Los held sway, too, in the country the pilgrims had just fled, even if it was an authority vested in him by a power higher still than himself, a man who like the pilgrims maintained a blurry identity, but whose wealth was a hundred million times greater than theirs, and who was therefore nothing like them at all. The men were filed into the room with the mattress, which was now leaned against a wall. Thick curtains had been drawn. The men arranged themselves without further instruction into rows on the floor. The women were steered into an adjoining bedroom. I retreated to our spot at the kitchen counter, leaving Vik in the crowded hallway, to gape wordlessly at what happened next.

They had hardly been inside the house five minutes. Suddenly one of the pretty women began to throw a tantrum. This, more than anything that had happened all day, seemed to trouble the men. They rushed past me into the bedroom. Vik watched the woman pull back the curtain and launch herself again and again at a window, the glass quivering with each assault but not breaking, and he realized: *it's not glass*.

Nike and Tommy Hilfiger toppled her and pinned her legs. Polo grabbed her arms while AE re-shut the curtain. Her screaming and grunting intensified. Snot was smeared across her upper lip and cheek. Los pushed past Vik. He was carrying a syringe and a vial and he sunk the needle into the septum and eased back the plunger while the woman glared up at him, shouting.

Suddenly there was yet another man in the room—one of the migrants. He wore a tattered denim jacket and was bald at the crown of his head. He pushed through the men, tossing Polo to the ground before tackling Nike and holding him down. He threw wild punches at the boy's head, bloodying his nose. The woman's screams intensified.

I could not see what was happening, and didn't want to. I thought: *someone must be hearing this...a neighbor, maybe...*

Vik watched as AE produced a knife and, without a moment's hesitation, drove the blade into the migrant's back, just below his ribs. The migrant arched his body and made a noise that sounded almost like ecstasy, followed by another, of sheer pain, distilled to its purest form. AE withdrew the knife, the blade bright with blood. The migrant crumpled to the floor, groaning. The woman went into hysterics. The man groaned and groaned. Reached out. He and the woman held hands. A puddle of blood grew beneath him. The other women in the room turned their heads as the life drained from the man's eyes. That was the first person Vik had ever watched die.

Watched murdered.

The woman did not stop wailing, nor did she let go of the man's limp hand until whatever Los then injected into her neck kicked in. As it did, she sat against the wall staring across the room at Vik, drawing others' eyes in the room to him as well, exposing him for his voyeurism. The look in her eyes, the way it implored...it mortified Vik. Here was someone so far gone as to believe he could help. He returned to the kitchen to find me at the counter holding my head in my hands. He would not sit down, though I implored. He was boiling inside.

They just—

I know, I said.

I saw it. I saw everything. And I just...

Don't. You can't think that way.

What did that man just die for?

Vik, seriously. *Stop.* It's not your fault. You didn't do anything.

Exactly. I just fucking *stood* there...

You didn't kill him.

Vik shook his head, *No.*

Los' men cleaned up the blood with towels. Soon after, the women and remaining men were taken away in the van. We never saw them again.

Now, Los said. He said it to no one in particular, without raising his voice, and still the young men gathered, as did

Vik and I. One by one we descended the plywood steps.

The tunnel was cooler than the house. Our group walked single file, the tunnel shoulder-wide. Two of the young men carried the migrant's corpse in a tarp wrapped with duct tape. I could hear an echo of water dripping, and the rhythmic clicking of rifle straps. I could walk without stooping. I tried to glimpse the tunnel's southern exit but could not. Electrical conduit ran along the ceiling between florescent bulbs. Metal cross-bracing, as in a mine shaft, supported the roof. I dragged a fingertip along the clay wall and wondered what was directly above. I tried to guess when we'd crossed over but there was no way of knowing.

I was still barefoot, and faltered on the rocky floor. This drew Los' attention; he barked an order. We halted while the youngest boy knelt. A pair of pristine Air Jordans were passed up the line. With everyone watching and waiting, I knelt too, and laced the shoes on. Thank you, I said.

We descended another set of stairs to a deeper section of the tunnel. Was the Rio Grande flowing above us now? Looking ahead over Vik's shoulder, I saw a man in cowboy boots sitting on the bottom step of another staircase. He had on designer jeans with a white belt. His t-shirt, taut around his biceps and chest, read REPUBLIC OF TEXAS. He wore a pistol on a holster. The severe tan lines on the side of his face matched the wraparound sunglasses currently atop his head. He was eating an apple and he rose as we approached and glanced at the corpse. He shook Los' hand.

This the IT guy? he asked, nodding at Vik.

It is, Los said.

The Texan bit into his apple and stood chewing. At least he's fuckin' Indian, he said.

Los grinned and turned to Vik, to see what he thought of this. Vik, meanwhile, couldn't keep his eyes off the corpse.

The house into which we then ascended was architecturally much like the one we'd just left, but smelled more like home cooking; here and there could be found a grandmother's flourishes: knickknacks, photographs. Decorative iron bars covered the windows. A gate separated a walled-in courtyard from a dirt road.

Vik was at that moment struggling to process the minuscule, and yet significant, degree of latitude we'd just traversed via the tunnel; his mathematical mind couldn't help but visualize an equation describing the cliff-like transition. It would have to be a step function, he'd decided. The Heaviside function, probably. With its disjoint in whatever variable one cared to plot: GDP; Christianity; Supply; Demand. Even average rainfall might prove unaccountably discontinuous. Vik had always struggled with step functions—not their implementation, more their *philosophy*. He'd used them in his code whenever he needed a variable to change abruptly from one value to another. Yet to try and account for what actually *happens* to the variable during such a transition seemed always to require hand waving, much like he'd seen professors use to explain 'quantum tunneling:' a particle comes to a barrier, then magically reappears on the opposite side; it just *tunneled*, see? For many years Vik thought the Heaviside function (the eponymous brainchild of one Oliver Heaviside) was actually called the 'Heavy Side' function. And, really, Vik's version makes more sense: a variable cruises along in some lightweight state, then plummets all of a sudden to a weightier one.

Does someone live here? I asked.

In Mexico? the Texan said. (This got a laugh out of Los.)

This house, I said.

Just a couple old beaners, the Texan said.

He led us past doily-strewn side tables and walls adorned in crucifixes and candles. We came to a sitting room where an old woman in a muumuu sat watching TV. The two men carrying the corpse turned down a hallway and disappeared. The old woman did not get up, but gave a warm, near-toothless smile. She beckoned me with a flick of the wrist. When I did not move, the Texan put his hand at the small of my back and provided an impetus.

Be polite now, he said.

The old woman reached up with both arms. She took my face in her calloused hands. I stared back into her milky eyes. She spoke, her lips barely moving. The Texan translated: She says she don't see too many ladies going ya'll's direction.

169

She says you are beautiful.

I forced a smile and said, Tell her it isn't by choice.

The direction? Los asked. Or the beauty?

The woman nodded toward one of the boys. *Mi nieto*, she said.

I followed her gaze. The grandson looked away, blushing behind his Kalashnikov rifle. I lay my hands tenderly atop the old woman's for a moment. I wanted somehow to thank her for her small kindness. Then I backed away. The woman spoke again, this time in English.

Baywatch, she said, jutting her chin at me. This got a rise out of the men.

That's enough, Los said. He kissed the old woman's forehead and said, *Gracias, Rosalita. Hasta luego.*

She sucked her cheeks and batted a hand in the general direction of the men and their ways, then returned her attention to the TV.

29

In a Mexican garage antipodal to the American one, we loaded into the back of a run-down taxi. The 'taxi' light atop the car was not lit; the driver was waiting with one hand draped over the steering wheel. He didn't turn around when Vik and I were loaded in. Dangling from the rearview mirror were a cluster of tiny flags, shell necklaces and a picture of some haloed saint. The Texan rode shotgun. The front and back seats were separated by a Lexan partition with a rectangular slot for cash and an array of holes for words, neither of which were exchanged as we drove out of the dark garage and into Juarez.

Los followed behind us in a white pickup with two young men riding in the bed. The taxi's rear doors were child-locked, but the front windows were down, and the city diffused into the backseat: the smells of meat and exhaust, the pulse of music, the barking of dogs, the buzz of scooters, the honking of horns. The Texan hung his hand out into the flow of it all.

It was evening, the light spotty—some blocks cast in pastoral darkness, adjacent ones aglow in commercial signage and streetlight. Vik and I again found ourselves staring out our respective rear windows, acclimatizing in our own ways. The taxi's suspension creaked; its upholstery exhaled cigarette smoke. We came to a group of men urging a car out of deep sand. Its rear wheels spun without purchase. The

Texan muttered something to the driver, who veered into on-coming lanes and bypassed the scene. Vik lay his hand on mine.

Juarez seemed not so much a foreign place as an altered one, its familiarity unsettling. The omnipresent ALTO signs, with their four-lettered command in white letters on a red octagon—STOP signs, yet *not*. Spanish words we didn't know touted brands we did: Coca-Cola, Bud Light, Ford. Tattooed on the taxi driver's neck were the comingled 'L' and 'A' of the Dodgers logo. This was California, and yet *not*. The fun-house-mirror effect of it all put me in a state of heightened perception and suspicion. For days I'd been content to let the world wash over me; suddenly I became more alert. Vik, too, turned his head to track things as we passed.

There were tires everywhere. Columnar foursomes outside storefronts; shredded loners amidst the weeds and palm trees of the boulevard; a spare strapped to the roof of a slouching sedan.

The streets teemed: a young girl in a tube-top lugging a baby, two boys on a scooter, a pack of schoolgirls in uniform, a woman hawking bottled waters at a stoplight, an old woman sweeping a sidewalk, a man bent under the hood of a mini-pickup. Well-dressed elders occupied graffiti-ridden benches in a public park; teenagers leaned into the windows of idling cars. So many people, going about lives they'd led long before Vik and I bore witness from the backseat of a taxi. Lives they would continue leading after we were gone.

The Texan turned around, watched us taking it all in. He smiled in a belittling way that seemed to say: *I'm American, too, remember. I know what ya'll are seeing right now, because I used to see things that way, too.* I glared back at him through the bulletproof plastic, hoping to wordlessly convey my reply, which was: *I don't give a shit what you see, in Mexico or in me.* Vik had turned to stare off into the unlit hills above the city. He was wondering where the migrant's body had disappeared to.

The driver downshifted in preparation for a grind up a steep road, the taxi straddling a channel of runoff eating away at copper-colored dirt. The hillside neighborhood was composed of what looked like tiny citadels in varying shades of pastel. Some of the homes looked perpetually incomplete, with rusted rebar jutting from their facades, tarps flapping in the evening breeze. Others were fully realized, and well-occupied, judging by the number of cars parked outside.

The road leveled off. We pulled up to the gate of a property surrounded by a 10-foot stucco wall with exquisite decorative tile. The driver rolled down his window and spoke a few words into an intercom. Moments later, the gate clanged to life and rolled aside, granting the taxi birth into an expansive courtyard. The house was massive, with iron-work flourishes and a Spanish tile roof. A man in a tracksuit emerged from the front door. As the gate rolled shut, I realized Los was no longer tailing us.

The taxi driver stayed put while the Texan came around to open Vik's door. I slid across the bench seat and got out on his side. In the courtyard, water streamed tranquilly down a polished, up-lit stone sculpture. Were we to have both suddenly lost our memories, we'd have believed *we'd* picked this destination.

The Texan ushered us toward the house, two men flanking the footpath. Something cat-like moved atop the perimeter wall, and we turned. It was a boy, no more than 10. He crouched against a tree trunk and looked down at us. The Texan made an angry gesture; the boy returned his attentions to the street-side of the wall.

What is this place? Vik asked.

La casa de huéspedes, the Texan replied.

Wezz-ped-ezz, I repeated, the word so foreign in my mouth that I'd parroted the Texan, despite his having murdered the pronunciation himself.

Our *guest* house, the Texan translated, turning to grin at us.

We were led through the front door into a spacious entryway. Tile floors echoed with the calming white noise of another water feature. The men inside sized us up. I felt as though I'd left something in the taxi—a piece of luggage? a passport?—but it was just the lingering nerve endings of my normal, amputated life. I kept my oversized sweatshirt on like a cloak of invisibility.

Looking at me standing there, Vik felt as sorry as he ever had: sorry for me; for my family; for his mother; for the murdered migrant. For Jurarez. For himself. He wished Los was still around. If nothing else, Los provided continuity, even hospitality. Vik felt abandoned. Sentenced.

The Texan left with a curt, *Adios*. As the front door shut, one of the men typed a code into a keypad on the wall. A confirmatory, two-note chime sounded throughout the house.

No leaving, okay? said the man, smiling. He wore a goatee that only partly obscured a jagged scar near the corner of his mouth. Unlike his cohorts, who openly brandished AK-47s, he did not appear armed.

You no need to go, he added. Here is everything for you. Everything you are need.

La casa de huéspedes was furnished like a department store showroom, with a jumble of décor styles on display in close proximity. From what I could tell, no specific taste had been applied, except perhaps *expensive*. As we were led through the house, we passed a game room with gold-leaf ceilings, flat-screen TVs and a Tecate bar sign casting a neon blaze over a white pool table; we passed a bathroom with marble walls, Harley-Davidson towels and a Dalí painting; a bedroom with a low-slung, white leather daybed beside an oak dresser; a long room with upholstered walls and a dozen, Native-American-patterned chairs around a medieval-looking, iron-and-glass conference table. But the bones of the home shone through—cracks on the ceilings, shoddy trim work, leak stains. The man leading our tour, if that's what it was, seemed keen on confirming our positive reactions along the way. Vik and I obliged, offering the occasional, *Nice*. Or more appropriately, *Wow*.

We descended into a basement, then through a kitchen with a massive range and a stainless steel hood fit for a restaurant. A woman chopping onions glanced up as we passed. The men ignored her but Vik raised a hand in greeting. He was hoping she'd see he was not aligned with the men from whom she took orders, that *he* took their orders too. She returned to her cutting.

We came to a tiered theater with La-Z-Boy recliners in all styles and colors, plus a plush sectional couch, even a carved-wood throne—as if each audience member had been allowed to pick their seat from a catalogue. The theater had fabric walls upon which hung photos of *futbol* players and porn stars, each lit by its own wrought-iron scorpion sconce.

Who stays in this place? Vik asked.

We are, the man replied, as if confused by the question. Also the guests.

Is there a room, then, for guests? I asked. Where *we* can go?

Of course, the man said. This is up-*eh*-stairs.

He kept walking. I looked at Vik. He could only shrug.

We were shown to the end of a dim basement hallway. The man with the scar paused at the door until we were front and center, then opened it. I felt a draft of cool, captive air and peered into the darkness. The man flipped a switch, and there, set up in the corner of a windowless storage room, was Vik's workstation, with its semicircular desk and ergonomic chair and everything else, configured exactly as it had been at Lake Tahoe. His iMac, his MacBook Pro. The keyboards weathered by *his* fingertips; *his* crumbs still strewn in the grooves. All of it risen from the ashes. Vik crossed the room with the cautious thrill of a child who, under his parents' gaze, approaches gifts under a Christmas tree.

How..., he started to say, but stopped himself: the answer was obvious enough. They'd taken care, that's how. They'd made it a priority. Someone had.

He crossed his hands atop his head and just stared. The men looked on proudly, whispering to each other. Vik, meanwhile, had momentarily fallen behind the curve, like some jetlagged time traveler. *These things are mine,* he almost had to say aloud to believe. Spared from arson to become instruments of indentured servitude. *Here is my file basket.* The scratch-paper stack of the junk-bond trader's unopened mail had been meticulously recreated. *And here is the trash bin I puked into, out of welling fear.* Now empty.

It was all undeniably *here*, and therefore corrupted, all of it. Vik's, and yet *not*.

Like his life.

Like me.

30

Vik leaned across his chair and tapped the keyboards. The monitors did not light up.

Is okay? the guide asked.

It's how I left it, Vik said. I'll say that.

The man nodded sternly.

What about internet? Vik asked.

The man didn't seem to understand. One of the other men said the word again, with accent: *El internet.*

Ah! Si, si, said the man with the goatee. Sorry. Internet. Yes.

You have it down here, Vik said.

In Juarez?

In the basement.

The man looked over his shoulder at an acne-scared young man standing off to the side. I hadn't noticed him before. The two men exchanged glances. The goateed man turned back to Vik.

Not for you, the man said.

Vik nodded acceptance, secretly antsy to hack his way onto whatever nearby network he might find.

You are work now, said the man.

Vik pointed at me. What about her? he said. What's she supposed to do?

There is TV, the man said. There is anything. Only, she is stay in the house.

I'm staying with Vik, I said.

In here? Vik asked. But I'm just gonna be…

I know, I said.

The men looked at Vik. The call seemed to be his. He was already anxious about writing such critical code under duress, in a storage closet. But he was the only thing left for me to cling to, even if he, too, was drowning. I glanced around the room with fresh eyes. Nothing had changed, of course. There was no place to *be*, really, other than Vik's one chair. So I edged through the gathered men and plunked down in the only possible place, a four-foot square of bare concrete. I tucked my knees up to my chest, hoping the physical argument I was making was convincing enough: having shrunk in stature right before their eyes, I'd proven just how small I could become, what little space in this world I'd come to expect.

We're good here, Vik said. Both of us.

If it is how you want, said the man with the goatee.

Necesita una cama de perro, one of the men muttered as the group pushed back into the hallway.

We are out here, the man added, when you are need something…

At this, he demonstrated a knock against the door.

I need my notebook, Vik said. It's in my backpack.

Where is the backpack?

You tell me, Vik said. You guys took it.

The man shook his head and took his leave, easing the door shut. We heard the dead bolt engage. Vik huddled beside me. Without my consent, a single tear streaked down my cheek. I indulged in a sniffle. This tiny outpouring was all I allowed myself. I cleared my throat, swallowed, and it was over and done with. Vik rest a hand on my knee and planted a kiss on my temple. I leaned into it ever so slightly.

Work, I commanded. Forget I'm here.

What are you going to do? he asked. Just sit there?

Maybe, I said. I might sleep.

There's music on my laptop, Vik said. Or, there *was*.

It's fine.

You've got to do *something*.

Work, I commanded.

Vik got up, took the single step to the door and knocked, nice and loud. Seconds later, a voice on the other side: *Si?*

I need something else, Vik said.

No entiendo.

Jesus. Just, go get the other guy!

(Grumbling.) *Momento...*

A few minutes passed. When the door finally unlocked, there stood the man with the goatee, holding Vik's backpack. He handed it over.

Gracias, Vik said.

Is fine, the man said.

Now I need something else though, Vik said.

Chingada....

I tried asking *him,* Vik said—gesturing at the sentry. He doesn't understand.

Maybe you try ask him in *es-Spanish.*

I don't speak a lot of *es-Spanish*, Vik said.

Que lastima, the man replied.

Si, Vik agreed, adding: But I'm guessing *you* don't speak combinatorics. *Correcto*? So how about you do your job and I'll do mine?

The man said nothing to this. So Vik proceeded to make his request, which required some pantomiming and was followed by a few tense minutes of waiting. Then all was well: I was nestled against the wall with Vik's laptop on my lap and a pair of Vicente Gamboa's noise-cancelling headphones on my ears.

While I tried to let myself get lost inside music only I could hear, the man stood in the doorway with a look of disgust on his face, his well of hospitality now clearly exhausted. He was no butler, after all. He stepped over my legs and jabbed a finger into the power button on the iMac. To Vik, the startup chime sounded newly ominous. He'd never loaded a profile picture; the icon on the login screen remained an anonymous male silhouette. Vik said thanks, but did not yet sit down—trying to make it clear that he was ready, now, to be left the hell alone. The man nodded at the computer, as if to

179

say, *Now finish your masterpiece, motherfucker.* Then he left.

Vik looked at his computer clock. It read 10:33PM. *Where?* he wondered. *Tahoe?* He would have believed it was almost any time at all. It was nighttime. He knelt beside me.

I peeled off the headphones.

Sorry, Vik said. I need to check something.

He took the laptop. Navigating menus, he found the Wi-Fi disabled, with an error message: "No hardware installed." He flipped the computer upside-down and inspected the star-pattern screws along the perimeter of the aluminum chassis. Having never needed to remove those himself, the tiny abrasions he found were proof enough that the Wi-Fi card was, indeed, no longer inside. He checked the other computer. It had been similarly neutered.

He smiled at his cell mate, then got to work.

We were supine together on the concrete floor—Vik's head near my feet, me still wearing the headphones, both of us staring up into the filament of the light bulb, and slow to snap out of our private trances—when the men stormed in and stood looming over us, Los and two others: the quiet, acne-scared one and an older one.

Romeo y Julieta, Los mused.

Sesenta y nueve, the older man countered.

I peeked at the laptop: 1 AM.

Los clucked and said, We bring his chair all the way from California and he lays on the floor.

Nevada, Vik corrected.

Lies, I added. *Lies* on the floor.

Que? Los asked.

You're an ignorant fucking arsonist, Vik said.

Ah, Los mused, *Nay-bada.* Sorry. Yes. No state income tax!

He stood looking at the floor, deep in thought, then clapped once, nice and loud.

So, he said, what are we doing in here, on the floor?

Even I knew Los enough by then to sense that he was

pissed to have found us this way, although not surprised, as if the reason he'd come was *because* he was pissed, and it struck me that there was surely a camera hidden somewhere in the room, tucked inside an air duct or stashed amongst the clutter on the shelves. The type of camera without a little red indicator light, the type I should have by then expected to be trained on us at all times.

Vik is thinking, I explained. (For I had posed a similar question to him half an hour earlier, when he first lay down next to me.)

I'm paying him to write code, Los said.

So you *are* paying me, Vik said.

Of course, Los said.

I want thirty five, then.

Percent? Los said, aghast. We agreed to thirty. Just like last time.

This isn't *just like last time*, is it?

Los frowned and said: An *inconvenience* tax, then...

Vik got his feet under himself and stood, eye to eye with Los, and might have dug in his heels over this dispute had he not noticed the neon bottlenecks clutched in Los' lowered fists: Lime Jarritos. Los handed one to each of us. The caps were already off. I took a long pull. Vik set his down on the desk. A teenaged girl came through the doorway carrying two plates of tacos with rice and beans, garnished with radishes and *pico de gallo*. There were napkins and forks in her shirt pocket.

Having disappeared so completely into his work, Vik was slow in reconnecting with his own body. He stared at the plates as if confused what food even was. The girl could find nowhere obvious to set her delivery down. I stood and took receipt.

Los stepped past Vik to the desk and picked up a piece of notepaper. He inspected it. Vik said nothing—just let the moment stagnate: Los frowning down at formulae outside the scope of his comprehension, as if he might—what? offer a suggestion? call out some mathematical oversight? The longer Los stood there, the stupider he looked, and perhaps this occurred to him, too. He let the paper fall to the floor as if it hadn't even interested him in the first place. He posed the only question he had license to.

How much longer, *cuate*?

Vik took his time answering. For he was relishing a long-absent sensation: leverage. He looked at me, as if confirming I'd detected it too. I held his gaze. *Yes.*

You know what I'm going to say, Vik replied (for this was not the first time Los had demanded innovation on a timetable).

How long does it take to catch a fish? Los replied, in his best Vik voice.

Now it was Los looking to me for commiseration. And rightly so: I was perhaps the only person on earth who understood Vik as well as he did. Everyone in the room was watching. I cocked my head to a taco and bit in. Chewed meditatively. Making it clear to Los that I'd thrown in my cards; I wasn't in on this hand. Los got up in Vik's face, close enough to kiss him, and gut punched him, sharp and square. Vik doubled over, sucking wind.

You and me, Los said. We are in a funny position.

Vik coughing, clutching his stomach, trying to get wind enough to speak...

I want something from you, Los said, and so you think I need you. That you can play games. That you can lie around down here with your girlfriend.

I don't..., Vik managed—straightening up.

Los struck another blow, this one to Vik's kidney. Vik crumpled to his knees.

Yes you are, Vik, Los said. Yes you are. And I'm telling you, it is a little dangerous. For you, *and* her. Believe me when I say, I know you are good at what you do. You have done amazing things for us in the past, it is true. But you are not the only one who can do such things. You are replaceable. Just like everybody, at any time. I can just—

Just what? Vik taunted from his crouch. However, he did not truly want to hear the honest answer—that *he*, like his program, was executable. Nor did Los, mercifully, see fit to speak it.

I saw fit to fill the silence. Trust me, I said. Vik's been

working. It's boring as hell in here.

Across the room, Vik's open terminal window, the expectant blink of its cursor...

He's going to get it done, I added.

Rapidly? Los asked.

Yes, I said.

So you are his agent, now?

I shrugged, then turned to Vik, begging with my eyes for him to speak up, to argue on his own behalf. He got to his feet. Stood staring at Los. Ready to take another punch, if Los wanted to deal him one. Los turned to me with a devilish grin.

Julieta, he muttered.

Nothing more was said. So this was going to have to suffice—this temporary truce I'd brokered. The terms being: *Vik will deliver, and soon. And Los will wait, but not much longer.*

Thirty five, Vik muttered.

Fuck you, Los countered. *Twenty.* At this, he raised his brow, daring Vik to dig an even deeper hole for himself. Vik said nothing. Los' hand shot out, and Vik flinched, only to realize it had been offered out to shake.

Slowly, Vik took it.

Los shook, and turned to go. *Buen provecho*, he said on his way out the door.

Vik was already doing the math. He'd just given up at least $200k a year. Or, maybe, nothing at all. Now in the cartel's clutches, where could he even go with his share of the spoils? What freedom did money even buy? It was credit at a prison commissary.

Vik and I huddled together against the wall. Vik was sore, and full of hate. He nodded at the food.

Think they drugged it? he asked.

No, I said—though the possibility had crossed my mind. But what drugs would they use? Adderall for Vik, Xanax for me? Drugging us wasn't in Los' self-interest, and there was no surer way to know Los' mind: self-interest was *his* optimization engine. Vik picked up the laptop and opened a blank new program file.

Well, I said. Nice talking to you.

At the top of the terminal, where Vik would typically comment out the line and enter a new script's working title and revision number, he wrote: *i think theres a camera in here.* He kept the computer on his lap, but angled it toward me. I read the screen. Then lofted my middle finger at the empty room. That's exactly how I felt.

Vik, meanwhile, felt like typing to talk. He wrote more: *i'm angry too you know*

I started dragging my fingers around the keyboard, producing a train of incoherent letters.

C'mon, Vik pleaded.

What? I said. Fucking *talk.*

Vik took a breath. Remember Tahoe? he asked. He wasn't sure how to put it any better than that. What he meant was, the whole summer; the ride to Marlette; me, before...

That seems like a long time ago, I said.

And with that, Vik was sunk. Because implicit in the distance I felt from our former lives was a heartbreaking reality: we were no longer *ourselves.* How could we be? Vik started backspacing, one-by-one, through the letters, then held down 'delete'. The cursor accelerated; our little one-sided conversation vanished. He took my hand. I looked at him. Saw the need in his eyes. I let my head fall to his shoulder. We sat like this for awhile, staring out at the little red eye that could not be seen, but surely was there. *Maybe we aren't our old selves,* I thought, *but that doesn't mean our new selves can't love each other.*

We heard a commotion above us, men shouting in the big house. It was hard to tell if the shouts were in sport or anger; it sounded like a boxing match. I put the headphones back on and zoned out, absently humming the song. Vik knew the words. He whispered along. I couldn't hear him.

He lasted another half hour or so at the computer with diminishing returns. He could no longer think clearly. He saved his code and turned around. My eyes were closed, my chin on my chest. I was breathing slowly. He tapped my knee and I threw up my hands, my eyes wide with fright.

I'd thought he was them.

31

Vik knocked on the door. The man with the goatee appeared, accompanied by a boy.

Terminado? the man said. You are done?

For tonight, Vik said. We'd like to go to our room if we could.

Por supuesto. I take you.

And back we went, single file past the empty theater, the darkened kitchen. Up the basement stairs. A taxidermied coyote snarled at us from an artfully lit alcove. A pop song accompanied us everywhere, playing from speakers in the ceilings and walls. There were more men about the house now, and women. A group drinking in the game room. An amorous couple up against each another in a hallway, the woman's bloodshot eyes devouring us as we passed.

I asked the man leading us if I could have a toothbrush, pantomiming brushing my teeth.

Of course, he said. There is everything for you, in the room.

At the front of the house we were reunited with the Texan from the tunnel, recognizable only from his sunglass tan. His designer jeans and t-shirt had been stripped off; he swayed, naked, barely able to stand on his own, in the middle of the foyer, upright on account of a noose, the leading rope of which was looped over a crossbeam twenty feet above and tied off on the staircase's iron railing. His wrists, ankles, and mouth had been bound with duct tape. Streaks of dry blood ran from his nostrils and ears. His left eye was purple and black and swollen shut. The letters 'FBI' had been written in permanent marker across his chest; the word '*soplón*' written on the duct tape over his mouth. A young sentry sat at the bottom of the stairs, playing a game on his phone.

We did our best not to gawk. As it had been in the taxi, the Texan and I shared a look, but his eyes were not judging me this time. They were full of fright.

I looked away. Vik, though, felt an obligation not unlike fellowship to maintain eye contact for as long as the Texan needed. In fact, Vik wanted to stop and talk to him, ask him what he'd done to deserve this, though it was clear enough. What Vik really wanted to know, then, was how the Texan had gotten caught.

Without a word from our chaperone about the spectacle, we were led to the second floor, then down a long hallway with doors on both sides. At the end of the hall, a door was opened for us and Vik and I passed through, then halted in the welcoming downdraft of a ceiling fan as we surveyed the suite, with its king-size bed and mahogany headboard, its adjoining bathroom. Wall-mounted reading lamps flanked the bed, and had been left on. There were bottled waters on a side table.

Best room in the house, said the man.

I made my way to the window and stood staring blankly out at the palm trees, the stucco wall.

There are clothes, said the man. All sizes.

He pulled open the closet doors to show us. Vik looked, nodded. I remained at the window with my back turned until the man and the boy had left.

Do you think they're going to kill him? Vik asked—giving voice to the conversation we'd begun downstairs with only our expressions as we beheld the tormented Texan narc.

Do you think they're going to kill us? I asked.

No, Vik replied—too quickly. His heart speaking up before his head could. No, he said again.

We sat side by side at the foot of the bed, not touching, and stared at the floor. Each of us waiting for the other to weigh in, but there was nothing really to add. Every possible pronouncement would be mere prognostication. Neither of us could make any promises. We were powerless, and felt it. I couldn't sit any longer. I got up. Escaped into the bathroom. Found a stack of folded towels on the countertop. They smelled faintly of mildew. I pulled down my pants and sat on the toilet. The ensuing burble as I urinated was a kind of intimacy—albeit the intimacy of siblings, or cell mates.

You're okay with this arrangement? Vik called from the bedroom.

With you hearing me pee? I replied, and I laughed.

I felt like I was emerging from a dark tunnel, and feeling fatalistic. We had no power over fate except to laugh in its face. Mine was a short-lived, unhinged laugh. It might have frightened Vik. It frightened me. For it cut to the rotten core of things. This whole affair was a cruel joke.

I flushed. Took my time washing my hands, tilting my face at the mirror. Trying to recognize myself.

I mean the one bed, Vik said. I can sleep on the couch, or we could ask for another room.

Vik, I said. It doesn't matter.

I tried to laugh again. Vik didn't. This did matter, to him.

It's fine, I added—and when that didn't seem enough, I told him the whole truth: I want it this way.

Okay, he said. Good. Me too.

With the door to the hallway shut, the music and occasional outbursts emanating from the house were muffled enough to create a feeling of seclusion in our suite. I went to the closet and stood touching the clothes. I still had on my hoodie, the summer dress flaring out the bottom. Vik and I both kicked off our borrowed shoes at the foot of the bed.

Vik headed to the bathroom and took his first shower in nearly a week. He shaved with a razor he found in a drawer and brushed his teeth with bottled water and the toothbrush from his backpack—one of his sole remaining possessions. These things made him feel a little better. Some unsupportable sense of righteousness had crept into his thoughts about the Texan: *the cartel has a code, and he broke it...asshole had it coming...*

I took off the push-up bra they'd issued me and selected a big, fresh t-shirt. I turned off both reading lamps and
lay on the bed with my back to Vik as he rooted around in a
drawer full of new packs of underwear—all sizes; all briefs.
He opted instead for a pair of board shorts; he'd go com-
mando. They fit okay if he over-cinched the drawstring. He
slipped into the bed softly and did not touch me.

You smell clean, I said.

I thought you were asleep, he whispered.

Not that lucky, I said. How's a shower feel? I bet I stink.

Vik scooted across the bed. Took a sniff of my shoulder.
Yep, he said.

He started to roll away, but I reached back for his arm
and yanked it across myself like a bedcover, drawing his bare
chest against my back.

I floated momentarily above myself. I saw our bed in
the video feed of some unseen voyeur, our bodies green-lit by
a night-vision lens, our pupils dilated, alien. Vik shifted his
hips ever so slightly to hide his arousal from me. We lay still.
My mind began to settle.

Vik's, though, was still lit up. Since stepping off the
boat, he'd experienced an unprecedented vividness to things.
Seared into his memory were the faces he'd seen. They paraded past now, unbidden: the pawn broker, the waitress and
her daughter, the vagrant thieves, the cops—all surely still
going about their normal lives, like the people of Juarez, while
the noises downstairs grew more and more raucous, and my
breathing fell into a rhythm, and my hand lost its grip on his
arm.

We awoke to a knock on the bedroom door. The room
was warm and brimming with light. Vik's head was buried
in a pillow; he was still asleep, or trying to be. I got out of
bed and pried open the door to find a tray on the floor: juice,
coffee, bread, jam, butter.

What is it? Vik groaned.

Room service, I said. I brought the tray into the room and set it on the table by the window. Poured two glasses of juice; took one to Vik.

I should get working, he said.

He sat up, his hair flattened lopsidedly. He took the glass. I kissed his shoulder.

You can come along, he offered.

We sipped the juice together. Vik raised an eyebrow: the juice was fresh-squeezed.

No, I said. I think I'm good. Just, come back in a bit, okay? Visit me.

Of course, Vik said. He wanted to lean over and kiss me. He refrained.

This is so fucking weird, I said.

Yeah, Vik said.

I mean, this is a *nice* room. This juice is *amazing*. And it seems like, so long as you're working, we'll just keep being—*guests...*

You're saying I should drag it out, Vik said.

But seriously, I said. What happens when you're done here? They just let us go? Take us back through the tunnel and say, thanks?

It's possible, Vik said.

No, I said. It's not.

It is, he insisted, insane as it sounded even to him.

They'd have to trust us, I said.

They've trusted me for years.

They don't trust me. I talked to the cops.

I don't know, Vik said. You're part of the deal now. You're with me.

I'm baggage.

You're not *baggage*.

Then what am I, Vik? I'm only worth anything as...*chattel.*

You're my partner in this, he said.

Bullshit, I said. Don't flatter me.

Vik looked out the window. He said: If you weren't here, I couldn't do this. I *wouldn't* do it...

No, I said. Don't you dare say that. You're not doing this

for me.

I'm doing it for *us*. For a future. A real one.

You actually think there's an 'out' here?

You don't?

A body bag is not an out, I said.

Then we're in agreement, Vik said.

For he had been asking himself these same valid, discomforting questions, and hadn't liked the answers he'd come up with either. If his new program worked as well as he expected, it would buy us some time, but little else. It would not bring an end to this. Not a true end. Whereas, if the program were to flop—or even if Vik somehow rigged it to surreptitiously compromise Gamboa's operation—how would that change the outcome? Vik had the same lifecycle as his code: useful, then obsolete.

I'm not saying things can stay the same, Vik said. Just—people *adapt*.

I wish you could hear yourself.

This situation's fucked, Vik said. I get it. But try and see beyond it. *Try.* Ask yourself, what's our alternative? Give up?

I could only shake my head. More in disbelief than disagreement. Was Vik really so deluded?

I believe we can survive this, he continued.

But I don't want to just *survive*, I told him.

Me neither, he said.

We caught eyes, weighing one another's commitment to what seemed this tacit pact.

Vik got up from the bed. Dressed. Poured two cups of coffee. Slathered two rolls with butter. He delivered mine to me in bed. There was nothing left to say. He took his breakfast and, planting a kiss on my lowered head, headed back to his dungeon.

The two men at the end of the hall let Vik pass unimpeded, each muttering *buenas dias*. Vik replied in kind. He suspected that, were he to head in any direction but the basement, he would be met with less civil greetings.

The Texan's corpse dangled in the foyer like a ravaged piñata. Scattered about were the implements of his obliteration: a blood-spattered pipe, a golf iron, a samurai sword. Flies buzzed about his wounds. Plastic sheeting covered the tile floor. Vik was repulsed by the gore, but also, somehow, felt some warped sense of dispensation: he couldn't help but believe that the Texan had been left there for *him* to see—as a warning, yes, but maybe also a perverted kind of tribute. *Look what we did to your countryman.*

Vik passed a floor-to-ceiling window and slowed for a moment to look out across Juarez. A ring of buzzards wheeled in a crystal blue sky. Painted in massive white letters upon the mountainside above the city were words: '*Cd. Juárez. La Biblia es la verdad. Leela.*' He walked on. He had been raised casually Hindu, but knew Christianity's wilder stories: the parting of the seas, the rising from the dead, the slaying of a giant with a well-slung rock. He tended to like the vindicating notion of a heaven and a hell. Of winners and losers, Mexicans and Texans, narcos and narcs. Of men who held to codes and men who break them.

The Republic of Texas was not *Vik's* republic; the Texan did not feel to him like a countryman. If anyone, Los was closer to fitting that description.

A man followed Vik to the basement, though not into the 'office.' Vik expected to hear the door shut and lock behind him, but no. So he eased it closed himself, for concentration's sake.

The rules of our captivity seemed to Vik in flux, and inexplicit. Best he could tell, his work ethic was being rewarded, disconcerting as that was: the eyes and ears of *la casa de huéspedes* were paying full attention.

Vik sat for a moment and tried to clear his head. He hunched over an envelope and, in the faint light cast by the monitors, picked at an equation that had so far proven impenetrable. With a fresh angle of attack, the problem soon cracked open, Vik's derivations spilling over to the address side of the envelope. He'd managed to hypnotize himself yet again. A crowded barroom was my element, but a claustrophobic Mexican storeroom—or anywhere, really, where you can hear yourself think—was Vik's. He'd soon climbed back into the intertwined branches of his program, high above the world.

By the time he remembered his promise to check in on me it was past noon.

32

On the way up from the basement Vik passed the man with the goatee. They bid each other *buenas dias* and Vik continued on his way, only to turn back.

Los around? he asked.

Los...

Yes, Vik said. Is he here?

Who is this?

Los.

*Los...*what? said the man.

Sorry, Vik said—realizing the problem. The man I work with, he explained (further realizing that '*with*' was delusional, and maybe even more confusing). From *California*. Dresses like he's on a sailboat...

Señor Javier?

Is that what you call him?

That is his name.

We call him Los, Vik said. (We *who? Gringos?*) The man made no reply. Vik asked: Where is Señor Javier right now?

The man pointed through the window overlooking the valley. Vik couldn't tell: did that mean Juarez? Or beyond?

Business? Vik asked, tapping the side of his nose, a joke for him alone. He might have even laughed were he in a different mood, a different country.

No, the man replied. *Family.*

Family *business*? Vik asked.

The man remained grave, and Vik was left to acquiesce. He continued up the stairs.

Señor, the man called. Your lady friend, she is not up there.

Vik's stomach dropped. Where is she? he asked.

La piscina.

Vik pointed down a hallway that he guessed led outside, to the pool. The man shook his head and pointed down a different hallway, seeming to relish all this direction-giving, all this disappointing.

She is bad to have here, the man said. My men. They are finding reason to go outside.

To look, Vik said.

Si.

Vik left the man without another word and stepped outside into the sweltering air. He spotted me from across the courtyard. City sounds spilled over the wall—car engines, the shouts of nearby laborers. And there I was, reclining on a lounge chair in the relative sanctuary of the courtyard, reading a book beside the shimmering pool. Wearing mirrored aviator sunglasses. There were plenty of patio umbrellas, but I'd situated myself well outside all possible shadows. I'd wanted to bask in the full sun, though I wore a t-shirt with the sleeves rolled up and baggy red basketball shorts that hung to my knees. It was not my intention to flaunt.

At Vik's approach, I looked up from my book and held aloft an icy glass (*More juice?* he wondered. *A margarita?*)— toasting my shift in attitude and environs before Vik could comment.

I had not seen, as he had, the Texan's corpse. The foyer had been empty and clean by the time I descended the stairs.

Hi, honey, I said, puckering up like a Stepford wife. Vik played along and planted a kiss on me.

You look..., he began.

I waited.

...*comfortable*, he said. Like, you belong in an ad.

'*Enjoy Coke*,' I quipped.

Nice glasses, he said.

They were a gift, I told him. (A nice young man had brought them to me when he saw me squinting in the sun.)

I see, Vik said. You're having an effect around here, I hear.

Oh, they come out, I said. They sweep. They stare. I'm the newest animal in the zoo.

La Americana, Vik said.

I sucked at my straw. My skin's as dark as theirs, I said.

Yes. But you're forbidden fruit, Vik said.

I patted an empty lounge chair. Stay a sec, I said. Keep me company.

Vik sat down stiffly—his guard still up, his shoes and clothes still on. He lay back. Interlaced his fingers across his belly and shut his eyes. Let the sun beat down. Breathed. I did the same. The hot sunlight became our sole sensation, our singular thought.

Until it wasn't. Fear and uncertainty crept back in almost immediately, and I went back to my book, trying to distract myself. Vik studied me, as other men had done all morning. Then he got up.

Where you going? I asked.

Nowhere, he said. Just a walk.

Where?

Around.

I watched him cross the patio to a pathway of decomposed granite that paralleled the outer wall. Taking slow steps. He was soon out of view.

He circumnavigated the property, lost in thoughts like those I had already been struggling with all morning. He was luckier: he got to get lost in his work.

Our respective notions of Eden were not so different from the situation we'd found ourselves in at the *casa de huéspedes*. We were together in an exotic place. It felt like an all-inclusive resort, walled off from everything but the local climate and labor force. On vacations, I liked to lay by a pool and read all day. That's exactly what I was doing. Vik had difficult work to do; but so be it: coding relieved his incessant need to grind away at something. He'd *earn* his siestas. We'd take dips in the pool; dip chips in guacamole. And at night, we'd share a bed. A near-idyllic day we could re-live, over and over. One we might even get used to.

But no. Of course not. What had already become clear to me became clear to Vik the further he walked (in a circle). The spectrum from bliss to agony is like the numbers on a clock-face: the extremes (1 and 12) are adjacent. It is in fact perfection's close proximity that makes the torture so exquisite.

Eden was just a garden of obliviousness until Adam and Eve discovered the fruit that had been hanging there all along. It wasn't paradise until it was lost. Vik and I had both considered Tahoe to be Eden, but it couldn't have been, not fully. We'd yet to 'honeymoon' in Juarez.

Vik stopped by the pool to tell me he was going back to work. I envied him that escape.

I kissed his brain for luck.

The basement was cool and dark. He got to work linearizing what had been a weakly polynomial equation for the prices of sales in the range between a gram and an eight ball. He re-weighted the data he had for price versus time of day, which he'd come to believe were too heavily centered, and overly-fit, on evening hours. He bolstered his error handling to better handle corner cases. In doing so, he teased out a bug in one of his floating-point calculations: it had been rounding prematurely at the seventh digit; in the case of very small purchases (less than half a bump), it would have set off a chain reaction of bad math, resulting in a price equal to one divided by infinity—an undefined quantity. (One cannot divide by an *idea*, according to Vik's high school algebra teacher.) He considered disallowing such chump-change sales altogether, but opted instead for double precision, with its lavish 15-digit computations. Who was Vik to deny the destitute?

He'd begun to thrill, despite our situation, at the prospect of releasing Kavi into the world. She (for Kavi was female, like a boat) amounted to just under 13,500 lines, ten percent fewer than Dora, even with her new functionality and bolstered security. Kavi was not *absolutely* perfect—certainly not—but even by Vik's standards she was nearly so. She was by far the most elegant and powerful script he'd ever written. He sat testing and re-testing the critical routines, mentally adding up the milliseconds he'd shaved from the their respective runtimes. Milliseconds no one would ever notice. And yet each one brought Vik satisfaction.

He went upstairs and helped himself to a celebratory bottle of Lime Jarritos from the beverage refrigerator in the game room. Outside, the sun re-engulfed him. He made his way down the driveway to the main gate, where he spotted—and was spotted by—the boy we'd seen the night we arrived. The boy was yet again perched atop the wall, peering out from the shade of a tree with curious eyes. Man and boy studied each other. Vik sipped his soda, then held up a finger—*hold on*. He turned and jogged back into the house. Returned to the refrigerator. Levered the cap from a second bottle.

Back at the wall, he offered the soda up to the boy, who hesitated, looking back at the house. Vik held the bottle higher. A small hand stretched out from the canopy and snatched it.

Salud, Vik said to the boy, toasting the air separating them. The boy climbed higher into the tree with his prize. Vik did another lap around the property on his newly discovered, and sole remaining, path.

33

Tell me a story, I said.

We were in bed, having earlier dined on *carne asada y cerveza* at one end of an otherwise empty conference table. Our interactions all night had felt stilted, like a first date. We drank beer, which helped. I'd been feeling happy, I suppose, and feeling guilty about that. I had even closed the bathroom door to primp for dinner. Brushed my hair. Used one of the available perfumes. And Vik was feeling good about Kavi. He was exhausted, and had what he called the 'good kind of headache'—mild, and well-earned, like a sore muscle.

You're the writer, Vik replied.

C'mon. Everybody's got stories.

Vik considered that. He had stories, yes. He'd already told me a few. He could not think of one that ended in redemption, or a punch line. I'm drained, he said.

Please, I pleaded. Just start talking. Tell me about software. I won't last long, I promise.

Vik yawned. The ceiling fan creaked in a ceaseless rhythm. He got an idea.

I prompted him: *Once upon a time....*

Right, Vik said. Once upon a time—and by that I mean the *nineties*—there was a video game. Called *Civilization*.

The nineties, I said wistfully. I was a little kid...

Well, *I* was an awkward teenager.

Who played *Civilization.*

Who's telling this story? Vik asked.

I apologized. He continued:

The way it worked was, you'd be the ruler of a civilization. But you're competing with other civilizations. Each led by some historical person. Shakespeare, or Leonardo di Vinci, or whoever. Anyway, to make the game work, the devs programmed in attributes of each ruler—with variables for things like 'cooperation,' or 'backstabbing.' I learned all this later, in grad school. When I was a kid, I just thought it was this cool, weird game.

I smiled to see the light in Vik's eyes.

Gandhi was the most peaceful ruler you could pick, he said. His aggression was set to 1. But the way the code worked, when a civilization became a democracy its aggression variable went down by 2. Which worked fine, except with Gandhi. It made his aggression go *negative*, which caused something called a variable overflow and reset his aggression to the highest value possible—something insane, like 200. So out of nowhere, Gandhi would turn into this fucking *warmonger*. He'd be the first one to threaten all the other civilizations with nukes. (Vik could still picture the graphics: Gandhi—shirtless, donning Steve-Jobs spectacles, palms pressed together in supplication—declaring war on him...)

That is kind of funny, I said.

The devs thought so, Vik said. Even after they found the bug, they decided to leave it in.

Why?

It's called a 'misbug', Vik said. When a bug becomes a feature.

I resituated my head on the pillow so I was facing away from Vik. I talked toward the window. *See,* I said sleepily. You know stories.

I slid my ass backward, settling into him. The sounds downstairs were even rowdier than the night before, and I was reminded of high school keggers, and stealing away with a boy to an empty upstairs bedroom. I swallowed. Before better judgment could thwart me, I began to move against him. He responded. Put his lips to the back of my neck, his arm across my breast. I reached a hand back and tugged loose the drawstring of his borrowed board shorts.

We remained sideways, both of us facing the window. Gangly palms teetered in the evening breeze, out of sync with the rhythm building in the bed. It felt wrong not to be facing each other. Reckless. I could sense hesitancy in Vik, too, a hesitancy which became haste, some unspoken agreement to skip past any conscience-laden foreplay—the mind fuck—and just go at it like the animals we'd been reduced to: the cartel's little pets.

Suddenly the hairs on my neck stood on end. A shadow was moving across the room. I turned to look and saw a man in a mask against the wall.

My skin turned to gooseflesh. I whispered, urgently: *Stop.* No response. Vik in the throes. I rolled away from him, and turned to face the figure but it was gone. I felt the bed shake.

A pair of arms hooked Vik and he was dragged to the floor, naked and tumescent and wide-eyed, a knee pressed to his throat, a pistol in his eye socket.

The barrel was body temperature, Vik remembers.

Levántate, said a voice. But Vik was pinned. The command had been addressed to me. I was still in the bed, clutching a sheet to my chest.

A man standing in the middle of the room said my name. That's when I realized there were two men. They were both wearing the same mask.

I glanced at Vik. He looked disturbed, breathing through gritted teeth. The man holding him down stayed put while the other man went to the foot of the bed and tore away the sheet I was gripping. I shrieked, and crouched back against the headboard. The house was otherwise quiet. No one stirring.

The man began methodically shutting the blinds until the room was pitch black. He flicked on the lamp on my side of the bed. I shielded the light from my body with my arms.

Cálmate, said the man. His mustache protruded from his mask. He wore a loosened tie and a dress shirt, unbuttoned to reveal a ribbed white undershirt. Black slacks. Lizard belt, lizard boots. Other than the mask, he looked as though he'd just arrived home from a formal affair and had begun to undress.

I recognized the mask immediately, and realized I'd sensed Gamboa's presence as soon as the shadow appeared in the room. Vik had sensed it much earlier: when Los first uttered the man's name on that fateful call from Mexico, those many months ago.

Gamboa muttered something. The man holding Vik gnashed his knee into Vik's temple, then stood up, releasing him. Gamboa held a hand out to me, palm up. I looked into his face; it was inscrutable. But his request was unmistakable. I unfurled my legs off the side of the bed and stood, quaking under his gaze. I fell under some storybook spell. I took his offered hand.

Vik got up too. Gamboa guided us toward the covered window, as if he were merely trying to reunite us, to right this terrible wrong. As if he hadn't been its author.

Please, he said. Join me.

The man who was not Gamboa—and was therefore, like Vik, just another hired hand, an asset—kept his gun leveled at Vik's chest.

Gamboa was taller than I'd envisioned, and heavier, but possessed some irrefutable charm, despite the mask, or because of it. Some magnetism. We paraded naked across the room, helpless to resist its tug. It seemed a force borne of self-assurance, of knowing the answers before the questions ever got asked. There was inevitability in it, which I found oddly calming, like giving myself over to God's will. *Whatever this has come to,* I thought, *please just get it over with.*

Vik and I didn't know what to do with our hands. He gripped his own wrist. I hugged myself. We stood against the curtained window. Gamboa drank in the sight of us. He stepped toward Vik, into the firing line of the gunman's pistol. The gunman stepped sideways to regain a clear shot.

A hush had befallen the house—one borne not of inactivity, it seemed, but suppression. No amount of screaming or struggling would summon anyone, that seemed clear. The men of the house had, like the farcical referees of *lucha libre*, turned blind eyes to the one-sided bout in the honeymoon suite. The ring was Gamboa's. He cleared his throat to speak.

Vik preempted him: I know who you are, he said.

Gamboa seemed neither pleased nor surprised to hear this, and moved ahead with aplomb.

Likewise, Mr. Singh. I have wanted to meet you for some time. I have been rather busy.

Likewise, Vik said.

Gamboa lifted a brow. And yet I find you here, he said, glancing to me. Taking pleasure.

Vik made no reply.

It is perfectly fine, Gamboa added, waving at the air. It is as it should be. This is a house of pleasure. But it is built on profit. You know this, of course.

Yes, Vik said.

I couldn't get a handle on Gamboa's accent. It was neither Mexican nor American. It sounded almost bland, internationalized. A mask in its own right.

I have taken great interest in your work, Mr. Singh. It has been a healthy dose of...*the New*. I want you to know, you are among people who appreciate you. Myself certainly included.

At this, Gamboa turned his attention to me. He had yet to peek down at my body the way the gunman kept doing. I forced myself to stare back at him. He had *something* he wanted to say to me, it seemed, but didn't say it. He turned back to Vik.

I say I know who you are, Mr. Singh, Gamboa continued. What I don't know is, *what* you are.

Your humble servant, Vik said.

Gamboa nodded. Are you Indian?

Vik didn't know how to take that. By blood, he said, yes. What else is there?

I'm American, Vik said.

America is a continent, Gamboa retorted. *I* am American. So is he...

Gamboa nodded at the gunman.

I suppose I am Mexican, Gamboa continued. But I was raised in Argentina. My parents are German. To my countrymen in Buenos Aires, I am *un emigrante*. With the 'e.' But to my brothers in arms here in Juarez, I am *un inmigrante*. With the 'i.'

So what do you consider *yourself*? Vik asked.

All of the above, Gamboa said. And none. Lines are drawn in sand. The wind blows, the lines move. Tell me, Mr. Singh: why are you here?

Vik somehow turned surly, as if he'd forgotten he was naked, and at gunpoint.

Because you *invited* me, he said.

Gamboa nodded. Of course, he said. But why did you involve yourself in the first place? Is it because you like money?

Fame, Vik replied.

Finally, the mouth within the mask cracked into a smile, and laughter poured out. The man leveling the pistol cocked his head curiously, unable to comprehend either what Vik had just said or the risk he'd taken in saying it. I had the sense that Gamboa's laugh was not something the gunman liked hearing. Vik decided to answer the question again, this time with sincerity in his voice.

I do it because it's very hard, Vik said. And because I'm very good at it.

Gamboa nodded in his mask. Yes, he said. What you say rings true. I know this feeling.

He stood in private contemplation for a moment. *Fame*, he mused. For me, it has meant living in basements, riding in the trunks of cars. *La pista secreta.*

Vik nodded cautiously.

I have become nocturnal, Gamboa said. Even though I love the sunshine.

I know *that* feeling, Vik thought, but did not say, for he was torn: his instinctual repulsion from the monster before us was somehow succumbing to the monster's inexplicable allure, and Vik felt this was a failure on his part. A fatal flaw.

I wonder, Gamboa said, if we might alter our arrangement. Make it...*no se...mas simpatico para todos.*

Alter, how? Vik ventured.

I mean: you, remaining here, working for me. Taking

whatever pleasures you wish, but continuing your important work. I see no reason why such an arrangement wouldn't work. Do you?

I have a house, Vik said. Or, I did. I'd planned to keep living in it. I loved it there.

Gamboa nodded. He turned to me.

Y tu, he said. I wonder, *Señorita*: what is *your* purpose? Do you know it?

I don't, I said.

Gamboa clicked his tongue, in disapproval or disappointment. He said, They are calling you *Julieta*.

I'm sure they call me lots of things, I said.

You are Persian, Gamboa said.

Half, I said.

Gamboa nodded. You are a confident woman, he said. It is plain to see.

Maybe, I said. I *used* to be.

You are still. Look how you stand.

I looked at the floor. Gamboa took a step toward me. Vik risked half a step into his path. This seemed to unsettle everyone in the room.

Gamboa opened his arms, settled things down. It is a pleasure to have met you both, he said.

I offered Gamboa a small nod. Unintentionally, it looked and felt like a bow.

Duerman bien, he said, and turned to go. The gunman followed.

They slipped back into the darkened hallway and were gone.

34

The air came rushing back into the room. I wanted to go to Vik, but in our nakedness and shame it seemed all each of us could manage was to go and fetch our clothes. We dressed. Vik switched the light back off. I ducked into the bathroom and cried. I heard Vik come to the door, say my name. I turned on the shower but did not get in.

Vik sat against the bathroom door, staring into the dark, teetering on the brink of a grave choice. Gamboa's visit had provided the break statement to bust him out of the 'while' loop he'd been stuck in:

while you believe this can still end well
  keep doing what you're doing

The conditional statement was no longer true.

After a while, I got in the shower. When I returned to the bedroom, Vik was sitting at the table.

Can we talk? he said.

I'm tired of talking, I said.

Exactly, he said.

In El Paso, I had asked him, *How does this end?*, and he had failed to produce an answer. Since then he'd seen far enough ahead to know that all our remaining paths merged into one. He was doomed to remain an imprisoned conjurer of spells, perhaps the cartel's greatest asset but also its greatest liability. His hands were on every transaction. Whether

Kavi worked miracles or wreaked havoc, we would never be let out of our lavish cage. We could never return to our old life.

What was left of that life anyway? There was no cottage to go back to. My continued employment at the hotel was contingent on my continued cooperation in an investigation into Vik. I had almost no money, and the bulk of Vik's assets were frozen in a Swiss account with Gamboa's name on it. The cartel would never allow us to be truly free, where the authorities might snatch us up.

There was no old life left.

These daughters of Vik's—Dora and Kavi—had by necessity become his surrogates. For while he could model the real world with increasing accuracy, he could no longer live in it. Vik had been such a clever kid. His parents and teachers had supported this cleverness so much that he'd come to believe he could outthink any problem presented him. Which had been true at a suburban high school in Sacramento, an elite college in Pasadena, and start-ups in Los Gatos. But those were paper worlds, where scissors ruled. For scissors are cleverness incarnate. However, the game is not binary. There is a third player, a brute, with no cleverness at all. Only force. Which cannot be out-thunk. Which is brutal, unyielding— matter over mind. Paper is said to beat rock, but that is only in games, only in courtrooms. Paper cannot conquer, only cover. It cannot crush.

On the morning following our visit from Gamboa, Vik left the bedroom before our breakfast tray came. We'd spent the entire night whispering to each other across the pillows. Half-delirious and completely terrified, I'd blamed him for dragging me down into this, and he'd accepted the blame. He'd apologized, which softened my defenses ever so slightly, enough that I'd been willing to at least hear him out. We both knew we had to do *something*, but it was the *something* we couldn't agree on, not until just after dawn, when sunlight flooded the room, harsh and unavoidable. I'd needed time to see the play from all angles, and to recognize it for what it was: our best and only option. Now we were decided. We were all in.

The key variable in Vik's Kavi algorithm was the price that a dealer would charge. Boiled down, price was the only thing Kavi told you. It was the variable that meandered through a chain of calculations before arriving at its final value. Or, *near* final. One last adjustment was made by a function Vik had dubbed the 'bump.' This function tweaked the price one last time based on: (1) the potential upside of such an adjustment, and (2) the customer's tolerance for it. For example, the remoteness of a transaction from the nearest population center served as an indicator of the difficulty a given buyer would have finding an alternate dealer. He'd dubbed this the 'desperation quotient,' or DQ. He had built in the means to compound DQ, depending on the time of day (or night, as was more often the case), and the amount of time expected to elapse between the placing of an order and its fulfillment. Late-night buyers with no time to wait could expect decent 'bumps.' However, there also existed scenarios where the 'bump' *lowered* the price a bit: buyers scheduling multiple purchases over time—arrangements Los liked to call 'prescriptions'—or high-volume single sales, arranged more than 48 hours in advance. The bump function had two key outputs: (1) a multiplier—0.03, say, to adjust a price by three percent—and (2) a polarity, which made the adjustment either positive or negative. It was a clever little function.

It was also a quick and dirty way to take the gold spun by Vik's algorithm and subject it to a reverse alchemy.

The trap could at least be *baited* with cleverness.

There was a guard stationed at the end of our hallway, leaning against the wall, his gun in his lap. At Vik's approach, he rose to his feet, then shadowed Vik at slight remove to the basement.

Squinting into the brightness of his monitor after the sleepless night, Vik searched out the line in the code that determined a buyer's tolerance for a bump, then hard-coded it so that, instead, *every* buyer would receive one. He then appended a *-3* to the bump-determining equation—thereby overruling all his careful optimizations. Now, what would have been a price boost of 4% would instead be a drop of 12%. He believed this discrepancy would be small enough to overlook on an individual transaction, but big enough to snowball into a real problem over thousands of transactions.

Vik sat staring at the *-3*.

How quickly would the damage be done? he wondered. *How quickly would it be noticed?*

Vik's high-school teacher had told him you can't divide by an idea, but of course you can: the numbers themselves are just ideas.

Vik had envisioned the *-3* while waiting for me to come out of the shower, but it was a different thing altogether to see it phosphorescing on the monitor. He could see past the pixels to the processor that would crunch the compromised numbers. He could see deeper still. Into the future. And the further he saw, the more impatient he became. There wasn't time for subtlety. He inserted a '1' between the negative sign and the three—changing the 'bump' multiplier to a negative *13*. Mathematically, the '1' represented an order of magnitude. It also represented a wrench in the works, an extraneous leaf woven into an otherwise-perfect rug, a stick of dynamite, a middle finger.

Kavi had been Vik's masterpiece. As perfect a thing as he might ever hope to create.

But he'd ghetto-rigged her to serve a different purpose. She became *jugaad*.

He couldn't help but recall elementary school, that feeling of rising from his desk to turn in a test. He opened the door and called to the sentry.

Please get Señor Javier, he said. *Por favor.*

No esta aqui.

Vik gave no reaction. Then call him, he said.

Un minuto, the man said. He pulled out his phone while Vik stood by. An urgent-sounding conversation ensued. Eventually the man nodded at Vik, in apparent confirmation of his request. Vik stepped back into his cell and slumped to the floor against the wall to wait.

The man with the goatee appeared, drinking a can of Red Bull.

Where's Señor Javier? Vik said.

California, he replied.

Vik tried to remain calm. He ought to have expected this. Had he thought it through. Had he slept. There was much for Los to handle up north. There was peace to be kept, for starters. Dealers doing God knows what without the code to do their thinking for them.

'Family business,' Vik muttered.

Yes, said the man. His daughter. Very sick.

Vik considered this. Well, he said. You can tell him I'm done.

You are stopping?

The program is finished, Vik said. It can be released immediately.

The man took a sip from his can, then barked an order at the man who'd just fetched him, who rushed off and soon returned with the acne-scarred young man we'd only ever seen lurking in the corner. The young man's hair was mussed. He was barefoot. He palmed his head and, without a trace of accent looked at Vik and said, I need to see your code.

35

Are you a programmer? Vik asked.

No reply.

You're American, Vik said.

The young man shrugged.

So, what? Vik said, growing angry. We're gonna do a fucking code review now?

Nothing official, the young man said. I just need to run a few tests. Look things over.

Where are you from?

At this, the young man smiled, baring his orthodontically flawless teeth, and Vik was reminded of the wayward, middle-class misfits who sometimes crop up overseas, embedded in terrorist cells, the nightly news juxtaposing pictures of the bearded freedom fighter and the clean-shaven prom-goer: *what went wrong?* Good family, good upbringing, and yet somehow *rotten. Radicalized.* Vik, meanwhile, had gone to the underwear drawer that morning and selected a new pair of white briefs; they were exactly what he'd been looking for, although their chemical rigidity was making him itch. Also, the jeans he'd grabbed were (purposefully) big, so he'd added a woven leather belt and a roll to the cuffs. He'd topped off the outfit with a loose, tropical-print shirt that hung past his ass. He looked like an American on vacation.

I'm like you, the young man said. Kind of. I'm a fan, actually. What you did with Dora—it's messy, but...impressive.

Vik glanced at the two Mexican men who'd been side-lined by this conversation. They would have to wait. For here was the person Vik had long ago given up finding, someone credentialed by the cartel *and* capable of appreciating Vik's code, not just exploiting it. He'd been sleeping under the same roof as us for days.

What's your name? Vik asked.

The young man shook his head.

What do I call you, then? Vik persisted.

Nothing, the young man said.

Doctor Nothing? Vik asked, trying to establish at least an educational pedigree.

The young man frowned. You have questions, he said. I understand. But it's really not that complicated. I perform a service. Like you.

I write, and you edit?

Review.

Revise? Vik asked.

Depends.

Are you a statistician? Vik asked. The little jolt of pride he'd enjoyed moments ago was gone. If this young man could truly comprehend Vik's calculations—if he could look Kavi straight in the eye—then he'd surely see her last-minute change of heart.

The young man helped himself to Vik's chair. I can add, he said. And subtract.

He inserted a pin drive into the USB port on the desktop. Vik watched as he downloaded a pair of applications. One Vik recognized, one he didn't.

What's Dumpfuck? Vik asked.

Sorry...I give things weird names sometimes.

Me too, Vik said. What's it do?

Simulates.

Simulate what? Vik asked. The dealers?

The world.

The world, Vik said.

Suddenly there was a cockiness in the air. Both men a little too mum for comfort; a Mexican standoff of false modesty. Vik believed his code spoke for itself. Señor Dumpfuck, therefore, would need to flip over a card or two—show at least part of his hand—if he expected to be taken seriously. Prove his tight lips were not just his way of hiding that he was a hack.

The young man seemed to sense Vik's skepticism.

From the perspective of *your* program, he said, I guess you could say that mine simulates the *inputs*.

So, fake buyers, fake sellers?

Pretty much.

The young man started opening files, creating terminal windows. Rearranging Vik's workspace. Okay, he said. I think I'm in business.

Okay, Vik said.

And, actually, there's no need for you to stick around. I don't know how long this'll take.

Oh.

Once I dive in though, I might have questions, the young man said. So don't go too far.

He turned around, an unreadable smirk on his face. Vik couldn't tell: was he being made fun of, for being a prisoner? Or was this a kind-hearted joke, an attempt at camaraderie? Surely, the young man realized he was no less fucked than Vik, *didn't he?* They shared an employer, after all. They were in that basement together.

I'll just take a little walk, Vik said.

Good idea, said the young man.

Vik headed to the kitchen, where the usual woman was pressing out tortillas while a man leaned against the counter with the presumptuousness of either her superior or her suitor and plucked chunks of fruit from her prep bowl and tossed them in his mouth. He smiled at Vik in a knowing way.

Gamboa's visit had stripped away whatever hope Vik (and I) still had. It had been enough to make Vik contemplate the kind of act he'd only ever succumb to in the heat of the moment. But this thing we'd planned was not that: it was *not* a matter of seeing red and throwing wild punches. It was something hatched in the quietest hours of night, a violence born not of the heart but of the head. There was a new length we were now prepared to go to regain some semblance of a life.

The code had now been successfully sabotaged. How long would it take, then, for this to come to light, for red numbers to supplant black? How long would it take for the news to reach the man at whom the buck stopped? Vik had predicted it would take a few days, but that was before another clever young man sat down in Vik's chair and started picking through his code.

Vik headed to the courtyard, now baking in midday sun. He walked. I was still in the bedroom, and caught a glimpse of him through the window. To anyone watching, he might have been mistaken for someone merely wandering. I knew better.

What's this section for?

The young man had called Vik back inside. Vik stood looking over his shoulder. On the desk was a notepad where the young man had jotted down a string of numbers, corresponding to specific (problematic?) lines in Kavi. Vik pointed at the screen.

This part, here? he asked.

Sure, said the young man. We can start there.

This is where—let's see. Vik peered at his code. Yeah, so this is where I calculate the distance from a dealer's current location to the location of a pending sale.

These are GPS coordinates.

Exactly, Vik said. But I have to get them into longitude and latitude first, then convert to radians. That's the haversine formula, there. You know it?

The young man shook his head; his stress level was palpable now that he'd lifted Kavi's hood, and Vik felt a small wave of relief. Interpreting someone else's code was never easy, especially code compressed to such a degree by pressure and hard thought. Kavi was simply too intricate to comprehend at a glance.

For the next three hours, the two men dissected Vik's brainchild. Vik's voice grew hoarse from all the talking, as it had when he'd worked as a TA, tutoring undergrads. The young man jotted notes and asked intelligent questions. Vik began to feel a kinship with him.

Okay, so...encryption-wise, the young man said—scrolling adroitly to that section of the code.

Sure.

It looks okay, I think.

Vik almost took offence. He'd modified a gold-standard encryption method, adding an extra layer of his own design. Glad to hear it, Vik said.

Then the young man asked to see the repository where Vik cataloged all prior versions of the code. And Vik realized: even a rudimentary diff checker was going to place its damning little red dots alongside the only two lines of code that had changed since his penultimate revision. Vik's traitorous final keystrokes would be as plain to see as a pox.

I need to eat, Vik said. Mind if we take a break?

Sure, the young man said. Sorry. Once I get going, I'm just...

No, no, Vik said. I'm the same way.

We can't change it now, Vik muttered, dipping a tortilla chip in salsa. It's already in motion.

We were eating lunch on the patio. The sounds of a jackhammer and playing children spilled over the wall. *Was it a school day, then?*

It's moving too fast, I said.

Yes, but in the right direction.

How?

If this guy figures it out, there'll be repercussions, Vik said. But if he doesn't, same thing. Either way, it's what we wanted—right?

I assessed him. He wolfed down more chips.

What I need is some *sleep*, he said.

He left the table and went to a pair of lounge chairs below an umbrella. He lay down. I went to join him, extending my hand across the gap separating us. He took it.

I'm scared, I said. Last night, I...

I am too, Vik said. But we're past being scared now. We're doing something about it.

Yeah.

His eyes softened, and fell shut. He left his hand in mine, and I held it until suddenly it quivered and went slack and stopped holding back.

A shadow loomed over our lounge chairs. The young man had just tapped Vik's foot to wake him up. He blinked at the daylight.

I've been waiting, the young man muttered.

Vik apologized and asked the time.

Almost two.

I opened my eyes. I'd fallen asleep, too, but awoke at Vik's voice. Vik's cheek was imprinted by the chair fabric. Mine probably was too. I nodded at the young man.

Hey, he said.

Vik says you're an American, I said.

Not anymore, he said.

He did not expound.

Vik stood up. Back to the dungeon, then? he said.

I reached out for Vik and ended up hugging his leg like a child. I didn't want him to go. But whatever fears I harbored, I would do my best to quell them. I felt I owed Vik that.

Get more sleep, Vik said.

This, the young man said. He tapped his pencil against the '-13' on Vik's monitor.

Yeah, Vik said. What about it?

It's the last change you made. I'm wondering why.

To be right, Vik said.

It seems counterintuitive, though. My sims show you're gouging reliable customers, but giving the bad ones a break.

I do what the math tells me.

And it told you to do this?

It did.

Well, could you explain that?

I could, Vik said. But instead I think you should try and explain something to our boss.

The young man leaned back in the chair.

You should tell him, Vik went on, that there's over thirteen-thousand lines of code in this program, and I thought long and hard about every single one. So are we going to sit here and second guess them all, or are we going to get on with this shit?

The young man started whacking the pencil against his thigh.

I wrote every line with the same goal, Vik said. Make Vicente Gamboa rich. Because that makes *me* rich. Right? I bet *you* have a stake in this, too...

I do. That's why I want to make sure it works.

And I'm telling you, Vik said. There's only one way it *will* work. And that's through trust.

I think maybe you're taking this the wrong way. I'm just...

You're just the messenger, Vik said. Fine. So, do your job. *Go.* Tell them they've trusted me before. Tell them I've made them millions of dollars, many times over, and that I did it without anyone looking over my shoulder. Without fucking code reviews.

I'm only trying to get some clarity.

It's fine, Vik said. Truly, it is. But deliver my message first. Before we do anything else. Please.

The young man scratched the back of his head and grimaced. I'd prefer not to, he said.

Vik laughed. Then don't, he said.

But then it's on *me*, the young man said, if your code's fucked.

The code's not fucked, Vik said.

Dora was good code, the young man admitted.

Dora was a hack job compared to this, Vik said.

The young man hung his head, stymied.

Tell them I'm being stubborn, Vik said. It's true, I *am*. But if they want this thing deployed as soon as they say, then we don't have time for this shit. There's *way* too many calculations to second-guess, and trust me, I've already second-guessed every fucking one. I've third-, and fourth- guessed them. That's what I do. That's *my* job. And I'm telling you, this thing's airtight. It needs to get released. *Today*.

I guess we can always modify it, the young man said, if we find it's not performing...

We certainly can, Vik said. It's only *code*.

The young man stared at Vik like he'd just blasphemed —and, truly, he had: Vik didn't believe what he'd just said.

The young man then did something Vik had seen his parents do countless times: he rocked his head back and forth, sideways. Neither a nod nor a shake. Pure equivocation. For the young man could still envision alternative futures. For him, decisions remained to be made. Plans could still be altered to suit circumstances. Not for Vik.

Okay then, Vik said, concreting the lingering silence into consent.

36

There was nothing left to do but nothing at all. Two days went by during which Vik did not hear from the young programmer again, nor from anyone else. The radio silence was disquieting. Vik had expected they would require his help to release Kavi, but what if they hadn't? What if Kavi was already out in the world, distorting a billion-dollar drug market?

If so, fine: the trap was baited. When it sprung would depend on the tightness and tolerance for error in the cartel's feedback loop; it depended, therefore, on just how greedy and micromanaging of a motherfucker we were dealing with. *That*, Vik thought he knew.

The days were both tense and dull. Vik and I tended to stay up late, and sleep in. I tended to awake first and watch him, envying his unconsciousness. We took our breakfasts outside, for mid-morning was the nicest time of day—the heat not yet full blast, the sounds of the city productive and routine. Few sirens. We would eat slowly, making small talk. The big things no longer needed saying. We would jokingly critique the food as if we truly were on honeymoon, with only nits left to pick. We would pretend to plan our day. *Should we hike to the waterfall? Snorkel? Shop?*

No, we'd decide every time. *How about let's just stay here...*

I had discovered a shelf stocked with books, some in

English. I settled into *Mexico* by Michener and was pleasantly distracted for hours by tales of bullfighting and human sacrifice. Vik jokingly picked out a romance. He'd guffaw every few pages, and read the more lurid scenes aloud for me to enjoy. This was as close as we came to making love. Still, we were as close as we'd ever been. Saccharine as it must have looked, we often held hands as we walked the property, impervious to gawking.

Meals were milestones. We usually retired to the air-conditioned *hacienda* for lunch—unless the power was out again—and ate at the long conference table. Then came the best part of the day, for me: poolside siestas under the umbrellas. Ever since I'd been kidnapped, sleep was the closest I came to escape. In the evenings, we put on the nicest clothes in the closet and descended to the dining room, where we sat at one of the three tables, and ate meat.

This is a fucked-up honeymoon, I remarked on the third day. We were sitting at the edge of the pool, dangling our feet in the water.

Agreed, Vik said.

Or maybe not, I said. Maybe this is what one feels like. You jet off somewhere all by yourselves and just...*hang*. It's a bizarre time, I bet. You're not in the real world (I nestled the term in air quotes). And there's not really a *purpose* to whatever you're doing, besides...I don't know...

Taking pleasure? Vik suggested, quoting Gamboa.

Eew, I said.

We brushed our teeth together in the evenings, our mouths rabid with foam as we eyed each other in the mirror. The deeper we fell into that hole, the deeper our comprehension of each other. We'd volunteered to share a fate. Though unblessed by any church or recognized by any government, we may as well have been married.

The third day came and went no differently. We ate a late dinner, then lay together in the cooling dark well past midnight. The nightly ruckus, to which we had now become inured, peaked and then subsided, the residents of *la casa de huéspedes* sleeping another one off.

Not so its two guests. I could hear Vik breathing. I knew

the sound well by then, and could tell he wasn't asleep yet. In the house and the city beyond, it was the quietest hour of the day, before the birds resumed their chatter. I thought about Tahoe, and the ever-present call of the chickadee, the golden light in Vik's cottage in the morning, high above the lake…

I awoke to find Vik shaking my shoulder. I had apparently just shuddered violently—a frightening, reflexive spasm that, according to Vik, accompanied my cross-over into sleep every night.

Sorry, I said.

Try as I might though, the fire in my head kept dwindling. It would burn down to the glow of a few tenacious embers, warm thoughts of my mother and father and brother, my once-normal life. These memories were comforting, and the fact that they were lost forever to the past made me sad, but not overwhelmingly so. *Sit up*, I told myself. *Don't give in…* I did, though. Vik too. And when Gamboa materialized for the second time in a week at our bedside, we had both succumbed to sleep. Surely it was no coincidence. It was uncanny, Gamboa's ability to know—and strike—when his prey were most vulnerable.

I came to. Someone touching my ankle; a presence against the bed. My eyes adjusted. I saw a man in a mask. *Gamboa.* Another on Vik's side. Vik was feeling around under the blanket. In his sleep he'd let go of the one thing he'd needed to hold onto.

The morning after we stayed up all night plotting, Vik had stopped on his daily walk around the courtyard at a birdbath set into a bed of decorative rocks. One of these rocks had, on a prior walk, reminded Vik of a huge jewel, with one side flat and the other comprised of multiple facets that came together in a point. It was about the size of a baseball. Vik knelt beside the birdbath to tie his shoe, then plucked out the rock and dropped it into the top of his intentionally-too-big pants. Standing back up, he'd put his hands in his pockets and re-situated the rock into a more tolerable position within the supportive fabric of his new underwear, only to look up and see the young boy perched on the wall above, staring down at him. Vik froze, hands in his pockets. He knew the boy could, at any second, cup a dirty hand to his mouth and cry out. Men would come pouring out of the house, all would be lost. The boy scratched at his neck. He glanced off at the house, then back at Vik. Vik's heart raced.

Salud, said the boy.

Vik had been slow to return the greeting. He'd grown so unaccustomed to luck that he didn't recognize it right away. Eventually he managed a heartfelt nod. The boy smiled back. Vik walked off.

Now Vik probed the warm bed sheets; felt something cool and hard near his hip. He wrapped his fingers around it. The sharp end was against his palm—not the way he wanted it—but he had no time. He gripped the rock tight. The man standing over him muttered something. Vik peeled back the blanket. Struck. As hard as he could. His hand arcing in a split second from mattress to skull. His target the man's temple. This unfortunate man, whoever he was. Whatever his name.

Vik's first blow landed near the man's eye socket. I pounced from my side of the bed and clawed at Gamboa's head, trying to twist his mask around as Vik landed a second blow against his man's ear. The man crumpled. Gamboa barked an order, his voice muffled by the leather stretched over his mouth. The room still dark. Vik felt along the downed man's arm to his hand and pried the pistol from his limp fingers and leapt up onto the bed. In two steps Vik crossed the mattress and stood towering over Gamboa and me. I was dangling from his side, gripping his misaligned mask with both hands, holding on for dear life. Vik jammed the barrel of the gun into a patch of black hair protruding through an eyehole, up against Gamboa's skull. I let go and fell away. Vik pulled the trigger.

The shot left my ears ringing. Gamboa's head lolled; he

buckled to his knees, arms dangling. He crumpled into a heap on the tile.

Vik tossed the pistol onto the bed and turned on one of the reading lights. The second man was moaning as he dragged himself toward the door, trailing blood across the floor. His mask was partly caved in. A bubble of reddish mucus expanded and contracted from the nose hole. One of his legs began to convulse. Vik picked up the rock again, sharp-side out this time, knelt beside the man as if to perform CPR, and smashed the rock into the base of his skull. I heard it crack.

Vik looked up at me. The look on his face absolutely harrowing. And I knew at that moment that the remainder of my life would be lived in complete disjoint to everything that had come before. Vik still had the rock in his hand; he stared down at it.

Oh god, I whispered. Oh god....

Are you hurt? Vik asked.

I inspected myself. My arm was spattered with bone and brain. I started picking it off.

Remi, Vik said, also whispering. Tell me you're okay.

I think so.

Are you sure? Because I thought I...

No, no, I said—composing myself. *Vik.* Your hand...

We have to go, he said. Now.

Look at your hand.

Vik held up his palm. In the dark room, his palm was darker. It was gashed. Blood was running through his fingers, down his arm. He hadn't truly felt the wound yet, but began to. I watched as he slowly opened and closed his hand. There came the sound of footfalls on tile. A small group ascending the stairs, toward the bedroom. A light came on in the hallway. It spilled under the bedroom door. Low voices. An argument. Still the door remained shut, though it wasn't locked. Finally someone posed a question, politely, in Spanish—then silence.

Vik grabbed the pistol off the bed and pointed it at the door. Surely they were speaking to Gamboa. But what had they asked? Whether he wanted help? (*No!*). Whether everything was okay? (*Si!*) A binary, with a potentially lethal out-put. Vik looked over at me, as if I knew the answer.

Help! I shrieked, out of pure instinct. *Please!* I smothered my own mouth with my hand and continued to cry out. I threw myself to the floor. Taking my cue, Vik lowered his voice and spoke a word he'd picked up from Los: *Tranquilo.* He said it twice, in a sing-songy way, all the while keeping the pistol aimed at the door. We looked and sounded insane. I made another dramatic plea, gave my own thigh a loud *slap!*, then ceased my solo struggle.

One of the men in the hallway spoke. One laughed. Their spokesman bid us *buenas noches* through the door.

The footfalls receded.

We got to work. I pulled the mask off what remained of Gamboa's head and tossed it to Vik across the room. A portion of the leather along its neckline had been blown off by the exiting bullet. I undressed Gamboa down to his under-wear, tossing his clothes into a heap at the foot of the bed. Vik removed the other man's mask and took them both into the bathroom. The sink basin went red, then pink. Vik ruined a white towel while I stood at the feet of Gamboa's man, yank-ing his pants off.

Vik returned to the bedroom. Rifled Gamboa's pockets. Found a phone. The login screen lit up. Vik lifted Gamboa's arm and pressed his lifeless thumbprint against the home button. A matrix of apps appeared. Vik reset the phone's password to 1-2-3-4, smearing blood all over the screen. I disrobed.

We emerged from the room different people. I was Gamboa: black pants, black boots, a black t-shirt and a brown leather jacket. My hair pulled up into the back of the mask. The mask was still damp. I tried to walk normally, but the shoes were clownishly oversized on me.

Vik was the unknown man: dark blue polo, the pistol tucked into the waist of his jeans. Gray cross-trainers that fit him perfectly.

Vik walked in front. The house was still cloaked in a pre-dawn gloom, very few lights on. We encountered a man at the end of the darkened upstairs hallway. Vik nodded at him. He nodded back, but averted his eyes. I felt cloaked in celebrity.

We descended the stairs and crossed the foyer. Vik opened the front door, let me pass, then eased it shut behind us.

The morning air was cool and smelled faintly of baking, of sugar. An unkempt, dark-green Ford Explorer was parked in the turnaround driveway. Vik started toward it. We hadn't seen this particular vehicle before, and could only assume that the key Vik had found in the unknown man's pocket would start it.

Fuck. There was a man in a mask standing on the other side of the Explorer. *Fuck fuck...*

Vik, I said.

Just keep walking, he whispered.

The man noticed us. He dropped his cigarette into the gravel and got in on the driver's side of the car. The engine started up. Vik quickened his pace, separating himself from me.

*Vik, wait...*I said as he zeroed in on the car. The man was watching us in his side mirror. Suddenly his door swung open. He got out of his seat to either greet Gamboa or confront an imposter, we will never know. Vik pulled out the pistol, leveled it at the man's chest, and fired. Then fired again. And again. The stillness of the morning shattered by each new report. The kick of the pistol hammered the open wound on Vik's palm. The man tried reaching for something near his waist as he bent, and fell, right where he stood. Vik had to step over the body to get into the car. I hurried around to the passenger side, imagining the dozens of eyes surely looking out the house's black windows at us.

The gate out of the courtyard was closed. Vik set the pistol on the dashboard and flipped down the sun visor, looking for an automatic opener. I checked the center console. My hands were quaking.

Go, I said. Just start driving.

I will, Vik said. He leaned over to my side and flipped open the glove compartment. It was crammed with paperwork. A spare ammo clip. Salsa packets.

Drive through the fucking gate! I said.

Vik looked at me. Saw I was serious. I locked the doors.

Let me just think for a sec, Vik said.

Go! I said.

He put the car in drive and drove toward the gate, still searching compartments, poking around under the seat. In the side mirror, I saw a light come on in the house. Magically —mercifully—the gate shuddered to life and scrolled open as if of its own accord, the car having triggered some sensor. When it was open wide enough for the Explorer to squeeze through, Vik pulled out into the street we'd been hearing for days, but never seeing. We looked up and down the road. Vik turned downhill, toward the twinkling sprawl of Juarez, still somnolent at this dark hour.

37

We peeled our masks off. My hair tumbled out. I took off my jacket and sat watching out the back. Vik didn't stop at the first ALTO sign. The streets were winding. We quickly got disoriented. At an intersection without a streetlight, Vik put the car in park and killed the headlights.

What are you doing? I asked.

Vik stepped out of the car. The morning was quiet. He turned in all directions, and discerned a faint glow along the horizon of one of the four possible directions we could go—the one we were currently going, in fact. He got back in the car. I watched, waiting. He took a left.

North.

He passed me the phone. 1-2-3-4, he said.

I entered the digits without a word. The screen glowed in the dark cabin. I queried the phone for directions to El Paso. A female voice provided them in Spanish. A map on the screen. I tweezed my fingers across the display, zooming out; I glanced back and forth—from the real road to its analog—trying to orient us, visualizing a route.

Left at the next intersection, I said.

Vik took directions, but seemed lost in thought, or perhaps its opposite. He gripped the wheel with his left hand, keeping his right cradled in his lap. We merged onto a major thoroughfare, heading north. There were other cars on the road here. People on the sidewalks. A woman carried big bags on her shoulders, a girl behind her, jogging to keep pace. A man in boots stood leaning against a big store window.

Okay, Vik said. Let's make the call.

I exited out of the map and brought up the phone's keypad. Brought up Gamboa's contacts. Typed in *Javier*. Found nothing.

How's it spelled again? I asked.

Try searching for '*1545*,' Vik said. I remember that part.

The search returned a single match. I didn't recognize the name, and held the phone up for Vik to see. He shrugged.

Try it, he said.

I placed the call, switched to speakerphone. We listened together to each ring, one after another, like pistol shots into the settled silence, three in a row. Behind us, one pair of headlights was swerving amongst the others, gaining on us.

You see them back there? I asked.

Vik accelerated.

On the phone, a voice offered a chipper, *Buenos dias*. The line had a low buzz. I watched the headlights behind us, then peeked at the speedometer. Vik was going 120 km/hr, slaloming the law-abiding.

Vicente? asked the man on the phone. His voice not quite recognizable.

Vik gambled: Good morning, Los, he said. How's the daughter?

Silence on the line.

Who is this? Los asked.

We stayed quiet.

Is that Vik? Los asked.

Vik looked at me. Yes, he said.

Veeek! Holy shit. My daughter, you ask. She is in good hands. Stanford, bro; best doctors in the world. How's our code coming?

That's not why I called, Vik said.

The traffic was getting heavier. We were approaching the floodlights of the border station up ahead.

Would you mind putting Señor Gamboa on for me? Los said. I need to speak to him.

That's not possible, Vik said.

Los' tone changed: You took his phone? Nice trick…

I took more than that, Vik said.

He gave Los a second to take that in—this evidence of a fundamental failing by Los' beloved organization, and a step change in life as Los knew it. For Los' guts to sense the free-fall. We'd agreed I would keep silent—no need to let Los know more than necessary. I tapped Vik on the shoulder, then pointed at the car gaining on our tail. Vik nodded.

I don't have much time, Vik said. So, call your people. Watch the news. You'll know soon enough the situation you're in. That we're all in.

The boulevard curved enough that the tailing car slipped out of view. Vik slammed on the brakes, then turned hard right onto a crossroad. The Explorer threatened to tip, but righted. Vik slowed down and drove through a neighborhood with tree-lined sidewalks. Most of the yards had metal security fences; most of the windows had bars. Vik turned again, then pulled into a driveway, beside another SUV in front of a garage. Killed the headlights.

This would not be a wise bluff, Los said.

I agree, Vik said.

I stared out the back window. We couldn't see the main boulevard, only the empty road leading back to it. We waited, hoping against the sight of approaching headlights.

There's an opportunity here, Vik said. I know that you of all people will see it. I'm calling as a courtesy, to you.

We could hear Los exhale as Vik backed out of the driveway and re-parked against a curb. A man had emerged on a nearby porch and stood, watching us.

We're all replaceable, right? Vik said. That's what you told me.

I did, Los said. We are.

And so I'm telling you now: a throne in Juarez sits empty this morning.

We got out of the Explorer. We left it unlocked, the key dangling in the ignition. We started walking back to the main boulevard. Vik holding the phone in his good hand.

That's it, Vik said. Make your calls. But then, before you do anything else—before you go back to your daughter's fucking hospital room—you need to call the best goddamn lawyer you know.

Oh yeah? And why do *I* need a lawyer?

You don't, asshole. *I* do.

Not following.

Get the lawyer to El Paso, Vik said. *Today.* Use the cartel's plane. No one will complain.

Is that so? Los said. Well then you listen to me, mother-fucker. Before this day is over, there will—

Vik dropped the phone down a sewer grate.

The streetlights were now competing with daylight. We ran without speaking, following a sidewalk beside the wide boulevard where hundreds of idling cars and trucks had queued. A tinted-out Lexus was parked askew on the shoulder, doors ajar. A trio of armed men trotted northward between the vehicles, their heads swiveling.

The road and the sidewalk ramped onto an overpass then diverged. We started sprinting. The men spotted us. They turned and ran back between the cars to reach the juncture at which the pedestrian portion of the overpass branched off. We were funneled into a canopied chute with chain-link on both sides, the Rio Grande below, just a stripe of wet concrete in a manmade channel. *One never crosses the same river twice.*

We reached the customs building. The men a hundred yards behind us and closing. Inside was a snaking queue of people waiting to cross the border on foot. Banks of monitors displayed regulations; announcements were being made over a PA; agents in blue uniforms sat peering into their computers. The crowd was subdued at such an early hour. Mostly men.

I started around the periphery of the room, circumventing the line. This earned us evil glances and angry mutterings. Vik followed. We heard the men burst in through the rear doors. I approached an agent's booth. She was examining the passports of a family of four.

Get back in line, she said—her shirt ballooned by a Kevlar vest.

We'd like to be arrested, I said.

The agent shot us a quizzical look.

I took Vik's hand and forced the issue, leading us together past the checkpoint kiosk, toward the American side of the building, at which point we were beset by two agents more than willing to accommodate my insane request. They ordered us to halt; to put our hands up. More agents came. We were made to kneel. We were handcuffed. The crowd gawked. A baby had started to wail. We were afforded our first good look at our pursuers. Two of the three men had phones out; one was on a call, the other held his phone above the many craning heads and shot video.

The agents escorted us to a detention room. Yellow cinderblock walls. Two other detainees slouched on opposing wood benches. One old and wearing a cowboy hat, the other much younger, and shaved bald.

I was still dressed in the clothes of the man Vik had bludgeoned, and Vik in the clothes of North America's most wanted man. Without wanting to, I started to cry. Vik sat down beside me. His hand shackled behind him, out of view. We beheld each other briefly—as though confirming we were both somehow still alive, still together. I took a breath. It felt like the first one I'd gotten all morning. I let the air out slow. Closed my eyes.

The shaved-head prisoner was American, or at least talked like one. *Welcome to limbo*, he said by way of greeting, to which we responded with polite nods, electing not to refute his assessment despite wholeheartedly disagreeing with it. Limbo was what we'd just escaped.

38

Vik and I shared the bench like casual acquaintances
—speaking little, never touching. This was how
we'd decided to play it. We suspected that someone would eventually puzzle out our relationship
—'LOCAL COUPLE MISSING'—but there was no advantage to
revealing ourselves to the men in the holding cell, nor to the
surveillance cameras. Love too soon becomes leverage in the
wrong hands.

A similar impulse kept Vik from making much of the
injury to his hand. It showed weakness; it suggested guilt. He
kept it dangling out of sight, behind him in the cuffs, every
heartbeat adding pressure to it. Inflaming it.

Eventually we were called out of the holding room.
A pair of agents led us down yet unseen corridors. The officer escorting me stopped at the open door of a room with
a table and chairs. Vik's escort, meanwhile, led him further
down the hall. Vik looked back at me. A curl crept into the
corner of my mouth. A slyness—not a smirk, but close. *Here
we go*. Though our paths were at present diverging, and being
dictated by agents of the United States government, this was
the path we'd chosen in bed in the middle of the night at the
casa de huéspedes. It was me who looked away first, holding
up my end of our futile charade—*we're nothing to each other*—
unaware that two months would pass before I got to lay eyes

on him again.

Over that time, this fleeting exchange became the thing Vik clung to. The more he re-lived it, the clearer it became to him that he'd looked back to get a glimpse of himself, to see his own resolve reflected in my eyes—or not reflected. He'd needed to see whether he was ready. Whether *we* were. What he saw gave him just enough swagger to keep walking.

They took Vik to a small room with a padded exam table. A tall, bearded man wearing a CBP uniform came in.

Bill's an EMT, explained Vik's escort. He removed Vik's handcuffs and re-shackled them on the front of his body. Take a seat, he told Vik.

Vik used the provided footstool to boost himself up onto the exam bench.

Bill washed his hands. Vik sat with his legs dangling and stared at his lap. He saw a pair of hands. *His.* One of them covered in dried, red-brown blood. Mostly his. He started to pick away at a dried rivulet near his wrist, though it clung to the coarse hair.

Bill plucked a pair of latex gloves from a dispenser. He squatted on a stool with coaster wheels and scooted up to the exam bench, straddling Vik.

Okay, he said—tugging on the gloves. Let's have a peek at that hand.

Vik lifted both hands, the injured one palm up. Bill took it ever so gently and probed at the periphery, turning it to different angles. Vik stared down at it, too, afraid of what it revealed. The impact crater told a tale if one knew what to look for. The gash was wet and dirty, and shaped like the sharp end of the rock that had made it. It spoke of desperation and haste, a choice made to strike, blunt side out.

Even premeditation devolves into improvisation. Into *jugaad.*

I murdered someone, Vik kept thinking. *I murdered three men...first Gamboa's gunman, and then... no, the gunman hadn't died first; the initial blow had only caved in his skull...*

You did quite a number here, Bill said. Despite being the tallest in the room, he looked up at Vik from the stool. Vik made no reply.

Bill persisted: What happened?

Fell, Vik said. On a rock.

Bill looked over at the other agent. He was against the sink with his arms crossed over his starched uniform. He smiled. Bill turned back to Vik.

We don't have an x-ray on-site, he said, but you probably need to get one.

He scooted on the stool's caster wheels across the room and started removing things from a drawer: bandages, gauze pads, ointments. He scooted back and set these things beside Vik on the bench.

How's it feel? he asked.

Vik looked into Bill's eyes. It was a pertinent question. One to which Vik did not have the answer yet. How *did* it feel?

Well. It felt...physical. It hurt. Hot and swollen and bruised. Bone and skin had committed to memory the fatal moments; they'd become infected.

Vik's thoughts returned to the gunman: *He'd had to die, hadn't he? Of course. No question. But why? Because he was with Gamboa? Yes. He'd made his choice; he'd sided with a socio-path; he'd pointed his pistol at us. He'd chosen to live in a world of kill-or-be-killed. I hadn't. My hand had been forced...*

No. The gunman and I have been living in the same world all along. There is but one...

Vik thought about Gamboa. *Who on earth had it coming more? How many lives had he ruined, how many death sentences had he pronounced from the mouth hole of that fucking mask?*

Vik had felled a monster. One who'd preyed on people in the dark hours; one who'd become complacent in his con-fidence. Bludgeoning the gunman had been a gruesome and barbaric thing, but shooting Gamboa would forever feel to Vik more...*conceptual*—an execution, not a murder. A sentence carried out. Math. A favor done for the world. *De nada.* Of nothing.

Discovering self-righteousness where he'd expected

guilt frightened Vik as much as anything.

As for the third man, the driver: shot on the spot, reaching for something; Vik had stepped past the crumpled body, electing not to look closer, not to see what the something was. Not realizing at the time that it would forever haunt him.

The exam room had gone quiet. Bill hadn't begun dressing the wound. He looked expectant. He was still awaiting an answer to his question. *How's it feel?* Vik regarded his hands again. The right had used weapons both modern and biblical to fell men both unlucky and diabolical. When compared to the left, it felt swollen and burdened.

It feels heavy, Vik said.

Bill nodded. He ripped into a package of sterile pads.

I'd imagine, he said.

39

They took me to an interrogation room. Here is what I told them:
1. my name.

PART V: THEFT

40

The lawyer wore a black sweat suit with red piping. His stubble was a couple days old and mostly gray, but still black on the mustache and chin. He was trim and tall, and he wore his hair slicked back. Gold wedding band. He looked to Vik like a former pro basketball player. (He was, in fact, a former college water polo stand-out.)

A CBP agent opened the door for him and he crossed the exam room to the circular table with four chairs where Vik had been told to sit and wait, fifteen minutes earlier. He carried a leather briefcase and a matching leather shoulder bag. These things, combined with his imposing frame, dominated what little volume the room comprised. He set his things down. Slipped his hands into his pockets casually and frowned in a genial way, as if he were standing in his own kitchen, sipping coffee. The CBP agent cleared her throat as if to re-possess the air in the room, but clearly it was the lawyer's air now. She showed herself out. Latching the door like the last word.

The lawyer peered down at Vik, sitting with his arms crossed at the table.

Howdy, the lawyer said. His voice was deep and level. He seated himself in the chair beside Vik's. As such, they would talk diagonally.

Vik asked where I was.

She's in a little concrete room, the lawyer said. Just like this one, down the hall.

Are we being recorded? Vik asked.

No.

How do you know?

The lawyer let out a small laugh. Because this isn't my first rodeo, he said. You—*we*—can speak freely, Mr. Singh.

Vik.

The lawyer nodded. So, *Vik*. Tell me what happened.

We got arrested.

Before that.

How far before?

Let's start when you realized you needed me.

Vik?

I'm thinking.

Hell. So start when you got arrested. How'd that transpire?

I think you already know that.

I did see some interesting video.

You did? Oh, from those fuckers that were chasing us...

Said fuckers.

Well, CBP split Remi and I up. They kept me in a detention room for a few hours. Some agents came, asked a bunch of questions.

When was that?

That was this morning. They did this... (Vik held out his gauze-enshrouded hand, which Bill had tenderly cleaned and dressed without another word said. The lawyer gaped at the hand, as if he knew what he was looking at, what it had proven itself capable of.)

Did you answer their questions? the lawyer asked.

It took you a long time to get here, Vik said.

Yeah, well, I didn't even fucking change clothes, as you hopefully realize. When Los called, I'd just put a gorgeous slab of ribs in the smoker. But, it doesn't matter. What have you told them?

My name, my birthday. They asked how I ended up in Mexico.

And what did you say?

I said I eloped.

And did they laugh, Vik? Did they get a real kick out of that?

They did not.

The lawyer sat back—point scored. What else? he said.

Nothing, Vik said.

Did they ask you how your hand got hurt?

Yes.

And?

I told them I fell.

The lawyer nodded in a way that seemed tolerant, even appreciative, of evasion. A connoisseur's nod. They'll likely ask again, he said.

I told them where I was born, Vik said.

Indianapolis...

Very good. And they asked where I live. So I told them.

And where is that? Where do you live, Vik?

Tahoe.

You have a home there.

I do.

Did.

Condolences...

Fuck you.

Vik, it is very important that you remember something, going forward: *you* called *me.*

In a way.

Yes. And in that way, I'm the one thing standing between you and them.

There are multiple *thems.*

That is true, Vik. That is true. And, have you made up your mind as to which one you intend to align with?

Pick a poison, you're saying.

Call it what you will.

I have made a decision, yes.

And when, may I ask, did you arrive at this decision? Was it before or after you ran into the loving arms of the CBP?

Do you not trust me?

I hardly know you.

Well, Vik said. Then I pledge allegiance.

Put your fucking hand down.

What do you want me to say?

Let's start with the facts.

The facts. Okay. I'm fucked.

Let me be the judge of that. But first: help me understand...I mean, what's your play here?

My play is, don't make a play, Vik said. Keep my mouth shut, take what's coming. Serve some time.

Do you have any idea what you're up against?

I did, a few days ago. I saw it very clearly. It was a life sentence.

Is that so? the lawyer asked. Do you see the cell you're in now? Do you see you're about to get fucked by the FBI, the DEA, the DHS? It's the *U.S. vs. Vik Singh* now.

The War On Drugs.

That's right, Vik. That's *exactly* right. It's been declared on you now. And yet I get this funny sense, when I look at you... it looks like there's a goddamn *twinkle* in your eye.

Yeah, well. I'm not in a barrel of acid.

Is that it, then? It's that simple?

It was when I made up my mind.

And is it still made?

Vik nodded. The lawyer scooted back in his chair.

I know what you're going though, the lawyer said. I really do.

Remi and I—there was no other way. Not for us to...not to *live*. Not that we could see.

No, the lawyer agreed. And I appreciate your candor. You and me—we have absolutely no time to sugarcoat. You need to know that I'm always going to give you the truth, and I expect that to be reciprocated for the entirety of our working relationship. Do we understand each other?

We do.

Good. Now, you're not charged with anything yet. But we can take an educated damn guess, can't we.

I've read the trafficking law, Vik said. He held up three fingers, folding them back one at a time as he listed off the punishable offenses: Manufacture, he said. Possession. Distribution.

The lawyer smiled.

Didn't see anything about *optimization*, Vik said.

No? said the lawyer. Then how about *knowingly furthering or facilitating, the sale, distribution, or trafficking of narcotics*? In other words, *conspiracy*. On a federal level. Did you see that, Vik?

How is writing software a conspiracy?

Oh, and they may *also* decide to bring some type of hacking charges. And I'm not afraid to say that I'm a little out of my depth on that aspect. I haven't figured out yet where it falls within the guidelines, if it even does. But I'll call in some experts. Big guns. There's a professor at Duke I like to use. Handsome devil, great on the stand. Plus I'll need co-counsel, a paralegal...

I have no money.

Nor do you pay my retainer.

(Who does, *now*? Vik wondered, but did not say.) It's not hacking, he said.

Why? the lawyer asked. Because you haven't broken into anything? Is that the distinction? I mean, I guess there's no virus, or whatever you people call it. For Christ's sake, it's just an app, right? Would that be an accurate description?

In the eyes of the law, Vik asked, I have no idea what the hell it's called. That's *your* job. And I'm sure you're good. Los has exquisite taste in contractors...

(At this, the lawyer couldn't help but share a smile, and for a moment, there they were: two men beholden to the same, enigmatic *jefe*.) Yes, the lawyer said. Well. I can tell you this Los isn't stuck sitting in a little room like this one.

Because of you, Vik said. Because you've done your job.

Like you've done yours?

Vik changed the subject. He asked what was going to happen to me.

She'll be fine, the lawyer said. She's gonna look like the victim here.

Which she is, Vik said.

To some extent.

She is to be left alone.

Not up to me, Vik.

I'll do what I can, the lawyer said.

Vik nodded acceptance. The two men sat for a moment, in contemplation of separate things.

Wouldn't *conspiracy* mean there's *co-conspirators*? Vik asked.

It would.

So—*Los*?

The lawyer winked.

Vik didn't know what to make of that. So, will they take *him* into custody, too? he asked.

Likely not, the lawyer said. They'd love to, of course. And I'm sure they'll try, but they don't need to, not to ruin *you*. Conspiracy has a low burden of proof. And mandatory minimum sentences. Fucking draconian. Tell me: have you ever been convicted of anything?

No.

I didn't think so. And that's good. It helps, just a little. But this is cocaine, Vik. And we're talking about a *bit* more than five kilograms...

I never touched the product.

And yet your hands are all over it.

Another question, the laywer said. Has death, or serious bodily injury, occurred?

Occurred, Vik said.

Yes.

Occurred..., Vik said, by *me*?

By you, Vik Singh.

Inside the United States.

Well, yes. Within the United Fucking States.

Not guilty, Vik said.

The lawyer shot him a look.

Well then, he said, we're probably talking ten years. *Mas o menos.*

If I'm guilty, Vik said.

If you're found guilty, yes.

I had a dog when I was growing up, Vik said. That's how long it lived—ten years.

And did that seem like a long time?

Yes. But. I was a kid.

The government's had eyes on you for some time, the lawyer said. There's surely a mountain of evidence.

A lot of which burned.

Well, then you have *something* to be thankful for. And just so we're clear, Vik: I'm not the judge here. I don't try you. I don't have to figure you out. I know whether you're guilty or not from day one. And you're guilty as hell.

Of certain things.

Yes. But, as you realize, that doesn't make you guilty in the eyes of the law. I'm going to fight like a dog for you.

For Los.

Mmm?

You're fighting for Los. That's who pays you.

Does it matter?

What's being done with my code?

Your code? It's been scrapped.

No, not the old version, Vik said. The one I just wrote.

Scrapped. Game over. It's too big of a vulnerability.

You're not serious.

I'm not in charge.

That code holds this whole shit-show together, Vik said.

Don't look at me, the lawyer said. Like I said...

You're 'not in charge.'

That's right.

Who is?

Excellent question, the lawyer said. I don't think anybody knows at the moment. Thanks to you.

Los *should* thank me.

You're going to get offered a deal. I can almost guarantee it.

By Los.

The lawyer blurted out a laugh. No, he said. By the U.S.

Attorney. A plea deal. They're after big fish. They'll offer you protection in exchange for a lesser sentence. In exchange for...information.

To be an informant, Vik said.

Yes.

Won't happen, Vik said. I've seen how narcs get treated in Juarez.

You're on U.S. soil now, remember.

The government sees the border. Los doesn't. I'm not sure I do either. Not anymore.

I'm telling you, as your lawyer: things are going to look mighty grim. The United States government can be hardcore too, you know. You're gonna feel like the whole world's caving in on you.

Which side are you arguing? I'm starting to lose track...

Yours, Vik. Always yours. I'm only trying to get a sense of your state of mind. You're a desperate man. I recognize them: I've seen my share. A desperate man will sit here with me, and vow to be silent, and then open their fucking mouth at the worst possible time because they think it suits them.

I understand, Vik said. But, silence suits me. I know that much for sure. And what I expect, in return for that silence, is for Remi to be left alone, and for me to be left alone, too, when this is over.

I'm not at liberty to promise anything.

Well then tell me who can. I need a guarantee that my loyalty will be rewarded. Who can give me that? Can Los?

You might try putting your trust in God, the lawyer said.

I'm serious, Vik said.

So am I. '*La biblia is la verdad...*'

I read that, too. On a mountain.

But you don't believe it...

Do you? Vik asked.

It's the book you put your hand on, in my line of business.

The ones who talk.

The ones who testify, yes.

Like I told you, Vik said. That's not my line of business.

41

Vik is awake in his bed. The air is stuffy, the lights are still off. Beside the bed there is a plastic chair and a desk affixed to whitewashed cinderblock. Upon the desk, a stack of books, a black-and-white composition notebook. Across the room, a stainless steel toilet/sink combo. Tucked neatly under the bed, a set of plastic bins containing an old iPod, a bar of soap, a half-length toothbrush, toothpaste, orange jumpsuits, and a letter from me that arrived after his first week in custody:

> *Dear Vik,*
>
> *Where to start? I want to ask you how you're doing, but that feels ridiculous and trite and anyway I bet I already know. You're probably doing okay, considering. But terrible, not considering. By which I mean it's relative—normalcy and all that, right? (You and I were getting used to being fucking 'guests'...)*
>
> *I'm just starting to feel a little more like...* <u>me</u>. *I've started writing again. I'm getting better about going outside. They've got me in a hotel. It feels like no one can find me here, and I hope that's true. I watch a lot of TV. Keeps my mind off things. People argue and worry and laugh and*

> *cry about the stupidest shit.   Do they let you*
> *watch TV? Do you know what I mean?*
>   *I'm told I get to move out next week. I hope so.*
> *I think of you all day. Write back if you can. Tell*
> *me how you're <u>actually</u> doing.*
>   *Love,*
>   *--R*

Vik had written back right away—though it had been tricky with his injured hand. I have an anonymous PO Box, courtesy of the witness protection agency, but Vik created a pair of email addresses we've been using instead. I'd guessed right in that first letter: he is doing fine, considering.

For both of us, the adrenaline rush of our escape has long subsided, leaving only flashbulb pops of horrific visions. I'd thought I'd want to immediately move on, to get away from it all, maybe even Vik, but it has been the opposite: I've needed to process it all, bit by tiny bit. I am trying to understand. I'm dying to talk to Vik, face to face. He is the only person I can relate to anymore. He says he feels exactly the same about me. We have become citizens of our own, separate country, population: two.

I CAN wait to see you, Vik said in his most recent message—referring to my upcoming, and first allowed, visit, still over three weeks away. *I have to wait*, he said, *and I can. In this way, I've changed. Things I used to do in an hour I make last all morning. I eat slow—even though the food's terrible. I breathe slow. I heal slow. I even have to <u>wait</u> slow. I used to wait so fast it wasn't waiting at all.*

Los' lawyer did all he could. And this is it, for the time being. I am in hiding, Vik is in a cell. But we have been recalibrated, Vik and I. To us, this constitutes getting away with it.

As predicted, the feds tried to get Vik to talk, to rat on Los. When it became clear Vik wouldn't, the prosecutor floated the possibility of a 10-year sentence for conspiracy; still, the evidence against Vik was actually quite thin, and the lawyer earned his paycheck arguing that the Federal Code lacked precedent for anything like Vik's code; *ipso facto,* no punishment for it would ever be found in the black-and-white sentencing schedules of the federal guidelines. Vik's transgression, if indeed there even *was* one, fell in a no-man's land of the law.

His transgressions north of the border, at least.

The judge was willing to buy some, but not all, of the lawyer's bullshit. She urged the prosecutor in the case to focus on a crime the government *could* confidently make stick and which *did* appear in the federal code, obscure though it seemed: 'knowingly employing, or using, a person under 18 years of age in drug operations.'

That sounds lewd, Vik had remarked to the lawyer when he first heard this charge.

No, the lawyer had said. It sounds *shrewd*.

The charge was built upon a chain of emails Vik had exchanged with one of Los' dealers, a 16-year-old wannabe-hacker named Salvatore. This had been early on—in the Dora development days. Salvatore had jumped at the chance to work with Vik. But recently, the now-17-year-old Salvatore had been arrested with half a kilo of coke and intent to sell. He'd handed over the emails in exchange for a lesser, possession charge. The emails pertained to one of Dora's many re-works. At that time, Vik had wanted a little customer ground truth before doing yet another full release. He'd asked Salvatore a bunch of questions about how much he sold per week, who he sold to, how they paid, what times of day, et cetera. There was proof that Vik *had* known Salvatore's age—one of Salvatore's emails made mention of a brand new Jeep Wrangler he'd bought, using cash, on the day he turned 16 and got his driver's license—but, back then, there had been hundreds of other, seemingly more relevant numbers for Vik to keep an eye on.

Vik took Salvatore's example and agreed to plead guilty in exchange for a lighter sentence. The alternative being: force the prosecutor's hand and go to trial, where the lawyer gave him coin-toss odds of beating the trumped-up conspiracy charge. For Vik, the decision had come down to this: our bond, forged in fire though it was, would probably not withstand a decade spent apart. He refused to become an improbability in my life. He would not flip that coin.

One year? he'd confirmed.

One, the lawyer had said. No parole, though.

Visits?

Occasional.

Take it.

We have no intention of returning to Mexico, nor has extradition ever been mentioned. The killings by Vik's hand that fateful morning at *la casa de huéspedes* have never been officially confirmed; the bodies of the men who died, Gamboa included, were not recovered. They are casualties in a war beyond the current reach of law. What Vik truly broke were *codes*. Rumor-ridden versions of what happened have circulated in the tabloids the world over. Of course, lacking the corroboration of the only two living eyewitnesses, these stories have been highly inaccurate.

This is the true story.

And sure. Maybe the sentence Vik is serving is just a stay of execution. Some form of justice has been done, but it is the justice of a nation—his debt just a number in a look-up table—while his debt to the cartel remains ill-defined. What does Vik still owe them, if anything? His life? Is he worth more to them dead or alive? Still, no matter how many ways we look at it, we always arrive at the same conclusion, and the same course of action: *name no names; pay down our debt with the only currency we have:* time.

Dora and Kavi are both dead.

Meanwhile, Vik recently met an inmate who'd been caught dealing coke he claims was supplied to him by the Gamboa cartel.

The king is dead; long live the king.

Who will say, then, whether Gamboa's alive or dead? He has his fans; some say he faked his own death. He had his minions, who are perhaps best served by his immortality. Either way, the Gamboa name lives on, even if only for brand recognition. Fucking *Los.* Vik will freely admit: Los is smarter than him. The day we threw ourselves at the mercy of the United States government, Los absconded, trading a life in his beloved *New* Mexico for a new one, in *Mexico* Mexico. Who knows: maybe *Los* wears the mask these days.

Vik has not heard from Los beyond a handshake and a few weighty words conveyed via the lawyer: Our mutual friend says, '*Hola.*'

At this, Vik had waved his busted hand 'hello' back, and asked if that was all Los had had to say.

He said to commend you, the lawyer said, for learning his language.

Spanish? Vik asked, before realizing, *no*. The lawyer had shrugged, as if he didn't know. A liar, the lawyer. World class. We are fortunate and grateful to have had him on our side.

No se, the lawyer said. I've given up trying to understand that man.

Vik nodded, weighing that, and asked: Do you think he considers our conversation over?

The lawyer frowned. I think that depends, he said. Do you have anything else you plan to say?

Does *he*? Vik asked.

He's paying me to be here. To defend you. He's paying *a lot*.

That says something, Vik allowed.

It says more than words ever will, the lawyer argued.

The writer in me disagrees.

Vik swings bare feet to bare floor. Stands. Crosses the cell to piss. Pulls on a clean pair of pants, leaving the matching t-shirt folded in the bin. The air smells of powdered eggs and disinfectant. It does every morning.

All the paperwork is done; I have finally been placed on his 'Allowed Visitors' list. Soon enough, I will be sitting beside him at a metal table, under casual surveillance: *almost* heaven.

By the time we came scrambling back across the border into El Paso, I had already been in the news for weeks —the missing darling *de jour*. Following my disappearance, an investigative reporter had dug up information suggesting (correctly, of course) that I had been co-opted by the DEA as part of a massive, ongoing investigation. This (of course) had come as news to my family, who could only deny—over and over, as they were hounded by reporters at the King's Beach motel where they'd set up something of a command center, trying to find me—that I would ever be part of something like that. By the time my parents were notified of my miraculous reappearance, DEA agents had already been trying to get me to talk for more than 24 hours.

Segregated to our 'his-and-hers' interrogation rooms, Vik and I had stuck with our plan. I told them my name. They worked out that I'd been kidnapped; and they could see I was back. I'd sacrificed far more for them than what I'd signed up for. The DEA had made me into a target, and I'd nearly paid with my life. I didn't owe them an explanation. I didn't owe them shit.

Facing quite the public relations fiasco, a higher-up at the DEA decided to grant me a brief, behind-the-scenes reunion with my family. Awkward does not begin to describe this visit. My parents—my mother, especially, but also my father, to an extent I've never seen—absolutely gushed. Tears. Words of love. Apologies for things long past. My brother too. I could only sit and absorb it all, for hours. They would not take their hands off me, at a time I was feeling a need to keep all hands off. I thanked them for all they'd done. Apologized for getting myself—and them—mixed up in something so terrible. I didn't know what else to say. I didn't tell them much of what had happened. There were agents about. I'd been living thousands of miles away from my family for years, but felt more isolated from them now, in the same room.

It struck me that they had been tortured, too, by my ordeal. Perhaps more than I had. My abuse had been physical, psychological, traumatic. Theirs had been entirely of the imagination—worst-case scenarios playing out in their heads for days on end. Fear of the unknown can be worse than fear of the known.

When the agents said it was time to go, I went.

I had been offered, and I accepted, placement into a witness-protection program. This offer was made despite the fact that I'd proven rather worthless as a witness. Still, my continued safety (from the press) became the agency's top public priority, and maybe, they hoped, I'd feel more like talking, later on...

Right they were.

I've started over in Seattle. I'd never been here before. It was far enough from Mexico for comfort, close enough to everything else. I tell Vik I'm trying to stay super busy, that I want time to fly by. A job was set up for me at a temping agency, and I've joined a local writing workshop. I take weekend road trips with an older divorcee I met there. I've bought a camper-trailer and a pickup to tow it.

On the last night we spent together in Juarez, Vik told me that a certain, half-burned cottage in Tahoe might still be worth robbing, if I still remembered how. A week later, while Vik was being transferred back to California, I slipped back into Incline Village in the middle of the night and traipsed through the forest to a familiar cul-de-sac, overlooking a silver, moonlit lake. The view had given me pause; alone in the forest, I'd begun to cry, thinking of Vik in his concrete box, unable to share it with me.

It was strange, I wrote him. I felt grateful, seeing it.

You got your tourist eyes back, he replied, referring to my habit of taking cruise boat rides just for the contact high of seeing *other* people see the lake for the first time. Vik's right.

I came away from the cottage with more than gratitude, though. At Vik's suggestion, I'd brought along a cordless sawzall and a backpacking bag. In my email the next day, I let him know I'd found the deadbolt of the storage closet already jimmied open. (Vik and I are forever speaking in code to each other. It's our little game.) I went on to say: *Sorry, honey. Your bike was gone. (Again. ☺) The only thing left in that closet was a water heater. Funny: it was still full.*

That was the week I bought the trailer and the pickup, cash.

From the start of his incarceration, Vik and I have been writing to each other. Long, luscious letters. His days are obviously far more routine and predictable than mine, so early on I prodded him to tell me about those parts of his life that *weren't*. You have nothing but time, I told him, and what better time to reflect. We can always live in our past, or our future, when our present becomes unbearable. He soon began to open up—to tell me his whole story, bit by bit, out of order. I craved every detail. I told him I wanted to sit on his shoulder all those days and nights when he was turning into the Vik I met at the lake, to see what he'd seen, hear what he'd heard, smell what he'd smelled. No matter how much he shared, I wanted more. When I told him I was working on a new novel, he asked what had became of the one I'd been working on before, at the lake.

It had a different author, I told him.

I know what you mean by that, he wrote, and by everything else you tell me, in a way no one else ever will, I think.

That's love, I've come to decide. Vik agrees.

This book of yours, he wrote. It isn't about us, is it? About what happened?

Of course it is, I wrote. But don't worry. I'm changing the names. And the places. The only thing I'm not gonna change is the truth.

Good, he wrote. Don't.

Maybe I'll have it published posthumously, or, as Vik jokes, when his statute of limitations runs out. Or, maybe when Los dies. If.

Vik: I told you I was a thief. And see: I have stolen your story, made it my own. Made your mathematics into metaphors, your algorithms into analogies. That's how my mind works. That's how I see the world, even when I look at it through your eyes.

Vik and I know we are in love. But it is a love that is far from perfect. How could it be anything else? It hasn't been given a fair chance. I have taken to calling our relationship to date a 'rough draft,' whereas Vik calls it as an 'indeterminate equation,' one he says will have many different solutions as time goes on, but will be forever solvable. He tells me that his faith in this keeps him sane.

He has been in prison for four months. His cell is the second to last in a row along the topmost level of a four-story building on the outskirts of a town with a Spanish name in the (present) state of California. His mother writes to him too. Vik tells me they are closer than they've been in years. Throughout Vik's preliminary hearings and all the way through sentencing, she was there for him (and for me—for that is when we met). We both needed her. She was our rock. All it took for mother and son to resurrect their former roles was for Vik to need her again. It helped that Vik had been proven so inarguably *wrong*; a son locked in a cage can no longer play the Know-It-All. Vik's brothers have sent the occasional letters too, but they have families, careers. Debts of their own to pay down. He understands that. He does not begrudge them.

Mrs. Singh and I both send Vik books. He dutifully reads them. He tells me he's becoming a better reader. I can see it in his writing. He writes wonderful letters. They are the air I breathe. Too long without one and I began to suffocate: I have not acquired Vik's newfound capability to wait. He tells me that, while the old Vik would have wasted hours carefully crafting his words, sleeping on them before sending them out —as he'd done with the very first letter he gave me outside the stadium—the new Vik gushes. His letters pour out unfiltered. He sends them the instant he finishes writing them. Then he waits, slowly, for my reply. Or starts another.

In the mornings, sunlight comes through his translucent Lexan window and casts a slender rectangle upon his cell door. He stares at it from his bed. The diurnal pace of its descent requires a certain patience to detect, a patience he has been honing. He's noticed the rectangle's longitude upon the door shifting day by day. Fall turning to winter.

He says this rectangle of light reminds him of Tetris, the videogame he'd played religiously as a boy. He'd internalized the game's Russian theme music. Internalized, too, the lessons of the game, geometric and otherwise. He'd learned to prepare for the long rectangle by constructing from its plummeting predecessors a chasm to accommodate its inevitable arrival, its foreseeable adherence to gravity. Played poorly, the rectangle gets you killed; played prudently, it earns you 800 points.

Anchorage. That is a place I daydream about going with Vik with the truck and camper. But Vik's been reading a bit of Thoreau—a dangerous philosopher for a prison library, don't you think?—and he says the Maine woods sound good to him, too. Maybe we can go there. Really, it doesn't matter where we go.

We.

The plastic sheath on the mattress crackles as Vik steps up onto it to peer through the Lexan. The shapes and colors he can make out are abstract, but familiar: he sees a blurry tower where a blurry man in blue looks down through binoculars at blurry men in orange marching double file across a yellow yard.

Vik drops to his floor and does pushups. His long nose tapping out the reps against flecks sprinkled into the polished resin. He stands, rolling his head around on his shoulders, shaking the blood back into his hands. The right one still hurts sometimes, he says—still hangs heavier. He says he thinks it always will.

He does sit-ups. Rests. Waits.

The rectangle of light moves across the floor. Vik kneels in it. Assumes the downward-facing dog.

ACKNOWLEDGMENTS

This novel was inspired and informed by
many works, but especially:
--*The American*, by Martin Booth [and the
movie by the same name]
--*Drive,* by James Sallis [and the movie by the same name]
--*The Information: A History, a Theory,
a Flood,* by James Gleick
--*Geek Sublime: Writing Fiction, Coding Software,*
by Vikram Chandra
--*The Signal and the Noise: Why So Many Predictions
Fail—but Some Don't,* by Nate Silver
--Quora.com
--The long-form journalism of *Rolling Stone*

This novel was encouraged and improved by many
people, but I am especially indebted to:
Jill Rogers
Christopher Coake
Adam Dedmon
Gabriel Urza
Curtis Vickers
Mignon Fogarty
Jason Ludden
Jack Fredericks
Biray Dogan

Finally, I give special thanks to my family and to my friends.

ABOUT THE AUTHOR

Ben Rogers' work has been published in *The Rumpus*, *PANK*, *McSweeney's Internet Tendency*, *The Portland Review*, *Arroyo Literary Review*, *Wag's Revue*, and elsewhere, and has earned the Nevada Arts Council Fellowship. He is also the lead author of *Nanotechnology: Understanding Small Systems*, the first-ever comprehensive textbook on nanotechnology, and *Nanotechnology: The Whole Story*, both of which earned the CHOICE Outstanding Academic Title Award from the American Library Association. He studied engineering and journalism in college and has worked as a business analyst, a reporter, a teacher, and a scientist at various labs, including Oak Ridge National Laboratory and NASA's Jet Propulsion Laboratory. He is currently the Director of Engineering at NevadaNano and lives in Reno with his family.

www.readrogers.com

ABOUT CQ BOOKS

For over 20 years, I made it my goal to find a home for my work at a Big New York Publisher (BNYP). I tried very hard to achieve that goal. So many times, it seemed like I nearly did. Here are a few of the rejections my agent received on my behalf from BNYP's:

> "Ben Rogers's novel is like nothing else I've read, which is usually a signal that I should go after a manuscript. In the end, alas, sales fears took over... I'll be pulling for Ben Rogers from afar, then. He's a wonderfully inventive writer."

> "I look forward to picking it up every night before bed...It certainly deserves to be published."

> "The characters...are exquisitely rendered and feel very much like living, breathing people....I'm sorry to say that I don't think that [BNYP]...is quite ready to publish something with such literary aspirations..."

> "With great admiration, we're going to pass."

> "I absolutely hate saying no to this...."

> "[Rogers is] a terrific writer and thinker, and I'll be wishing all good fortune to The Heavy Side from afar."

> "I heartily believe it's just a matter of time and a little luck until many other readers discover [Rogers'] writing. Wish I could be the one to introduce them to it, but there we are."

One night in November of 2019, I was lying in bed, frustrated by so many seeming near-misses and by how much time and effort I was putting into finding a publisher (when I wanted to just keep writing!) and I wondered: what if, instead, I put all that energy into building something myself? Into getting my work into the hands of readers, including those who've so kindly kept asking when I'd have something new to read (after two wonderful, small presses published, and then re-issued, my first novel, *The Flamer*)? I got out of bed, and before sunrise I'd created CQ Books.

'CQ' is what amateur ('ham') radio operators say into thin air, not knowing whether anyone is even listening on their frequency. It's an invitation to a conversation. It's a call of hope. It sounds like they're saying 'seek you.'

I am.

Ben Rogers
January 2020
Reno, NV

259

AUTHOR'S NOTE

Dear Reader,

Thank you for reading my novel! I hope you enjoyed it--that it entertained, informed, or inspired you in a meaningful way.

When I put a piece of writing into the world, I'm dying to know how it lands, whether it resonates, how it makes others think and feel. I write to form connections: connections between ideas, experiences, and, most of all, between people.

As such, please consider reviewing *The Heavy Side* on Amazon or Goodreads. Reviews close the loop of connection for me, and are the lifeblood of an independent author. I read every one and they help to make my writing better.

More about my work can be found at readrogers.com.

Thank you!

-Ben

ALSO BY BEN ROGERS

NOVELS

The Flamer

SHORT STORIES

The Young Man and the Mountain

Mayfly

On the Rejuvenating Effects of Arch Theft

NON-FICTION

Nanotechnology: The Whole Story

Nanotechnology: Understanding Small Systems

CPSIA information can be obtained
at www.ICGtesting.com
Printed in the USA
LVHW032322130121
676435LV00031B/500

9 781734 306705